THE
NATION'S
HIGHEST
HONOR

THE NATION'S HIGHEST HONOR

A NOVEL

JAMES GAITIS

CLEARWATER I FL I USA

For information, contact Kunati Inc., Book Publishers in Canada.
USA: 13575 58th Street North, Suite 200, Clearwater, FL 33760-3721 USA
Canada: 75 First Street, Suite 128, Orangeville, ON L9W 5B6 CANADA.
E-mail: info@kunati.com.

FIRST EDITION

Designed by Kam Wai Yu
Persona Corp. | www.personaco.com

ISBN 978-1-60164-172-4   EAN 9781601641724
Fiction

Published by Kunati Inc. (USA) and Kunati Inc. (Canada).
Provocative. Bold. Controversial.™

http://www.kunati.com

TM—Kunati and Kunati Trailer are trademarks owned by Kunati Inc.
Persona is a trademark owned by Persona Corp.
All other trademarks are the property of their respective owners.

Library of Congress Cataloging-in-Publication Data

Gaitis, James.
The nation's highest honor : a novel / James Gaitis. -- 1st ed.
    p. cm.
Summary: "A literary satire that targets dysfunctional government, the
military, cultural malaise and social inequality by pitting a peaceful and
innocent outsider with no ulterior motives against the
establishment"--Provided by publisher.
ISBN 978-1-60164-172-4
1. Political fiction. I. Title.
PS3607.A36N37 2009
813'.6--dc22
                    2009001443

To beautiful Dawn

What is honour?
A word. What is in that word honour?
What is that honour? Air. A trim reckoning!
Who hath it? He that died o' Wednesday.
Doth he feel it? No. Doth he hear it?
No. 'Tis insensible then? Yea, to the dead.
But will it not live with the living? No. Why?
Detraction will not suffer it.
Therefore I'll none of it.
Honour is a mere scutcheon:
and so ends my catechism.

Sir John Falstaff, *Henry IV Part 1*, Act V, Scene 1

CHAPTER I

1

The black government sedan came cautiously up the road that really wasn't a road at all but something less—a dirt track, an abandoned wagon trail perhaps—which had been carved into and through the desert apparently with the singular intent of traversing every embedded rock and undulation and obstacle that might have been avoided by routing the road with the slightest degree of care. A windblown landscape cluttered with cacti and mesquite and stony outcroppings and thorny brush. A wasteland, some would think. A vast and weatherbeaten region of a dying and near-dead planet.

With resolute patience, the driver did his best to maneuver the car along the ribbon of scratched roadway that twisted through the forsaken expanse of sand and rock and rising foothills that obscured and denied and deceived. But he could not avoid the rock and stone and washboard surface and deep ruts that grabbed at the tires of the sedan and tested its suspension and threatened to strand him there in the middle of God-knows-where.

He drove on, in spite of it, determined to complete his mission, at times reacting too slowly; jerking the wheel to the right when it was too late; cutting back to the left only to instantly set the sedan atop a rippled hardpan surface of caliche that vibrated his very core until he conceded his error and cut back hard the other way, back into the potholed craters that dropped the sedan on a sudden and slammed its frame to the ground. But he could do nothing to stop the dust that forced its way in through the vents he had closed and the air conditioner that was supposed to be self-contained, coating everything slowly in a fine sediment of grayish brown. So he drove on. Speeding up when he thought the worst was behind him, slowing to a crawl when he could see that the worst was yet ahead, twisting left to avoid one obstacle, veering right after only another hundred yards. And with each turn and lurch, rise and dip, saying "goddammit" again and again. With the inchoate road and the compliant sedan and the driver who became more and more unnerved all joining in a form of uncoordinated ritual dance, soaring up too fast and falling down too slow, overreacting in this direction and overcompensating in that, with the inharmonious beat of the driver's blasphemy keeping it all, almost, on track.

Five miles down the road. More or less. For five roadless miles. Until a sign attached with rusting baling wire to a crooked mesquite post emerged in front of him from out of a pile of rocks set almost into the road. In words burned crudely into the battered piece of sun-bleached barnwood, it read:

Pack Rat Haven
Gallery & Curios
Antique Treasures and Junk For Sale
8 mi. up Burnt Gully
(turn left at windmill)

So the driver took the sedan onward. He loosened his silk tie for which he had paid dearly and gripped the wheel tighter as if to prove to the road that he was more determined than it, the car lurching and the stones kicking up and denting the oil-pan and wheel wells, and the scenery of the isolated and cactus-strewn land passing by him for another mile, maybe two, when the driver slowed again and then stopped and waited for the dust to settle before he rolled down the window to examine his progress.

In every direction but behind him he saw that the land gradually rose, first slowly and then at sharper angles so that what was hill became foothill and then the beginning of mountain, treeless and broken and brutally formidable. He saw, also, suddenly birds, small birds, many of them, flitting through the tiny leaves of the brush and trees and standing on the needles of the cacti as though they were all but oblivious to pain and puncture. And lizards, scurrying along the sand by some design that failed to account for traction but which allowed them to move in a blur of speed nonetheless, like fish in water, skaters on ice. And something else, something unnatural, inanimate and incongruous along the side of the road just a way ahead.

He closed the window, closed out the faint scent of the greasewood and at least the excess heat that rose off the ground, and drove until he came up close to the object and examined it at length without bothering to lower his window. It was a face—that much was clear—set upon a crosscut slice of tree trunk no wider than a serving platter. With eyes and mouth and nose made out of parts of a rusted and antique cook stove, although the driver could not have known as much, could never have recognized the iron cooking plates and flaking chromium-plated handle for what they once had been. He looked at the iron and wooden face and found it to be devilish and crude, wide-eyed and lidless and grinning with an evil, belittling smirk; and he drove on.

At some point the road seemed to vanish entirely. The driver stopped the car again and got out and stepped onto the dry brittle soil and walked about searching for the road, snagging his suit trousers on the needles of a prickly pear he thought he had stepped clearly over, fighting a small doll-like segment of cholla that somehow had found him and somehow could not be removed from his pant leg even when he gripped it painfully with the needles penetrating his fingers, looking forward and from side to side until he finally found where the road continued ahead of him, past the sandy wash where it had temporarily vanished into nothingness. And only then did he look up from the ground to find himself enveloped by the beginnings of a canyon that started to rise up from out of nowhere, for no reason, from out of the sandy desert floor. And he saw that up close the walls of the canyon did not look like the walls of the mountain that loomed in the distance, that they were ornate and intricate and colored with an entire spectrum of yellows and browns and reds, and that the cholla and yucca and ocotillo and saguaro and prickly pear and cliff brake dressed the canyon walls with a cascade of desert flora that was unlike anything else on earth.

Onward. Now somewhat pleased with himself, in a way that was unfamiliar and new, he continued up the road more slowly, taking the time to notice that the colors in the stone ranged from soft brown to beige and umber on into vermillion and carmine and even into black. Over more of the same sharp rock, with similar ruts grabbing at the tires and the suspension and the driver no longer even trying to pretend that they could be avoided; and across another dried streambed and around a corner, through two gateless juniper posts, where he brought the black government sedan, covered in dust and rattling from some damage somewhere under the carriage or the hood or both, to a stop.

He turned off the engine and leaned forward. He peered through the windshield that was coated so thickly with the powder of the road that he could hardly see the road sign that had been planted there in another pile of rocks and which read, Slow, Children Playing. Fifty feet or so beyond it stood a barnboard shack, rectangular in shape with a shed roof and a porch running the length of the building, facing due south into the midday summer sun. Not an abandoned shack, but a lived-in shack, on the walls and under the eaves of which had been hung an assortment of rusted objects and bleached bones and oddly shaped branches and old cookware and a variety of other things that surely had absolutely no value, let alone any redeeming aesthetic quality.

He waited until the cloud of pulverized sand dissipated and settled, and then he got out of the car and went around to the other side and opened the door and took out his suit jacket and put it on and adjusted his tie and picked up the briefcase and strode toward the building, with the brittle ground crunching beneath his shoes that had lost all sign of luster and polish.

2

It would later be told that when Leonard Bentwood learned that he was to be a recipient of the nation's highest honor, emotional tears came immediately to his eyes. But it was really only the dust, which always kicked up when the city visitors in their road cars zipped by Leonard's sign that read Slow, Children Playing, and pulled in at excessive speed in their hurry and enthusiasm to examine what they had found at the end of the diminutive canyon. And, in fact, Leonard was already wiping the dust from off his face when the young man, dressed in a fine summer woolen suit, rose out of the sedan and stepped into the dirt and picked his way past the prickly pear and other cacti as he made his way up to the stoop that served as Leonard Bentwood's porch. Leonard nodded his head once, and the man presumed this was a greeting and said, "Good morning," with an uncomfortable smile as serious and reserved as Leonard had ever seen. "I'm looking for Leonard Bentwood," the man said as he stood at the bottom step, reluctant to come up if there were no need. "The postal office back at . . . back a few miles . . . said I could find Leonard Bentwood out this way."

To which Leonard Bentwood nodded his head in affirmation.

"You're Leonard Bentwood?" the man asked with a hesitant tone of disbelief.

"I'm *a* Leonard Bentwood," Leonard Bentwood answered with a soft smile that highlighted the creases in his tanned face. "I suppose there might be more than one of us."

The man smiled weakly and then reached deep into his attaché after dialing the combination to the lock—the briefcase looking perfectly odd and oddly collectible to Leonard Bentwood—and he pulled out a yellow envelope bearing a blue and official-looking address with an even more official-looking insignia, vaguely circular in shape and adorned with some form of banner and ribbons and some arrows or spears that were held in the talons of a raptor. And he held it out to Leonard Bentwood.

"Mr. Bentwood," the man said as his eyes slowly moved back and forth, taking note of the random assortment of rusting and dented farm implements; the broken kitchenware and bent tools; the worn-out tires and the bleached and crumbling cow and deer skulls; the crude attempts at sculpture and craft that adorned the outside walls and eaves and ledges of Pack Rat Haven. "My name is William Worthington. I am the Assistant to the Minister of Cultural Affairs. It is my privilege to advise you that you have been chosen by the President to receive the Nolebody Medal, which I am sure you know is the nation's highest honor."

Leonard Bentwood looked down at the envelope but did not take it. "The president of what?" he asked.

"The President of the nation, of course," William Worthington answered in somewhat of an astonished voice. "The Nolebody Medal," he said. "I am sure you have heard of it."

Leonard Bentwood looked at the man, and then past him as though he was searching for something on the ground or on the porch or underneath the sedan. "Okay," he said. "Be sure to thank everyone for me when you get back."

3

The Assistant to the Minister of Cultural Affairs was still holding the official-looking envelope for Leonard Bentwood to take, not realizing that while Leonard Bentwood was looking directly at him, his mind and thought were still focused on where he might have left his coffee cup which, Leonard Bentwood kept reminding himself, was still half filled with coffee.

The sun bore down on the southern exposure of the stoop, and the Assistant to the Minister of Cultural Affairs quickly found that his fine wool suit captured and retained the heat in a highly efficient manner. "May we go inside?" he asked. "There are some things we need to discuss."

Leonard Bentwood looked over at the bench at the edge of his porch, but his cup was not there either. "Beg your pardon," he said. "Did you say something? The heat gets to a man's mind after a while." And then he pushed open the plank door, which groaned heavily on its rusty hinges and grated loudly as it scraped against the warped and uneven floor, and he said, "Why don't you come in for a minute and get out of the sun."

Inside the shack were Leonard Bentwood's most valuable, or at least most vulnerable, collectibles. On the walls were masks made out of hubcaps and figurines made from broken coffeepots and mice skulls and the like. There were pictures on the walls—some held there by a nail, others set inside frames that had no glass—most of which were nothing more than glossy pages that had been torn out of books or magazines. A couple of worn out saddles with broken stirrups and cracking leather were thrown over what had once been a couch and an easy chair. Rusted and broken leghold traps, some large enough to catch a bear, sat piled in the corner. There was a steel drum turned sideways that served as a stove, and a five-gallon bucket that was three-quarters filled with a brownish water that dripped from a spigot fashioned from old pipe into which had been thrust a cork, the water smelling distinctly like old and rotting eggs. There was a table, and two chairs (one of which sat unevenly, as though a leg had been replaced with one that did not fit), and an endless assortment of other objects ranging from stacks of books with broken bindings to piles of magazines with torn covers and bent pages to old whisky and perfume bottles to stuffed birds from which half of the feathers seemed to have been lost.

"Have a seat," Leonard Bentwood said to William Worthington, gesturing with a backhanded flip of his hand toward the couch, which seemed covered with a layer of lint but which actually was cat hair. And then he pointed to the five-gallon bucket and said, "Would you like a drink of water?"

<h1 style="text-align:center">4</h1>

As soon as his visitor departed, Leonard Bentwood renewed his search for his coffee cup. But he only looked for a few minutes and when he did not find it, he went back inside and sat down at his table, on top of which was a smattering of objects—a packet of rolling papers and some tobacco and matches; several worn books with bookmarks somewhere in the middle; a variety of smallish paint brushes; some crusty bottles of acrylic and oil paints; a menagerie of cheap pens and chewed stub pencils; more books, mostly very worn and musty; a half-smoked cigarette; opened and unopened letters; the better part of a ream of bleached white paper. He picked up a dented remnant of a pencil that had been sharpened by a penknife and he pulled out a piece of the clean paper and began to write. He would scribble a word or a line and then stop and think for a moment and then shake his head and then write some more and stop and repeat the pattern. This time it took only four lines.

He rose and opened the door, which scraped along the floor planks as he pulled it open. He went around the corner to the side of the shack and then around the next corner to the back north-facing side where an old school desk sat, weathered and cracking in the heat despite the fact that it was largely shaded from the sun. And he picked up his cup, which rested right where he knew it would be, on the corner of the school desk that long ago had lost its last hint of varnish and color.

In the time since he had misplaced the cup, which was half filled with coffee, the cream had reformed into floating pale globules that looked vaguely like egg whites cooked in too much butter. In half that time, a moth had fluttered too close to the dull surface and had pasted itself to the inside wall of the cup where, in the time it took the Assistant to the Minister of Cultural Affairs to come and go, it died in a caffeine-induced stupor.

With his forefinger, Leonard Bentwood lifted the dead moth from the mug. He flicked it aside onto the desert sand and felt saddened by the moth's demise. He stirred the coffee once, with that same finger on which an imperceptible quantum of moth wing dust now rested, and then drank the remainder of the coffee down with a single draught.

The afternoon winds came up and, as they always did, funneled through Leonard Bentwood's narrow rocky desert canyon with an exaggerated and arbitrary force. They whipped up the dust, and enlivened the hard dry leaves of the crown of thorns and scrub oak, and then blew their way through the open door of Leonard Bentwood's shack, scattering the papers that the Assistant to the Minister of Cultural Affairs had left behind. The official letter with the official seal, advising Leonard Bentwood that he was to receive the nation's highest honor, and describing the reasons why the coveted medal was to be awarded to him, lifted off the crude table as though the raptor on the official seal had taken wing with the spears or arrows still in the clutch of its claws and the ribbons and banner trailing behind it as it sailed off into the glory of the moment. It drifted like a parasail, wafted this way and that before it slipped to the floor and then under the battered threadbare couch.

The instruction sheet, containing all the relevant directions on how to dress and the transportation arrangements and when and where Leonard Bentwood should present himself in order to attend the private opening reception and how much time he had at the actual award ceremony to say his thanks and what he should consider saying and avoid saying, also lifted off the table like a vague memory of a dream and then promptly lost the breeze and fell in a perpendicular line straight down to the floor and slid through a crack between the floorboards to become more nesting material for the mice who lived happily below.

Only the formal notice, reflecting the time and place of the actual awards ceremony, remained, exactly where Leonard Bentwood had left it—on one of the many plank shelves that lined the walls of the shack and on which stood endless rows of almost everything that Leonard Bentwood owned.

The paper on which Leonard had written some words just minutes earlier also lifted off from the table and fell to the floor where it landed face up. There were only four lines written on it, but they had been scrawled in a large hand and he had included some extra space between each line so that the four lines of writing took up a good portion of the page. The words said,

three cups of coffee, three times, three
a bird, a song I do not know
cheeseburger cheeseburger cheeseburger
a visitor coming, from down the road

Outside, Leonard Bentwood was busy at his work. For the rest of the day he sifted through his piles of junk, thinking of combinations, examining angles, considering repairs, walking around and around his collection and the desert environs with a slow and decided quietude that counterpoised the heat and intensity of the sun. Just as he always did. And the visit by the Assistant to the Minister of Cultural Affairs slowly faded from Leonard Bentwood's mind until he forgot about it entirely, if one can temporarily forget about something they will, at least in part, later recall. And he would have forgotten about the paper, also, had it not been lying there on the floor directly in front of the door when he finally came back into the shack. He stooped down and picked it up without rereading what he had written. And then he placed it face down onto a stack of other papers on which he also previously had written in the same large hand.

5

The next day was letter-writing day for Leonard Bentwood. Not that Leonard was a prolific letter writer. He was not. Leonard wrote one letter a week to his mother, who now was in the twilight of her years and yet had always been, and still remained, his guiding light. And Leonard loved her very much, even though he had not seen her or even spoken with her now for a period far in excess of a decade. Maybe more.

He had something of a ritual for writing letters to his mother, and it differed in no way on this particular morning. He made his coffee in the same cup as yesterday without bothering to wash it or wipe it clean. He opened his little rusted pearl-handle penknife on which was inlaid the name of the Capital City Manufacturing Company, and he vigorously sharpened a pencil even though the lead point was already more than sufficient for the task. He got himself a bowl of dry oatmeal, to which he added raisins and some honey and a little water from the five-gallon bucket, and placed it on the table. He smoked the remaining half of a half-smoked rolled cigarette and then stamped out the butt in the lid of a jar that served as his ashtray. And then he pulled several sheets of used paper from the stack on the shelf, being the same stack of paper on which only yesterday he had placed the sheet with the four lines containing the words he had written about the coffee cup and the bird and cheeseburgers and the car, and he sat down and wrote his letter to his mother using the clean side of that sheet, and others besides.

Dear Mama, it always began. And then it continued as it always did, with a detailed recitation of how his week had been and what he had made and what he had sold on the rare occasions when he had, in fact, sold an item from his collection to some adventurous soul who had come up the road that really wasn't more than a rough track scratched through the desert terrain.

He told her about the weather, which was blissfully hot. He told her about the desert tortoise that had come through the yard so slowly that by the time it completed its meandering traverse the temperature had peaked and then had fallen with the approach of evening. And he told her about a dusty novel he had pulled out of one of his stacks and read and much to his surprise had thoroughly enjoyed despite its cover and boring title. He mentioned the stars and a meteor that had crossed the entire span of the cloudless night sky in a blaze of reddish white with streams of sparks visibly flying off its tail. And of many other things. But he did not tell her about the Assistant to the Minister of Cultural Affairs and the nation's highest honor because from the moment the man had presented himself, Leonard had believed that it was nothing more than a sales gimmick of some sort, like they used to offer when he was a boy and he would answer the phone at his mother's home and the voice on the other end would tell him that he had won something that subsequently never arrived in the mail or on the doorstep no matter how long and how patiently he waited. And, as always, he told her in concluding that he loved her and that he would write again the following week.

He rose and folded the letter but did not place it in an envelope because he did not have an envelope. In fact, he never had had an envelope into which one could place a letter. Instead, he took the folded letter and stuck it sideways between the kerosene lamp and the drooping candle that sat on the shelf on the wall next to the door.

6

It is moments before true dawn. The faded darkness of night lingers like a furtive shadow over the desert. The eastern rim of the earth brightens in a faintly luminescent violet tinged with the darkest blue. The sudden scattered chatter and sounds of birds—quail and doves, a pyrrhuloxia, some sparrows, a lone thrasher; far off the shrill cry of a hawk and the final inquiry of a greater owl. Otherwise all is silent and motionless, breathless and waiting; the creatures of the night in full retreat and the creatures of the day on the edge of their advance. Until the sun breaches the horizon with a narrow sliver of intensity and the desert is flooded in a matter of minutes with a brilliantly searing light. The cloudless sky returns to powdery blue, with the heat quick to follow. So fast that on summer mornings

Leonard Bentwood is certain he can watch the mercury rise in the plastic thermometer that hangs outside his door.

At that early hour of the day, now two days past the visit by the Assistant to the Minister of Cultural Affairs, Leonard Bentwood prepared and ate his breakfast, the same oatmeal and honey and raisins and sulfur-laden water, along with the last of his apples and the last of his plums. When he had finished, he filled several bottles with water from the bucket and then went out into the yard and walked behind the shack where a dented pickup truck, which once might have been doe skin in color but now was faded almost to a dull unpolished white, sat underneath a large mesquite. The tree's branches extended out and over the truck and that was why Leonard always parked the truck there—to give it shade, shelter from the sun. Woodpeckers—flickers probably—had driven deep holes into the trunk and limbs of the tree, and the overhanging branches occasionally dripped a crimson-colored sap that dried like splotches of blood on the pickup's hood and windshield. But that did not matter to Leonard since he liked to watch the woodpeckers as they rammed their heads with remarkable precision and alacrity into objects that seemed quite solid. And the truck was just a truck, after all.

He opened the door by reaching through the glassless window and lifting the lever from inside. He swept out most of the yellow powdery mesquite catkins that littered the seat and then got in. The engine churned and sputtered and coughed and eventually started, and Leonard Bentwood backed up and turned the truck around and made his way down his desert driveway that someone long ago had cut through a land as desolate and unchanged as could be hoped for in an overpopulating world.

He took the same route he always did, down his easement and onto the graveled and maintained road that served as the highway frontage. He drove slowly, enjoying the endless vistas, the vast expanse of sky and desert, mountain and mesa. Watching as the cars and trucks on the highway rushed by at excessive speeds with their drivers blasting music on their radios and a piece of trash or the remnant of a still-lit cigarette occasionally flying out of a window to bounce or spark wildly along the highway before it came to rest on the shoulder or in the bar ditch that must have been dug for that purpose alone. At the first intersection he turned left onto the narrow paved road that came through the underpass of the highway and then he headed north.

He drove slowly, for a mile maybe two, until he saw a hawk a way ahead, sitting on a fence rail, absolutely motionless and absolutely alert. He slowed even more, eased the truck up to where the hawk was perched, just short of an object in the middle of the road. And then Leonard Bentwood stopped the truck and the hawk flew off and he got out and walked into the middle of the road and examined the furry carcass that showed a hint of undried blood beneath it.

He picked the dead animal up slightly by the tail, turned it lightly over, looked to see what damage had been done. And when he decided that he wanted it, he took it and laid it gently in the truck bed and then started the truck back up and continued onward.

After ten miles, he had collected two dead hares and a couple of sparrow-sized birds and a snake and several lizards. All of them now rested in the back of the truck bed where Leonard Bentwood had placed them—side by side, like victims of the plague or an execution or soldiers awaiting burial after a bloody battle. All of them placed up against the wall of the cab, indiscriminately mixed together—hare and bird and lizard and snake—so that they might not slide around unduly should he have to apply the brakes to avoid a hazard along the way.

At twelve miles, he turned left, off the pavement and onto another dirt road that pointed to the mountain that rose up defiantly out of the earth like an isolated island in the middle of an ocean. An oasis, coated in the higher elevations by the dark green of an evergreen forest but still containing glimpses of that same jutting rock that thrust toward the heavens in shades of burnt sienna and sepia. And he drove toward it, with the mountain at first in the background and then looming in front of him and growing as he approached and yet somehow also shrinking, becoming smaller and less formidable.

He parked alongside the road that now was mostly of dirt and mud and not rock and got out and walked around for the better part of an hour. Collecting things. A piece of bark that looked to be the petrified skin of an alligator. Tiny little pine cones with funny little points, globules of quartz, oddly shaped twigs, the partial femur of a deer, a turkey feather, seed pods from yuccas, an enormous leaf blown from a sycamore he couldn't even see. And then he returned to the truck and placed them in a cardboard box in the bed and moved the box over toward the roadkill and got in the truck and returned to his shack by the same route he had come.

7.

There were any of a number of ways to get the job done. There was the stove, of course, but that was messy and the smell of cooking skin and brains and eyes invariably got in

Leonard's sinuses and bothered him for days and sometimes, oddly, for weeks or even longer. As though the memory of the smell itself was insidious and irreducible. There was the penknife and bleach, but that could be awkward since he kept the knife sharp and it had a tendency to cut into the bones and shear off parts that Leonard would have preferred remained attached. So Leonard opted for the chicken wire and the little mesh cages he had constructed on his own and which were perfectly efficient as long as time was not the issue.

He retrieved the hares and the birds, the lizards and snake from the truck bed and brought them out back. He put the hares in separate cages, and the birds in another and the reptiles in a fourth and then climbed five or six feet up a palo verde that draped itself like an ancient willow over the fence beyond his shack. He wired the cages to the highest limb he could reach, beyond the grasp of any but the most industrious scavengers other than the insects he sought to attract. It would take a week or two, maybe even three if it rained, but in the end he knew that most of the meat and much of the tendon and sinew would be removed without any effort by him and that, in this way, he would have the skulls and little feet and other interesting skeletal remnants to himself, so that he might use them in his sculptures when he found the need.

He washed his hands outside in another five-gallon bucket that contained more of that same water that smelled like week-old eggs. And then he went indoors.

There was something else he needed to do, but he could not remember what. It was not pressing. He could sense that much. But it would become pressing at some point if he failed to recall it. He pulled out a clean sheet of the paper and rolled a cigarette and thought for a moment while it dried. Then he picked up a pencil and thought some more, and wrote: tomorrow, Wednesday, morning. A flash of sensibility came to him. He paused, considered whether that was all there was to it: that he had forgotten that tomorrow was mail day—the only day of the week on which Leonard Bentwood got mail at his rural and isolated location in the middle of the desert.

He shook his head, because there was more to it than that. Yes, tomorrow was Wednesday, mail day. But what had he done with his letter to his mother? That was the point. He lit the cigarette and thought and smoked and was still thinking when he snuffed it out after it had been half smoked. He took up the pencil again. This time it took five lines, in total. He put down the pencil and rose and walked over to the door and took the letter off the shelf and put it down on the center of the table, which not only was a safe enough place but was the place he normally put letters to his mother that were ready for delivery.

He made himself dinner, which was composed of beans and green chilies and onions, all fried together in oil and served on flatbread. Then he went outside with his plateful of food and ate while he sat on the rocker on his porch. After a while, he smoked the other half of his last cigarette and then, with a small tumbler of brandy in hand, he watched the evening collapse into night with the star-filled firmament slowly revealing the profundity of the illimitable universe.

8

The Assistant to the Minister of Cultural Affairs had been waiting in the receiving area only briefly when the receptionist advised him that the Minister could now see him. "Minister

Frasier has another appointment in fifteen minutes," the secretary advised him with an air of superiority as he opened the door.

He walked into the wide office and crossed the plush circular carpet that had been a gift of the native peoples of a faraway land and approached the Minister of Cultural Affairs who rose from behind her enormous oak desk and came around to the side to meet him. He was a great admirer of the Minister and long ago had concluded that she must have been alluring and beautiful when she was younger. And he had seen photographs to confirm that this was true. They exchanged greetings and a warm handshake and then, before he could even raise the subject, she asked, "Did you find him? Leonard Bentwood, I mean. Were you able to locate him?" And then she added, "I'm sorry. Have a seat, William, please," which she herself did by sinking deeply and tiredly back into the black leather chair behind the desk.

William Worthington eased uncomfortably into one of the antique side chairs that were positioned in front of the Minister's desk. They had been made in a different era and the legs were somewhat shorter than the standard of the day such that he felt low and diminutive facing the enormous desk and the Minister who seemed to authoritatively tower over him. "Yes," he answered obsequiously. "At least I think so."

The Minister frowned. "Did you say you think so?"

William Worthington looked up at the Minister of Cultural Affairs and then beyond her, past the national and presidential flags that framed the large window behind the desk and which afforded a spectacular view of the colonnaded monument to the war dead that sat on a rolling hillside across the river. "Yes," he said. "The man is an eccentric, to say the least. I had the feeling the whole while I was talking to him that he was not even listening to me, that he was not at all interested in the fact that he is going to receive the Nolebody Medal. It's hard to believe that this man is the same person who has half the world talking. If I didn't know better, I would have concluded that the Leonard Bentwood I met is not the same Leonard Bentwood who is to be awarded the nation's highest honor."

"Well are you certain it was him?" the Minister asked with a tone suddenly tinged with irritation. And when William Worthington said yes, that the woman at the local post office had assured him that the Leonard Bentwood who resided at the end of the desert canyon was the same Leonard Bentwood whom he had described, the Minister shook her head and sighed.

She had had misgivings about sending her assistant on the errand in the first place and was becoming increasingly frustrated by the entire exercise associated with the annual nation's highest honor ceremony. "Eccentrics," she said. "Every single one of them. You would think at least one of them would be a plain old everyday person who is no different than the rest of us." She rotated the enormous leather chair a quarter turn so that she could look out the window, out over the manicured lawns and gardens, the trimmed hedges and the stately oaks and cherry trees and firs and across the river to the solemn marble columns of the War Memorial. And William Worthington respectfully waited while she pondered the implications of her own observation, until she turned back to face him. "Yesterday," she said sternly and with a concurrent downward nod of her head, "I was informed by Katrina Solatairie's publicist that she will require a suite and a masseuse. And that we will need to accommodate her Pomeranian, also. And keep in mind, Ms.

Solatairie is only a category awardee. If the category award winners think they can act that way, think of what we can expect from the Nolebody Medal winner."

William Worthington smiled weakly. "I suspect I will have to follow up on Mr. Bentwood," he said. "As far as I can determine, he has no agent or assistant to take care of appointments and the like." And even as he spoke he noticed how in the window light the Minister's hair and the silken braids and tassels that fringed the flags that stood on either side of the window all appeared to have been dyed precisely the same royal golden color. Had he been more observant he would have noticed also that her eyes were the same ambiguous brown as the eyes of the raptor on the presidential flag. And that the shafts of the arrows or spears or whatever it was that was being held in the bird's talons were of that color also. And that her dress was more or less of the same blue as that on the banner and ribbons that flowed and draped around the raptor like the fluttering robes of the angelic figures in the frescos on the dome of the National Museum.

"Yes. I was about to ask you to do just that, William," she said, and her authoritative voice pulled him out of his reverie. "I would calendar a follow-up inquiry, just to make sure. Three weeks before the ceremony, or something like that. Hopefully, you will have found an easier way to communicate with him by then. To be honest, I do not much care for his work. But the public response over the years has been overwhelming. And the President has insisted."

"I'm not sure how I feel about it myself," William Worthington answered. He wanted to tell her about the dirt road into Leonard Bentwood's canyon and how he had boldly navigated it without concern for his own wellbeing. "There is a certain creativity to it, I suppose. But it seems so primitive. On the other hand, it would not be the first time ..." He stopped without finishing the sentence. Instead, he continued with a different thought. "I will admit, though, he certainly has found himself a remote enough place for his artist's hideaway. You would not believe what one must go through to get there."

The Minister of Cultural Affairs had resumed looking out the window while William Worthington was speaking. She had observed two men who seemed to be acting suspiciously near the War Memorial and was wondering whether they were up to something. After a while she noticed it had grown quiet in the room and she turned back to look at her assistant. She had tired of the subject. "Did you learn anything about him?" she asked. "Biographically, I mean. The President is going to need to say something about these people and right now we have no idea what to say about our guest of honor, Mr. Bentwood."

William Worthington twisted in his seat. "I tried to get some information. He's just not the talkative type. I asked him how he viewed his career with the benefit of twenty-twenty hindsight. You know what he answered? He said, 'Hindsight isn't twenty-twenty unless you've had your vision corrected.' That was the extent of the interview. I tried other ways to get something out of him too. Believe me. But in the end I had to be content just to make sure he knew about the award ceremony and the details." And then William Worthington added, "I don't see how anyone can live like that. He doesn't even have running water."

9

The Minister of Cultural Affairs would have been chagrined to learn that at that moment the President was conducting a closed meeting down the street, in the secluded and private confines of the library of his official residence, with the Home Secretary and several other high advisors present and no one taking notes or otherwise recording what was said. The Home Secretary had just made her recommendation and the President was less than pleased. "What kind of an idiotic statement is that? 'We need to sit tight and see what happens.' Sit tight my ass. I could have gotten better advice from Spangler, for God's sake." The President reached down and apologetically petted an old retriever lying on the exotic foreign rug in the center of the sitting area, right in the middle of the section of the library where the five officials had collected. "What about the rest of you? Is that all you can come up with? We're on the edge of anarchy and the best advice I can get is, gee, let's be calm and see what happens?"

A quiet filled the library, as if the meaning of silence itself was being absorbed into the pages of the archived volumes that were neatly arranged, row upon leather-bound row, on the dark maple, glass-fronted bookcases that towered over and around them. A silence absolute and regretful, as though something had been said that starkly offended the sensibilities of the patriarchs of the nation whose portraits adorned the walls and whose profiles and busts emerged from the shelves, from pedestals, from antique writing desks, from out of the ambiguity of the past.

The President paced back and forth across the length of the rug, each time stepping over or around the retriever whose eyes followed his progress with an uncertain distrust, back and forth, back and forth. The President turned on a sudden to face the Home Secretary. "What is it about martial law that frightens everyone so much? Can someone explain that to me? Why is it a better choice to have too few police when we can supplement the police with an army if and when it is necessary?"

The Home Secretary finally summoned the courage to answer. "I continue to believe, Mr. President," she said with an air of formality that belied the close relationship she maintained with the President, "that it would be premature to invoke martial law at this time. To date, there have only been a few disturbances and the local authorities have kept the peace in reasonable order. My concern is that the sudden appearance of troops on the street, the sudden revelation that we even have troops, will only catalyze the radicals and throw fuel on the fire."

The President said nothing.

Nor did the National Advisor on Internal Matters, who for several minutes now had been standing by the window and idly watching two men dressed in black who seemed to be loitering near the National War Memorial, which stood just to the left of the presidential residence. He turned back toward the conferees and smiled languidly. "I suppose Elaine is right for the moment," he said. "Remember, we are prohibited by treaty from having troops. Still, I suspect the time will come when what the President proposes will be necessary. Mark my words: there is no going back at this point. We can only continue with our original plan and hope it comes to fruition before the public rebels against us."

Followed by more of the same utter silence, in which

everyone in the room looked about at everyone else, deeply into each other's eyes with their mouths pursing and expressing their mutual discomfort with the present state of affairs. Until the President rose and said, "Well, then. That will be our decision for the moment." He shook hands solemnly with the four advisors who had risen in unison. He thanked each of them separately, and then he ushered them to the door and thanked them again and then turned back into the library, shutting the door behind him. "Shit," he said out loud once he was alone. "If I wanted that kind of advice I would have asked the Minister of Cultural Affairs."

10

Leonard Bentwood looked deep into Frieda Haster's eyes for more, but she had nothing more to say. "Your mother is ill," she had told him when he asked where his mother's weekly letter was, and then she had said nothing else even when Leonard waited patiently for it. So they sat at the picnic table where they always sat, twenty feet or so to the left of Leonard Bentwood's shack, shaded from the midday heat with the brushy acacia that rose up all around them doing little to cut the breeze that danced Leonard's thinning and longish hair in ways that caused the silvery gray to deflect first light and then shadow.

Tears formed and Leonard let them form and fall down his cheeks into his graying and wiry beard without bothering to wipe them away. Frieda Haster reached out and dried his face, softening the already soft and lined visage with the moisture of his own sentiment and telling him it would be all right, that he should not worry.

They talked some and then, after a while, Leonard rose without saying anything and went into the shack and came back out with the dented enamel pot and refilled their cups with more of the scalding black coffee, slowly so that the grounds at the bottom of the pot would not pour out also. He laced the coffee with the final remnants of the brandy, finishing the bottle off, one way or another, just as they did most Wednesday afternoons when Frieda delivered the mail. He sat back down at the table and he made a face that looked sad and was meant to show that he was sad.

She reached out and laid her hand atop his. "I've brought you some treats," she said. She got up and walked out to her truck, and Leonard could hear her fumbling with something in the cab, and then she returned with a box filled with the normal items—fruit and flour and beans, cereal, tobacco and nuts, raisins and vegetables and Leonard's art supplies, a block of ice she had kept in a cooler, and a new bottle of brandy, an unopened ream of paper—and also things she had never brought before. A hand-crank phonograph and some records, which Leonard told her he did not want and which she promptly placed back in the box. A hat, which Leonard thanked her for and told her he would wear. A star chart, which Leonard would later try and fail to master. Yesterday's newspaper with the current news.

They talked, as they always did, about Leonard's week and what he had done since they met seven days prior. What he had made. What he had observed. He took her inside and showed her his latest sculpture. She took her time, examined it from a sufficient variety of angles, noted his use of the dried and hardened webbed foot of a duck that upside down looked like an orange and armored wing of a bat, noted how the dried skeleton of the cholla looked almost like coral from the sea, commented on how the forest green of the lichen complemented the dark red stain of the rock. She told him she liked it, the way he incorporated the metal and the steel, and he believed her and they drank their coffee and brandy until she looked over the edge of the cup and asked, "Did you have a visitor this week, Leonard? I'm told someone came by the post office looking for you."

And that caused Leonard to remember the Assistant to the Minister of Cultural Affairs. "Just a salesman," he answered. "I let him ramble on, but I didn't offer to buy anything. I suppose I should have. I felt sorry for him. It looked like the road took a bit out of him, with his shiny shoes and all. But he had some kind of gimmick going and it made me uncomfortable. Reminded me of something from the past, although I can't remember what it was." He stopped for a moment, looked up into Frieda's eyes and, seeing that she did not react to his last statement, continued, "So I just let him deliver his lines, and then I sent him away."

Frieda smiled and they talked of other things and finished their coffee and brandy, with the birds flitting around them and the heat dominant and the light playing off Leonard's hair like the sun on an army of knights on parade, until Leonard said, "My letter is inside." Which meant that Leonard was now ready for her to go.

11

The opening chords of a concerto were playing silently somewhere in the depths of Leonard Bentwood's mind, soft and intimating and incomplete, as Frieda Haster drove off in her pickup truck bearing a rural mail carrier insignia which, too, boasted a raptor with weapons in its talons. If he had once known the full score of the music, its theme, development, cadenza, coda, it was now long forgotten. But the first chords were forever embedded in his mind. They came to him often and played in the unconscious background of his thought without his even knowing it.

He watched as the truck went through the gateposts that to him had no purpose; watched as the truck and Frieda jostled and rattled down the road and then out of sight. And, as always, he was sad to see her leave and he was glad that she had come. He followed the truck's progress by the cloud of dust that rose up and then dispersed westward like the steam from a locomotive riding the rails of the past into a diminishing and distant tomorrow.

The chords of the music repeated themselves again and again, and he tried to remember what music they were from and finally went inside and sat at his table with a piece of paper in front of him and wrote a line and then another and then yet another without ever succeeding in triggering the memory that he sought and which perhaps did not exist.

For well over twenty years now, Frieda Haster had delivered the mail to Leonard Bentwood once a week, every Wednesday, without fail. And Leonard Bentwood was always there, waiting with the sulfur water boiling in the dented enamel coffeepot on the stove and a portion of the bottle of brandy still remaining and a smile as broad and sedate as the desert sky itself. He could never have been aware of it, but from the beginning she had found him to be something of a curiosity, writing his letter once a week to his mother and waiting anxiously for the response and driving the fifty miles into town only when it was necessary to replenish his meager inventory of food and drink and the tools and materials by which he assembled his concoctions and displayed them on the splintered and cracking shelves and walls of his shack.

It was only some years later that Leonard Bentwood came to learn that some form of arrangement eventually had come into being between Frieda Haster and his mother, but he never learned the details and did not care to know. All he now vaguely recalled was that at some point long after he made his way into the desert and his canyon home, long after his faith in Frieda had become absolute and irreversible, Frieda one day had advised him that he was the beneficiary of a trust that provided him with enough money to sustain his particular lifestyle forever, if that is what he wanted. And with time, and at Frieda's subtle bidding, he had altered his regime so that while he still wrote his letters to, and received his letters from his mother on a weekly basis, he no longer drove into the dusty little town and instead relied on Frieda Haster to deliver his groceries and art supplies to him, all with the funds he never saw and with debits and credits to the accounts he never knew existed.

With the passage of time, Leonard withdrew in some respects and yet became more outgoing, more adventuresome in others. He took to venturing out on gathering expeditions, much as he had the day before Frieda Haster delivered the mail and told him that his mother was ill. And then one day he burned the words Pack Rat Haven, Gallery & Curios into a sign, and he placed it on a post along the dirt road that led to his shack. "Do you think that's a good idea?" Frieda had asked him rhetorically. And when Leonard had replied by saying yes, it was the only way to sell his sculptures and hangings without going into town, Frieda said, "Yes, I see your meaning." So the sign remained and on occasion it was spotted by some reckless souls who had made their way into the windswept land or had actually attempted to find Leonard Bentwood's shack after having heard about it from someone else.

After that, the years had gone by for Leonard Bentwood like the flowing water of an artesian spring, with nothing seeming to change while everything changed. The color slowly went out of his thinning hair and his strength imperceptibly withered and the lines in his face multiplied and increased in depth. He no longer went into town, had not used a phone or as much as listened to a radio in over fifteen years, spoke only to those who drove up through the juniper gateposts in a cloud of dust or, even more rarely, whom he encountered on one of his forays into the desert or up into the mountains or to the road-cuts where he collected and compartmentalized the fossilized, compacted, up-thrown, faulted and eroded geology of eons. Or at the local dump and junkyards where he ventured once or twice a year to replenish his supply of metallic and rubber and plastic objects. The rusty springs and bolts and screws and wires, broken dolls and colored bottles and this and that and these and those, and whatever else he fancied might be of interest once it was attached to something else.

Like the flowing water of an artesian spring. Changing, but only imperceptibly, by the slow accretion and avulsion of time itself and nothing else.

12

When she was gone he went back inside his shack and put away the things she had brought. The block of ice in the ancient battered icebox with chrome hinges, followed by the fresh vegetables and fruit. The dry goods in drawers where the mice could not get at them. The glue and wire and tacks in his box of supplies where he could find them when he needed them without having to try to remember where they might be. The hat somewhere to the side and the bottle of brandy on the middle of his table like the centerpiece to his existence that, in some ways at least, it was.

He turned to the newspaper and looked down at it and was unsure that he wanted to read the stories plastered across the front page and on the pages that followed, uncertain as to whether there was risk in knowing what had happened yesterday and what might transpire tomorrow, uncomfortable with being so close to what had just occurred and what was about to happen. Just as he was uneasy with the prospect that the present could be close enough to reach out and intertwine him in today when he had always settled for something more delayed and more removed. For Leonard Bentwood had not read or heard the current news for fifteen years. Maybe twenty. As he looked down at the newspaper he thus felt to be on the ledge of a precipice, peering down into depths he could neither fathom nor comprehend.

That is not to say that Leonard Bentwood was not generally aware of what had happened over the past decade and a half, or even in the last year or even in the last month or two. The news was discarded all over the world, lying everywhere that one might happen to glance, news along the roadsides, news in ditches, in the dumps and even drifting on the sandstorm winds that carried yesterday into today and today into tomorrow. So Leonard Bentwood would find the remnants of the news in outdated newspapers but more often in a torn and faded magazine that had been tossed aside by someone at some former time. And he would pick it up and fold it neatly and stick it in his back pocket or place it in his collecting box or on the passenger seat of his truck, atop the dried mesquite blossoms and leaves coated in the dust of the road, so that he might read what it said later, in the cool confines of his shack in the midday heat, or on his porch with the slow and sensuous rising of the sun or the fading capitulation of the day into the coolness of the evening.

Which meant for Leonard Bentwood that the news did not come in an orderly sequence in which one event logically followed another in accord with the progressive march of time. The news came as it came. Back and forth, with March sometimes following June and an even year following another even year and records being broken and then eclipsed by lesser records and people dying only to be observed in public later and freezes one day and heat waves the next, the moon full and then quartered within the same hour, with nothing in temporal harmony but Leonard Bentwood himself, who absorbed it all with an equanimity that rivaled the theoretical physicists of the day who contended that the universe in which he lived was not even a universe but something less, something smaller than a pinhead and, by dimensions, that much less significant.

13

He filled a tumbler with brandy and took the paper outside and sat on the porch. Placed himself in motion by the simple artifice of pushing back on the rocker and then letting gravity demand the release of the tension. Back. And forth. Back. Forth.

The sun, well past its zenith, moved deeper into the edge of evening. But it was not yet finished for the day; its angle was such that it undercut the eaves of the porch, and it burned with a false noonday intensity that would have been unbearable to the uninitiated. And that is where Leonard Bentwood sat and rocked in his rocker, in the last of the day's sun, sipping at his brandy while he watched a long-nosed lizard sitting motionless, frozen in the heat, waiting and alert, until it instantaneously was in motion, whipping across the sand and rock to snatch and swallow a tiny forlorn insect in a single deadly strike. And then the lizard looked up at Leonard Bentwood and must have concluded that Leonard Bentwood was massively alive and massively dangerous, for it bolted into the brush on an instant and was gone.

Leonard Bentwood picked up the paper and looked at the front page. He noticed first a flag on the upper right-hand corner, a flag of the nation, unfurled and proudly flapping in a fictional wind. Then he saw the stated price (which seemed high), the date (which he had not known), and the expected high and low for the day (which both seemed understated to him, although he did not care). Followed by a headline in rather bold print that said, **SCARE AT WAR MEMORIAL**. And this prompted Leonard to read the headline story, which told how yesterday afternoon two men were arrested on the steps of the War Memorial in the nation's capital only to be released after intensive questioning when it was determined that, despite their suspicious dress and looks and behavior, they had only stopped on their delivery route to eat a sandwich on the lawns in front of the monument and had posed no real threat.

He read the story again, and again, turning deep into the paper each time where the second half of the story was completed in two long and interrupted columns, but never finding what he was looking for since there was no explanation as to what they were wearing or what they looked like or what they were doing that would have triggered their arrest. At least as far as Leonard could tell. He read the story a fourth time, parsed through the few facts—that they had been dressed in black, that their hair was of a certain cut and they of a certain age, that they were nobodies—and again failed to understand. The use of the word "nobody" particularly troubled him. It reminded him of something his visitor from just the other day— the salesman or whatever he was—had told him. Something about nobody or no one or some such.

He shook his head, frustrated with himself. Took another sip of the brandy that had warmed by the deflection of the sun and then again by his own hand. And then he turned the newspaper to the second page and read a story of how unemployment had risen unexpectedly to a new high and how the government's chief economist enthusiastically was forecasting that the surplus of workers was bound to increase in the months ahead and that inflationary pressures and other adversities should thereby be kept at bay. He read some advertisements. One for sporty cars. Another for sharply tailored clothes. Another for paradise vacations where you and a loved one could realize the six days of your dreams for a single price that included everything you might imagine, plus other luxuries of which you probably were not aware. He read the sports page and could not come close to understanding it, which was always the case no matter how dated the sports material he was reading at the moment. Because Leonard Bentwood had always despised statistics, and he long ago had concluded that sports basically was not about winning and losing but rather about the aggregation of statistics. Of how many times or how fast or how high or how long someone accomplished some truly incredible feat. Not who won or lost, because that faded with time. How high. Fast. Frequently. Far. Many. Etc.

And then he decided he would stop reading, not because he had had enough as much as because he found the experience somewhat intriguing and invigorating and because he did not want to overindulge and ruin the sensation in that way. He put the paper down beside him and forgot about it.

The sun fell below the horizon, and the heat retracted by relative degrees. A covey of quail moved across the yard, five adults and almost twice that many chicks, with the adults on guard and the chicks scurrying mindlessly at their heels and all of them pecking at the ground, finding seeds, bugs. A single star shone; a planet no doubt. Then two. Then in multiples and exponentially. And the dark descended on Leonard Bentwood, who sat on his porch with the bottom of his tumbler of brandy still before him, inviting him to nurture it for hours to come, with the moon still to rise and a hint of humidity, a dry but definite and promising scent of creosote faintly rising in the desert evening air.

CHAPTER II

1

When the monsoon finally arrived at Leonard Bentwood's doorstep that year it was with the same unpredictable assuredness by which it always arrived. Assured because the monsoon always came to that part of the world in that season without fail. Unpredictable because it had first to build and lay its foundation of heat and humidity and seasonal flow in proper combination, so that it might arrive in all its fury and glory at the right time and in the proper mood. And it was only the integral, self-placating nature of the monsoon that determined that it was fully prepared.

Leonard Bentwood knew as much. He had already had his rite of monsoonal baptism many years ago, during his very first summer in the desert when he was initiated into the monsoon in utter unawareness and ignorance, immersed in it and nearly drowned by it without the benefit of warning or expectation.

That first year it had come from out of nowhere, the initial storm seemingly the primordial vestige of something concocted dually on the canvass of heaven and in the forges of hell, life-giving and deadly, dramatically furious and dramatically beautiful, imbued with arbitrary power and absolute mystery. And when that first storm had passed, leaving behind a deceptive quiet, Leonard Bentwood had wrongly concluded that it was nothing more than an anomaly that had come once and now was gone and lost to memory. He had gone outside and had stood in the fading mist of the receding rain while the water dripped off the leafless and still thirsting branches and the emaciated cacti, and he had been awed by the sudden calm and the brilliant sunlight that emerged from behind the thinning clouds. Only to quickly learn that the calm was momentary, transient, illusory; for in the days and month and more that had followed, the monsoon had perpetuated itself in endless waves of irregular onslaught in which the skies periodically stormed with an anger that was unsustainably torrential and then indifferent, only to clear, with the humidity and the sweet smell of the rain pervasive and enduring. And then in a few hours, or a day or two days later, the dew point entrenched at a higher level and the demeanor of the desert already more alert and yet not close to being sated, the clouds again would begin to build, off in the distance like faraway mountains of black and billowing smoke, growing larger and taller and spreading even as they marched in ranks across the landscape until one of them would lower its mass of darkness and drive down upon the land. With the wind up first, and then a spattering of light and playful drops of rain and then the real wind, whipping the branches and limbs of the trees and challenging the cacti to bend, break, uproot; the air filled with dust and leaves and pollen, fragments of seed pods, cactus petals, stamens, pistils. Followed always by lightning that did not flash but exploded all around and above, and the thunderous explosions would shake the roof of Leonard Bentwood's little shack and rattle the shelves and give suggestion of life to the sculptures and creations that adorned the walls of his would-be home.

In subsequent years he came to anticipate it, to wait for it just as did everyone and everything else that lived in the desert and arid mountains and the high plain savannahs graced with tall grasses and yucca, scrub oak and prickly pear, agave and antelope and deer. Sometimes impatiently and sometimes almost without any waiting at all when the monsoon came early, ahead of its appointed time.

Many times over the years he had deigned to join the storm, to become a part of it, to sit or stand or walk in it, in the battering gusts and the sheets of rain, beneath the curling dark of the thunderheads and insanely jealous winds. And he had, at times, slept through it, through a day of it, through night after night of it, with the rain blowing through the openings in the walls, and the wind becoming part of the atmosphere inside the shack, and the roof and the walls of the shack groaning and threatening to capitulate long before it stopped.

He had been through the long and heavy monsoons that washed out the roads and cut streams through the desert in places where it seemed water could never have flowed; when it had drowned the mountains with floods that flashed from out of nowhere and took out tree and rock and log and creature and even creek bed with a calculated indifference that demanded that the world be cleansed anew. And he had been through monsoons that were filled with disappointment, that teased and tempted and tantalized but never served up the quantities of desperately needed moisture they could only pretend to carry with them. And, almost always, he had been gladdened when it was gone, when the monsoon was done and the heat had returned in slight moderation and the desert was drying and then was dried again, and all had resumed to be as it had been before, with the rejuvenation of the desert guaranteed for at least another season.

2

In this particular year, the year in which William Worthington found Leonard Bentwood, the monsoon had come early and it had come on strong. With each passing storm, the rain lasted longer than the norm. And the winds blew stronger, with more avarice and destructive determination.

Leonard Bentwood sat on his rocker on the porch, watching as the storms again began to form over the highlands to the south, spotty patches of dark clouds that emerged from out of nothingness, like a menace bred out of a dark and unseen cauldron in the ether. At the moment, they were remote and unintimidating, little more than dark and diminutive caps drifting at low altitudes past mountain and over desert plain. But Leonard knew they had time, that it was only an hour past noon and that the storms preferred to unleash later in the day, after the combination of heat and convection and atmospheric pressure had sufficiently coalesced the potential for havoc into the reality of chaos. So he sat and waited for an hour and more, occupied himself by continuing to try to remember the same thing he had been trying to remember now for three days running.

He didn't even know what it was, but he knew that he had forgotten something that he needed to recall. He had tried. He had consumed page after page of a single side of the bleached typing paper, scribbling notes, jotting down ideas, searching for words that might reestablish the memory, stimulate recollection, remind of something tangential that might lead him closer to the answer. But it had been a waste of time and had wasted time that was needed for other purposes, in that he had not yet written his letter to his mother and it was mail day and Frieda would soon arrive and he had no letter to give her to send to his mother from whom he had not heard a word for two weeks.

He made one final attempt. He picked up the dulled pencil and wrote in his broad script the first thing that came to his mind, and then the next, and then the next—a body, my body, no body—until in frustration he wrote, I am tired of all this not remembering, and then he uncharacteristically and almost in anger threw the pencil out into the yard, onto the ground that even then was beginning to be darkened by occasional splashes of rain.

He began his letter to his mother in the same way he always did. Dear Mama, he wrote. And then he told her of all that he had done and seen during the week; and of the rains and the way the frogs and toads had suddenly appeared, although not in as great numbers as in some years gone past. He asked how she felt. He told her that he missed hearing from her and said how Frieda had mentioned that he might have to make the trip and go and see her soon. He said how Frieda had brought him a newspaper and he had read it, or at least some of it, and found it interesting in some ways and sad in others. And he would have said more, perhaps about his latest sculptures or maybe of a recent dream, had he not heard the muffled sound of a vehicle coming up the road and the splash of tires running over the muddy surface and the grinding of the gears that he knew to be the gears of Frieda's high-axled truck making its way along the sinuous track into his desert canyon. He picked up what there was to the letter and signed it affectionately and folded it three times and placed it under his coffee mug. And then he walked out from underneath the cover of the eaves and into the desert sand that was actually moist, and he waited for

Frieda Haster as an occasional drop of rain struck him lightly and coolly, like the moisturizing caress that it was.

3

The sound of the truck came closer, and Leonard Bentwood thought there was something wrong about it, that there was something wrong with Frieda's truck. That the incongruous combination of noises coming up his desert easement—the familiar and steady meshing of gears that he knew to be Frieda's pickup, and the irregular revving and racing, downshifting and upshifting that he had never before heard—implied that she was having some kind of problem with the differential or the linkage. But he should have known better and in fact he did know better. He had possessed his own pickup for far longer than Frieda had owned hers, and the only reason his was still running was because he had found a manual in the dump years ago and had learned how to keep it running. So he knew enough about trucks and had learned about them on his own; or, more aptly, with the aid of a man named Hoaggie, who owned the local dump and who traded him parts in periodic exchange for one of Leonard's sculptures or masks and who always appeared most grateful for the trade and patted Leonard gently on the back when they parted ways.

That was one of Leonard Bentwood's universities, as they say. His schooling in the vocation of early model, eight-cylinder, four-wheel drive, short-bed pickup truck maintenance. Several times a year he would make his way to the dump with several of his creations lying on the passenger seat or in the truck bed, and Hoaggie would listen as Leonard described the truck's symptoms and then tell Leonard what he needed to fix it.

And then Hoaggie would find the item in the vast and always growing graveyard of cars and vehicles and would take in exchange the sculpture or curiosities that Leonard had brought with him, telling Leonard that he gave the peculiar faces and figures and abstractions to his wife, who hung them on the walls of their home or placed them on display so that visitors to their household might enjoy the marvels of her ever-growing collection. And then Leonard would take the truck parts back to his shack and sometimes fix the truck by himself but more often wait for Frieda to deliver the mail and then help him with the valves or the seals or the cap or the pump or whatever it was that time around.

So Frieda knew trucks also, and she certainly knew her own, with which she had bonded long ago as she drove her rural desert and mountain mail routes in solitude and seclusion, month after month and season upon season, encountering and besting every absurd condition and event and improbability that one might expect to observe in the Sunday funny pages. Rockslides and avalanches in the mountains, floods, sandstorms in the desert, accidents and suicidal herds of antelope, and even snowstorms, ice, hail in the narrow months of winter, with the truck purring steadily along through the years, holding the road and rarely requiring more than the patching of a tire or replacement of a joint or the realignment of the frame that had been torqued and bent and straightened so many times that it almost seemed to be metamorphic in design.

Leonard thus really knew that Frieda's truck could not be the sole cause of the noisy contradiction coming up his road. He listened more intently to the tandem sounds as they rose and fell with a certain inharmonious consistency, winding their way through the shallow desert ravines and around the little foothills and approaching his desert canyon with increasing volubility. And then he realized that what he had already suspected was correct, which was that two trucks approached, not one.

Frieda Haster pulled up first, smoothly and slowly with her high-axled pickup easing through the gateposts on which it was likely that no gate ever would be hung and coming to an easy stop with the engine purring and Frieda all smiles and waving at Leonard through the windshield. And then the second truck came, too fast and still bouncing on its rear springs from the encounter with the last pothole just yards before, through the gateposts at too high a speed, mud splattered across its sides and over the entirety of the windshield and even across the hood and the roof, as though it had been doused with a dripping and grainy icing the color of the desert floor.

By then, Frieda had walked up to Leonard Bentwood and had kissed him lightly on his bearded cheek. The two of them turned and watched as the second truck came in and the engine was finally cut and the driver slid out from behind the steering wheel and onto the ground. This time not in a suit and not wearing shiny and polished shoes, but dressed in light khaki pants and matching short-sleeved shirt and wearing brown leather boots with heavy black soles that were made for trudging on forest trail and hard rock surface. Although he still had with him his briefcase with the braided leather handle and the brass combination lock which Leonard Bentwood again subconsciously noticed and subconsciously desired.

The man walked toward Frieda Haster and Leonard Bentwood, hurried toward them with a highly animated jaunt in his step, almost as though he had reason to believe that they were expecting and waiting for him. "I almost rolled it," he said with a nervous laugh as he strode up, his head bobbing about in a peculiar manner that itself implied enthusiasm, self-satisfaction. "At that last turn. After that face you've got stuck on the post. I'm pretty sure I was on two wheels. Thought I'd lost it." He looked back at the truck, the words on its side reading Ministry of Interior, Depot 213, For Government Use Only, and the governmental seal only partially visible through the muddy splashes and stain. And he smiled at it as though the truck were a fond pet with whom he had enjoyed yet another memorable adventure.

He came up directly, face-to-face with Frieda Haster and Leonard Bentwood, almost too close, too intimate, so that he could not have missed the way Frieda's hazel irises sparkled in the desert sun as though they themselves were part of the native surroundings. He began to say something to her but then stopped himself. He instead turned to Leonard and said, "Hello Mr. Bentwood. Nice to see you again." And Leonard Bentwood stared at him with a puzzled look that showed he did not recognize him.

"It's William Worthington," William Worthington said. And then he added with a hint of pride as he looked over to Frieda Haster who stood lithely by Leonard Bentwood's side, "You remember; the Assistant to the Minister of Cultural Affairs; I was here a week or so ago." He finally turned to directly face Frieda Haster.

"Good morning, ma'am," he said as he stuck out his hand. "I'm with the government." And then he looked over at Frieda's truck and saw the metallic sign that had been stuck on the side of her truck stating Mail Carrier and which was emblazoned with the same governmental seal as adorned his vehicle, the same banners and ribbons, the same bird of prey tightly clinging to the arrows or spears or whatever they were. "I see we have the same employer," he added.

And Frieda replied, "In a manner of speaking. I'm a contract mail carrier," she said. "I'm not legally an employee of the government. No insurance and unemployment and all that, I mean. No paid holidays. No retirement. I'm a nobody," she said.

And William Worthington said somewhat coolly in return, "I see."

The sky out of the south was now completely dark. It had lowered and spread itself out so that everything in that direction, and to the southeast as well, was black and moving northward, inexorably toward Leonard Bentwood's canyon, enveloping the desert around it and the mountains behind it in a shroud of marbled and roiling purple. It began to rain in earnest as they stood there and Frieda Haster and William Worthington and, less hurriedly, Leonard Bentwood instinctively moved toward the porch and then onto the porch and under the cover of the eaves. Thunder rolled, not far off, to the south. The sound of it tumbled through the dark mass of cloud unevenly and then faded away. The wind began to gust and the branches of the mesquite and the palo verde bent and swayed and danced, and the air filled with static, dust, moisture. Leonard Bentwood and Frieda Haster and William Worthington all leaned against the wall of the shack, backed away from the weather as far as they could without seeking the shelter of the interior of Leonard Bentwood's shack, and watched the storm pass through with the wind cutting across the porch and the moisture striking at their faces and skin and the three of them entranced and invigorated after their own fashion and with their thoughts entirely to themselves.

4

It lasted only twenty minutes, in which time a deluge of rain had fallen and the already saturated ground was saturated again and most of the mud had been washed off the truck that William Worthington had picked up at the airport government car pool, many hundreds of miles from where they now stood. The storm, or what was left of it, moved north, and the wind receded entirely, and the sun broke through and bore down on Leonard Bentwood's shack.

Leonard Bentwood and Frieda Haster and William Worthington walked out into the sunlight. They stood and looked around and someone might have made a meaningless comment about the power and brevity of the storm before Leonard looked over at Frieda and then at William Worthington and then back at Frieda, as much as apologizing to her for the violation of their privacy. "Any mail?" he said.

And Frieda said guardedly, "No, Leonard, she's still in the same condition. The doctor says she might be feeling better next week, but we will have to see. I have your groceries," she said. "And I brought you another paper, if you want it." She looked over at William Worthington who had been picking the mud out of the treads of his new boots while he politely tried to ignore their conversation. She looked back at Leonard Bentwood questioningly and then she turned back to Worthington and said, "Did you say you work for the Minister of Cultural Affairs?"

William Worthington smiled proudly. He tossed a piece of the mud into the brush. "Yes, I did. Minister Frasier. I am in charge of the Nolebody Awards Ceremony this year and have been sent out, for the second time, I might add, to talk to Mr.

Bentwood."

Frieda Haster moved toward William Worthington with the speed of a striking snake. Her hand darted out and she seized William Worthington by the elbow and led him away from the porch and then into the middle of the yard. She looked back at Leonard Bentwood. "Excuse us for a moment, Leonard. I think I have some mail that belongs to Mr. Worthington." And then, still holding the Assistant to the Minister of Cultural Affairs firmly by the arm, she led him over to her truck and opened the driver's side door and engaged him in a heated conversation that started with her speaking in a low voice and then him responding in a low voice and then each of them becoming more and more animated, apparently vigorously discussing something, their arms flying up into the air and their hands making gestures of surprise and emphasis for what seemed like a half hour but which really was only fifteen minutes. By which time Leonard Bentwood had given up waiting and had gone inside and poured three full glasses of brandy and had come back out and now was sitting in his rocker waiting for their discussion to conclude.

Frieda Haster and William Worthington finally came back to the porch in obvious silence and at a close yet safe distance from each other, like two fighting cocks that had engaged and had been separated but were not yet through with their encounter. Leonard Bentwood sensed the tension but could not understand it. He suggested they sit and join him in a brandy, only to feel waves of disappointment, rejection, confusion when Frieda replied by saying that she couldn't, that there had been a mix-up at the post office, that she still had deliveries to make, that the weather was creating problems for everyone, that she would not be able to stay and talk.

She looked over at William Worthington, expectantly, with a glare that demanded. And William Worthington finally said, "I'm afraid I will have to decline also. I came here to give you something, Mr. Bentwood. But I seem to have left it back in my office. I'll be back, though, Mr. Bentwood," he added, and he looked back at Frieda Haster defiantly. "I'll take you up on your offer then."

Leonard put his tumbler of brandy down on the wooden planks of the porch, under the rocker where he always placed it, and he rose but remained silent. The birds had come out after the rain, phainopepla and finches, a mockingbird, all of them singing and flitting about as though they had not been in the air and in the open for months, as if they had just been freed from cages in which they had been long restrained. A lizard crept out from under some object that rested against the wall of the shack and climbed vertically next to the window. William Worthington seemed captivated by the sudden activity, by the mechanical jerks of the lizard's head as it surveyed its surroundings from this different angle, by the cacophony of the birds and their reckless flight paths through the rising air and dripping branches. And then Frieda Haster said his name, calling him to follow her off the porch.

She led William Worthington back to his truck, opened the door for him and waited for him to get in. She closed it behind him and then she spoke. "I think we understand each other, Mr. Worthington," she said with a particularly firm, instructive tone. "As Mr. Bentwood's guardian, I am permitted to insist that all communications with Mr. Bentwood go through me. I alone will determine whether to show them to him and whether he will respond and, if so, what the response will be. Do we understand each other?"

William Worthington was not looking at her, but rather through the windshield and in the direction of the shack. There was something bothering him, more than one thing actually, but he could not put his finger on any of it. "I understand what you are saying, Ms. Haster," he finally answered. "I will not argue about it here. You know what my standing instructions as a government employee are. But I will tell you this much. I cannot accept your contention that Mr. Bentwood should not be awarded the Nolebody Medal. The government will not sit by and have you dictating policy and cultural decisions, Ms. Haster. No matter how much you might wish for it."

He rolled up the window of the truck, decided against it, rolled it back down and leaned out of it slightly, staining his khaki shirt with the last remnants of the mud that stuck on the door panel. Instantly he wished that he had done something that would have made him appear more sophisticated, more manly to Frieda Haster. "I will be back, Ms. Haster," he said. "And I will have the appropriate paperwork with me. You can be assured of that." And then he turned the truck and drove off at too high a speed so that the shocks and the springs of the truck did not have sufficient time to absorb the jolts delivered to them.

Frieda Haster turned to her own vehicle, opened the door and pulled out the box filled with Leonard Bentwood's weekly groceries and sundries, lifted it out and carried it over to the shack. She told Leonard what she had brought, pulling out each item one by one and telling him what it was. Leonard Bentwood became more and more perplexed as he stared down into the box, until she had taken out everything but the newspaper that lay on the bottom, and which Leonard Bentwood reached for and took before she could say anything against it.

"My letter is ready," Leonard Bentwood said as they carried the items inside.

And Frieda Haster answered, "I knew it would be."

5

The Nolebody Medal, of course, was named after Philip T. Nolebody, the great industrial magnate and philanthropist born late in the prior century and whose ambitious foresight and determination served as the foundation for the nation's growth and ultimate ascension to preeminence in the hierarchy of nations.

Philip Nolebody was directly responsible for the creation and efficiency of the nation's transportation sector; and it was Philip Nolebody who found ways to exploit the natural resources of the nation efficiently and to their full extent, the mineral and petroleum deposits, the forests and rangelands, the lakes and rivers and streams and coastlines, the very sky; and it was Philip Nolebody who wisely proposed that the nation's capital be moved to a more centralized locale where the needs of all the nation's people could be addressed and administered efficiently from relative equidistance. It was Philip Nolebody who provided the capital for the intensive research and development that led to the mass production of the antiviral vaccine PTN247 and the eradication of the millennium virus. It was Philip Nolebody who developed human resource processes by which the work of twenty could be performed in half the time by one. It was Philip Nolebody's manufacturing and technical prowess that supplied the armament that ensured victory in the great wars that interrupted and then invaded his life; and it was Philip Nolebody who provided the ultimate guidance for global reconstruction in the aftermath of the first war and whose legacy largely eliminated any need for reconstruction after the second and third. And it was only through the contributions and generosity of Philip T. Nolebody in his latter years that the arts, sport, the sciences, the very cultural and philosophical underpinnings of the nation had survived the wars, the pestilence, the economic malaise and societal upheavals of the time in which he lived and which he dominated as its greatest influence.

That was the official history of Philip T. Nolebody anyway. The history that was recited and recalled in the books and biographies and classrooms and governmental brochures and encyclopedias and portrayed by portraitists and muralists and sculptors, by those who named streets and schools and bridges and a plethora of animate and inanimate objects after the memory of Philip Nolebody. The Philip T. Nolebody Tunnel. The Philip Nolebody School for the Blind. The Nolebody Sportster. Nolebody Avenue. Nolebody Borough. The Nolebody Doctrine. Nolebody Creek, and Draw and Spring. Nolebody This. Nolebody That. And then there was the other history— the real history of Philip T. Nolebody—that lay hidden and all but lost amid the scraps of subtle evidence and brittle and crumbling fragments of the truth, buried in dusty basement archives or moldering in libraries and attics and scrapbooks, long ago faded and gradually disintegrating into a rusted flakey brown of nothingness. Into nothingness with the passage of time and the accumulation of intentional misinformation and negligent omission and conveniently forgetful oversight.

The truth, then, of Philip Nolebody—the real, honest-to-God, in-actual-fact unaltered truth, that is—was that he came to his riches by a fortuitous chemistry that involved the normal measure of immorality and greed, mixed with an extra dose of corruption, amalgamated and catalyzed to perfect and supersaturated crystallization by the heat and precipitant cooling of mathematical accident. By the purest form of luck, compounded by the most statistically unlikely run of good fortune, exacerbated by the most fortuitous twists of fate, all enhanced constantly by a rapacious and imperious dishonesty and disinterest in anything other than personal aggrandizement and accumulation. All of it culminating in the invention and patenting and ultimate sale to the government, on financial terms that exceeded precedent and forever would alter the thinking of economists, of the Nolebody Vaccine, which brought an instant and permanent end not only to war as it was then known but to virtually every other manifestation of mass violence, whether in the form of organized rebellion or protest, or in the guise of spontaneous eruptions in the form of riots or panic- or greed-driven stampede.

Philip T. Nolebody thereby became the most singularly and spectacularly rich and powerful private person in the world and, indeed, that the world had ever seen. He wallowed in his success, playing host to the leaders of the world, courted and entertained and solicited by them; building mansions beyond description, with so many rooms that measures (both sophisticated and mundane) had to be taken to ensure that visitors and staff did not become permanently lost within their walls; proposing with an imperious insistence that the very framework of society be altered to accommodate the new world order that was reinforced by the Nolebody Vaccine. Only to slowly and then with increasing rapidity lose his faculties—

first his coordination and then his memory and then his mind at an early midlife age. Initially forgetting merely the trivial, and then, one day, something of far greater import, and finally his name and where he was and how to speak and write and stand and maybe even how to understand words if indeed he heard them at all.

After which, after a mental death in which he still lived in an oblivion of unawareness, his wife, who never loved him and whom he had never loved, defeated the attempts of his friends and enemies (for he had plenty of both) and neighbors and relatives and even the government to pilfer his estate by every conceivable argument known under the laws of probate and fraud and contract and taxation, by giving it all away, creating a foundation in his name. Just to spite him. For in his conscious knowing life, Philip T. Nolebody had never given as much as a single silver coin or gift or compliment to another person.

"The whole purpose of capitalism," Philip Nolebody said more than once in speeches, in interviews, in his writings, "is to get other people's money." To which he easily could have added, "All of it," without straying in the least from the pinnacle of his ambition. But he was not known for that; he was known for his charity and constructive foresight. And the Nolebody Medal helped to ensure that he would always be remembered in that redeeming light.

A few years after the death of Philip Nolebody, during yet another of those periods in which humanity was tested by unforeseen and inexplicable trauma—trauma largely self-inflicted by the human species' penchant for the theatre of the self-impugning absurd—the then-president had decreed that thereafter, on an annual basis, one or more of the nation's most influential citizens would be named as the recipient of the

Nolebody Medal, which would be the highest honor that could be bestowed upon a civilian member of the population. The announcement, and the awarding of the medal, was meant to be a palliative to the people, a sedative of sorts, an amusement, a distraction. It purported to recognize Philip Nolebody's contribution to society by recognizing that of others.

In the year in which the award was created, a dozen recipients were named. They were and they became the heroes of the nation, made paradigms of sportsmanship and inventiveness and creative expression as the result of their service in fields of medicine and discovery, for a contribution to the maintenance of the peace. And so on and on into the future. But as time passed, it became more and more evident that the sheer number of awardees was undermining the meaning and the purpose of the Nolebody Medal, which was intended to placate the public by giving them something to anticipate and debate and, ultimately, with which to relate. Two types of Nolebody Awards thus were created—the more numerous Nolebody Category Awards, which were allocated according to twelve vaguely defined vocations—sport, medicine, music, engineering, the graphic arts, and so on—and the Nolebody Medal, which was given to only one person in any given year. To be named the recipient of the Nolebody Medal thus gained even greater meaning, both to its recipients and to the general public, which the government perceived was greatly in need of heroes and role models and the like.

The Nolebody Medal itself was something to behold—the gold medallion sported a relief of Philip T. Nolebody, his name, the span of his years and, on the reverse side, the omnipresent seal of the government with the proud raptor staring sternly and boldly into space and its weapons of war clutched in its talons and its banners of victory and glory flowing around it like the robes of an emperor from the distant past.

The number of those who had been honored with the Nolebody Medal was not so great that enthusiasts with a good memory and a little study could not recite the name of every recipient and perhaps provide some minor biographical details to go along. And given that those who were honored were typically in their later years, it was always the case that the number of living honorees amounted only to a dozen or so at any particular time.

There had been doctors of medicine and doctors of philosophy and doctors of this and that. There had been an occasional athlete and musician and writer and once, on an off year, a socialite and twice, in times of political contentiousness, former politicians, and once even a religious figure, albeit of the lowest rank, and a steady stream of other luminaries and dignitaries from most, but not all, echelons of the rich and not so rich but always famous. Always famous.

Naturally, the Nolebody Medal was not to be granted to someone who was against something else. The award commemorated affirmation, not rejection. No atheist had ever been awarded the nation's highest honor. Nor, understandably, had any critic of literature or the arts. Nor had anyone who advocated revolutionary political thought. No equalitists nor plebicists nor libertarians. Nor had they and their ilk ever been considered; and, indeed, no such person had ever been knowingly invited to the awards ceremony and none would have been knowingly admitted had they appeared with a purportedly official invitation in hand and attempted to gain admission to the spectacle. Because while the awarding of the Nolebody Category Awards and the Nolebody Medal—the nation's highest honor—was advertised as a celebration of the people, it really was nothing of the sort. It was the vestige of an idea of a presidential counselor from a different era who once advised that the nation needed some good old-fashioned uplifting and who proposed that the spirit of the land could be reinforced by handing out medals to the civilian sector, just as had been done in the past for the military sector, back when there were still wars, and a means had to be found to maintain morale and recruitment and support for battles yet to come.

6

William Worthington sat uncomfortably in his office chair, a high-backed cloth-upholstered abomination that had been designed with no regard for the physiology of the human back or the human pelvis and instead had been conceived and fabricated based on government specifications designed to minimize cost and maximize production. The same chair, in the same bland gray durable fabric with the same awkward rollers, awkward adjustments, awkward appearance, sat at that moment in ten thousand government offices throughout the nation. They had been produced at a factory that once manufactured parts for tanks and military aircraft. The invention and deployment of the Nolebody Vaccine and the resulting Permanent Peace had rendered the factory, or at least its products, obsolete, so the factory had been refitted to produce chairs and tables and children's toys.

William Worthington stared at the government-issue calendar blotter that lay atop his desk, at the date on it marked with a large red star and the letters LB. He thought of the desert road that was really something less than a road that led into the canyon where he had found Leonard Bentwood's barnboard shack, the road on which he had now driven four times, twice in and twice out. He recalled the way the washboard surface had grabbed and shaken him and the government sedan about, vibrating him and the car as would a kitchen appliance incorrectly tuned to a highly specific culinary task; of how, on the second occasion just days ago, the government truck had slid and cut through the muddy ruts in the road and the washes that flowed with water when before there had been only sand and dirt and ground the density of granite or something even harder. And he wished that he were there, alone in the mystery of the desert where there was so much to learn and explore and observe in contrast to his sterile office at the Ministry of Cultural Affairs where the business of the day was to instill cultural norms in a culture that was nowhere close to normal.

He bent down next to his chair where his briefcase rested. He dialed the combination of the lock and pulled out the photo he had taken of the truck with the mud still splattered on its sides. He placed it on his desk, leaning it against the drinking glass in which he kept his pencils and pens, all of which bore the official imprint of the government. As he stared at the photo, scenes of the harsh desert landscape flashed through his thought and a broad smile spread across his face. And somewhere in those scenes, deep within some subconscious realm of his mind, he saw also Frieda Haster, the seductive shape of her mouth, the thickness of her graying hair, the way her tanned face matched the desert's hue, how womanly and natural and alluring she had seemed in her faded jeans and cotton shirt.

There was still more than a week before the deadline for

responses would come and pass, but William Worthington now knew that Leonard Bentwood would not meet it, that there would be no written response stating, yes, Leonard Bentwood was honored to learn that he had been selected to receive the Nolebody Medal and, yes, he was pleased to confirm that he would be present at the ceremony. Because Frieda Haster had made it clear that she would not allow it.

A great deal had transpired in the past two weeks. The false arrest of two innocent bystanders at the War Memorial had catalyzed a subtle remobilization of the nonviolent protest movement. The ensuing work stoppages had brought commerce largely to a halt. The President had dismissed several of his main domestic advisors and then had advised the nation, in a rare speech lasting all of four minutes, that it was merely coincidence that they had all resigned in the same week for family or personal or professional reasons that remained unspecified and unimagined. Martial law, or what was better known as martial society, again had been imposed to ensure that essential goods and services were provided to the degree necessary to keep the government in operation and the people fed if not placated. Which meant that the secondary, public economy had again shut down, leaving only the primary governmental sector functioning in its standby mode (to use the phrases coined by Dr. Melingore, one of last year's recipients of a Nolebody Category Award).

All of this was highly disruptive for the normal government worker and even more so for William Worthington, who was involved in the more sophisticated workings of the government, at the ministerial level. He now had to prepare his own meals at breakfast and lunch and dinner instead of dining on the catered meals to which he and his fellow officemates at the

Ministry of Cultural Affairs had become accustomed. He had to wash his own dishes, empty his own garbage, clean his own toilet. On his flight back south and then his drive to the desert and canyon land where Leonard Bentwood lived, he had been forced to buy his gas at government stations and his food at the government dispensaries and to stay at the modular hotel that catered only to government employees who were traveling on government business. Even his personal life was implicated by the imposition of martial society, for so long as it lasted he was prohibited by law from socializing or even communicating with those from the private sector, which included his neighbors and some of his friends and indeed most of the population of the capital city.

His phone rang and he ignored it and it rang again and again until he finally picked it up. "Yes," he said abruptly, impolitely. And the voice on the other end said, "William, this is Marsha Solinsky. Minister Frasier's secretary. You are late for your appointment. What shall I tell the Minister?"

"I'll be there in three minutes," William Worthington answered in a flustered voice. But Marsha Solinsky had already hung up.

7

The Minister of Cultural Affairs was not waiting for William Worthington when he opened the door and stepped into the Minister's reception area. She was already in the process of leaving without him. He came through the door half out of breath with his tie in need of adjustment and briefcase in hand and ran directly into the Minister who said, "I'm glad you could make it," before she walked right past him and through the door, and he followed behind her like a sad and neglected dog.

They took the Minister's private lift down to the main floor and then walked through the marble vaulted foyer, across the mosaic of the government seal and past the marble guard desk and then through the electronic doors and out onto the building's apron. Only then did the Minister stop. She turned to William Worthington and said, "Tell it to me again. All of it, I mean. Who this Haster person is. And where she gets her authority. And what Leonard Bentwood has to say about it."

William Worthington drew a breath and then sighed. Beyond the Minister of Cultural Affairs and along the entire edge of Nation's Park, he could see the throngs of people who had been gathering in greater and greater numbers every day for a week. They stood and sat in silence, on the steps and beneath the columns of the Justice Center and along the many thoroughfares that crissed and crossed the capital complex, in the gardens of the National Museum and National Conservatory and the People's Library, gathering in silence, men and women, teens, the elderly, children in strollers and cribs, on bicycles, with walkers, on crutches, some with dogs, at every place they could find room, including on the steps of the Cultural Affairs Building, on top of every fountain, every statue, every tree.

"Frieda Haster is a contract mail carrier; a nobody. That's all I can learn about her. The Office of General Counsel says her filings and documentation are valid. That she is Leonard Bentwood's legal guardian. As for Leonard Bentwood—I couldn't say, since Ms. Haster will not allow me to talk to him." William Worthington shrugged his shoulders, indicating that he would offer more information if only he could and silently wishing that Frieda Haster were not involved in what was rapidly becoming an unpleasant situation.

The Minister of Cultural Affairs shook her head in disgust. "We'll see about that," she said, and she turned and headed down the marble steps, with William Worthington following behind and the capital security forces ensuring with little effort that the passive crowds stayed behind the barriers and that there was room to pass. As they walked down the long, uninterrupted flight of marble steps, no one said a word; not the protestors who carried no signs and offered no facial expressions and instead stood or sat and watched in utter silence; not the Minister, who took each step with her indifferent gaze fixed directly and ambivalently toward the front; not William Worthington, who twice tripped as his head moved from side to side taking in a sweeping panorama of the crowds; not the security officers, who did nothing other than to stand in silence, facing the crowds and staring over them, out into the skies along the horizon where their eyes met neither the humanity below them nor the heavens above.

8

William Worthington had always had an uncomfortable feeling about the Justice Center, although he was never quite sure why that was. In a physical sense, the Justice Center was not significantly different from any other government building in the capital city. The marble with which it had been dressed had come from the same marble quarry as was used to cut the stone for the other government buildings; its style was of the same classical design in which the other government buildings mimicked the architectural genius of an earlier civilization; it had the same scale and proportion of windows, the same long lead of marble steps at its façade and the same hidden doors and private parking to the rear. He certainly had never had any business at the Justice Center that might have affected him personally; so that was not it either. And he did not know a soul who worked there; so it was not that. But there was something about it, perhaps about what it stood for, about the fact that while its occupants dealt with abstractions just like the government employees in every other building in the capital, the officials in the Ministry of Justice for some reason got to characterize their solutions in absolute terms—in terms of final judgment and unappealable order and permanent injunction and justice finally done and finally served—such that the power wielded there, in the Justice Center, had a much greater potential for the definitive, the arbitrary, the capricious.

The Minister of Cultural Affairs and William Worthington walked into the courtroom on the third floor of the Justice Center to find their lawyer, a pool attorney from the Office of General Counsel, sitting inside an enclosed area, front and slightly to the right of center before the elevated bench at which the judge obviously sat and the elevated chair where witnesses obviously were placed to be questioned and interrogated in the full view of anyone else in the room. The lawyer stood when he saw the Minister enter the room; he bowed slightly, waved them over, and opened the little swinging oaken half-door so that they might enter the special area that had been segregated for attorneys and their clients. He sat them at the table, to his right, and they huddled together and talked in quiet, raspy whispers so that the other attorney, who sat at a twin table to their left and who also was employed by the Office of General Counsel, could not hear what was being said.

After a while the door into the courtroom swung open again, and William Worthington turned his head and saw Frieda Haster enter. She took several steps toward the bench and then stopped when she recognized William Worthington. "Good morning," William Worthington said to her in a friendly tone from across the room and she ignored him. The other attorney rose and walked over to her and introduced himself, and they, too, hid their faces and talked quietly and secretly only to each other. All the while, an obvious buzzing sound filled with static emitted from the small black speakers that had been set in the high ceiling corners of the room.

A few minutes later a scratchy, stentorian voice that must have been recorded years ago blurted out of the speakers, too loudly, too practiced. "All rise." And with no fanfare, the Chief Judge of the Fifth Judicial District entered the room through a door hidden in the paneling behind the high bench. She adjusted her robes and sat down in her enormous black leather chair. She shuffled a few papers and read one of them to herself and then picked up the gavel and whacked it once loudly on a piece of wood plated with brass. "The court will come to order," she announced. The courtroom, which not only was already quiet but was entirely empty except for the judge and the attorneys and their clients, quieted more and William Worthington suddenly heard the soft whirr of a machine and then noticed that there were microphones on the tables and that the proceeding was in all likelihood being recorded. There were also cameras hidden in the walls, and while William Worthington could not see them, he should have known that they existed and were in operation, just as was the case in every building and in fact on every street in the capital city.

The Chief Judge of the Fifth Judicial District read over something on the piece of paper in front of her, and then read it a second time, out loud. "We are here on the Emergency Petition of the Ministry of Cultural Affairs—Ministry of Cultural Affairs vs. Frieda Haster. I will take your announcements."

The lawyers introduced themselves, said whom they represented, and then Frieda Haster rose and said in a loud and confident voice, "I object, your honor."

The Chief Judge of the Fifth Judicial District looked down at Frieda Haster benevolently and said, "You are not entitled to object, Ms. Haster. That's your lawyer's job. Please sit down."

"You don't understand, Judge," Frieda Haster answered, still standing. "I object to this person, Mr. Tooley, I think his name is, representing me. He works for the government. It is the government that has brought me into this courtroom for whatever purpose they have in mind. I object to being defended by a government lawyer against claims made by the government."

The Chief Judge looked at Frieda Haster and then over at Mr. Tooley, who shrugged his shoulders and said nothing. "Your lawyer has no objection, Ms. Haster," the Judge said. "And you are not entitled to object. Your objection is overruled. Now please sit down, Ms. Haster. A limited amount of time has been allocated for this matter. Justice delayed ... well, you know."

The process that followed was more than a little confusing to William Worthington. It started with the Judge stating that preliminary motions would be considered. Frieda Haster's lawyer then asserted some objections relating first to the lack of adequate notice, which the Judge overruled by observing that Frieda Haster was there in the courtroom so she had obviously had notice, and secondly to the fact that the Ministry of Cultural

Affairs did not have standing to seek the nullification of the guardian papers, which the Judge overruled by noting that the Ministry had to have standing because if it did not then it could not obtain the relief it sought, and thirdly to the fact that the Judge was related to the attorney for the Ministry of Cultural Affairs, which the Judge overruled without explanation, but only after fining Frieda Haster's lawyer a not inconsiderable sum for contempt.

The matter proceeded to the merits of the government's claim and it took all of thirty minutes for the Chief Judge of the Fifth Judicial District to enter her final decree declaring that the papers under which Frieda Haster claimed rights of guardianship over Leonard Bentwood were null and void *ab initio* (a phrase that the Judge had to spell into the microphone to ensure that the recording system recorded it properly) and that William Worthington, and anyone else for that matter, was free to talk to Leonard Bentwood whenever they might please. The Judge picked up the wooden gavel and whacked it again on the plate of wood capped in brass and said, "The court is adjourned," and then she pushed an unseen button and the scratchy stentorian voice again came over the speakers and said, "All rise," and the lawyers stood and their clients followed suit and the Judge stood and turned and was about to leave via the hidden door in the panel when Frieda Haster said loudly, "Judge, may I ask a question? Unofficially, I mean."

The Chief Judge of the Fifth Judicial District turned back to face Frieda Haster and said, "Yes, Ms. Haster, by all means."

"Does that mean I can't be there when Mr. Worthington shows up to talk to Mr. Bentwood?"

And the Judge paused for a minute, thinking, and then answered, "Well, no. I don't think it means that. No one raised an issue about that. In fact I wish I could talk to Mr. Bentwood myself. I am a great fan of his, to tell you the truth. I will be looking forward to the awards ceremony. The judiciary is always invited, you know. I haven't missed one in fifteen years."

CHAPTER III

1

It was only the third instance in which the President had assembled his entire Cabinet at one time. The first meeting of the Cabinet, which had been held shortly after the President ascended to power, had been just that—a "meeting" in the most literal sense, a social gathering in which the Cabinet members were introduced to, and became acquainted with, each other over coffee and tea and cakes. They met in the ornate Cabinet Chambers amidst much pomp and posturing, affirmation and self-congratulation. They became acquainted, or more likely renewed acquaintances, exchanged pleasantries, demonstrated their mastery of the requisite social graces and political skills and then were sent off to occupy their own little fiefdoms after they and the President generally agreed that the state of affairs was sufficiently stable and static that there would be little for any of them to do during the President's term.

The second meeting of the Cabinet had differed only in that a general social strike was in progress at the time, with the result that the Cabinet members were typically overwhelmed by the daily tasks that had beset them once again—cleaning their own homes and cleaning their own dishes, walking their dogs and cutting their lawns, driving to work and driving back home, buying their own groceries, and all of that. On that occasion, the Cabinet had been called to order merely so that a general consensus on rationing could be reached. That objective had been accomplished within a matter of a congenial hour, and the ministers had blithely adjourned to ensure that their own departmental employees were advised that the luxuries to which they were accustomed would be slightly less available, although not for long and certainly not to a particularly inconvenient degree.

This third meeting of the Cabinet was altogether different. Another strike was underway, yes; and rationing had been automatically instituted once again. But that was not the reason for the meeting. It long ago had been agreed by the President and his advisors that strikes, which at that time were commonplace, and rationing, which was nothing more than a petty nuisance, did not warrant a Cabinet meeting, particularly because the standard response always eventually outlasted and thereby resolved the problem. It was thus clear that it was for some other purpose that the Cabinet members had been abruptly and rather impolitely summoned to the President's private residence with little warning. It was something more significant that had caused the President to demand their presence without exception. The starkly typed message, appearing on a single page of the presidential stationery and hand delivered under seal by the presidential courier, bore the heading, Emergency Cabinet Meeting. It stated the date of the meeting, which was the following day. And the time, which was the first business hour of the morning. And the room, which naturally was the Cabinet Chambers, which otherwise served merely as another place for Spangler, the presidential retriever, to sleep, and the presidential cats to hide and climb, scratch and play and, with a certain deliberate instinct, slowly destroy the furniture and furnishings that had been bought and installed at great public expense. And the message concluded with the signature of the President and a personal handwritten note stating, *attendance absolutely required.*

All twenty-six of them now sat around the elongated handcrafted conference table, inlaid with tropical woods from forests now long gone. Their seating was arranged in the normal fashion, by rank of importance, with the Minister of International Affairs and the Home Secretary seated on opposing sides of the President's chair at the head of the table, and then in diminishing importance down each side of the table in two lines which met at the opposite end with the Minister of Conservation and the Minister of History, both of whom seemed so distant from the vantage of the President's chair that they might have been figurines or table settings or something less. Behind the President's chair someone had set up a large easel. On it had been placed a chart that contained a graph with a bell curve. Some points had been highlighted on the graph and a dotted line had been drawn down from those points to the horizontal axis that plotted time, so that specific points on the graph could be associated with specific dates. The very center of the curve, being the highest point on the graph, was marked with a black X; above it, in large block letters, was set forth a date that corresponded to that point on the graph. And the date was only several weeks away.

The Minister of Cultural Affairs sat halfway down the table. To her right, closer to the President's chair, sat the Minister of Government Transportation, who bore more responsibility or power than she; to her left, in a lower chair, so to speak, sat the Minister of Museums, whose role could not be said to be of the greatest importance to the government. On down, and on up, the line.

The Cabinet membership had all assembled by the appointed time. They had been escorted into the Cabinet Chambers by a haughty receptionist who showed them no more than the necessary courtesy and who told them the President would be along soon. They all now were engaged in cross-table and sidebar conversations as they waited for the President, who traditionally was always late. The Minister of Museums had just asked the Minister of Cultural Affairs a question that had caused her to look up at the easel. She looked at the graph, squinting to see the smaller print that identified the axes, and then she finally said, "Yes, you're right. That's the date on which the Nolebody Awards Ceremony is to be held this year. But I don't understand the graph and, frankly, can't imagine that it relates to the ceremony. We've never used graphs to analyze the ceremony. What would there be to graph?"

She turned and looked back at the Minister of Museums who continued to look at her quizzically, as if he were demanding a justification for why he had been required to come to the Cabinet Chambers on a Tuesday morning when Tuesday morning was the time in which he always played golf with the Minister of Health. And the Minister of Cultural Affairs guessed enough of what he was thinking, saw it in the way his mouth formed accusation, demanded explanation in a way that matched the irritation in his eyes.

"I hardly think the President has called us together to discuss who will be attending the ceremony," she said. "It's just a coincidence. Nothing more." She looked over at the door and wished the President would arrive so that she could learn more about the chart and more importantly why the chart bore the only date that really mattered in the performance of her duties as Minister of Cultural Affairs. The last thing she wanted was to be the center of attention and the whole Nolebody Awards Ceremony did just that for the week each year during which it captivated the nation's attention. She would rather that it were over and done with, yet again.

The doors of the Cabinet Chambers swung open and the President stepped through. He was accompanied by a second individual who was uncomfortably dressed in a worn woolen pinstripe suit that did not fit him well and in which his body did not fit, as though body and suit were equally alien to each other. His eyes darted to and fro, and he seemed surprised by the number of people in the room and overwhelmed by the fact that he was in the presence of the President and his entire Cabinet. The President came to the head of the long conference table and generally greeted the ministers without bothering to call any of them, other than the Minister of International Affairs and the Home Secretary, by name. He led the man who was not a minister over to the easel and directed him to stand to the left of the graph while he stood to the right. He picked up a marker that lay on a tray underneath the graph and he drew a large black circle around the date that had been written above the point where the graph peaked. "Ladies and gentlemen," he said, and then he paused for the usual dramatic effect. "The day of reckoning has come."

2

It took some time before the ministers quieted, even after the President had raised his voice and waved his hand and called out several ministers' names. "I would like to introduce you all to someone," he finally said in a voice that was too loud and too impatient. And then he mundanely turned and smiled grimly at the man who had most unwillingly followed him into the room and who stood uneasily before the easel with his ill-fitting and out-of-fashion pinstripe suit hanging off him like the sopping clothes of a scarecrow after a heavy summer rain. "Before I do, though, I would like to ask everyone in this room a question."

This was an unusual approach for the President, and it took the ministers by surprise. The President rarely asked questions, and the ministers therefore were not especially practiced in the art of answering them, particularly in the presence of other Cabinet members. A dead hush fell upon the room as the ministers waited anxiously to learn what it was that the President wanted to know. The President continued: "Have any of you noticed anything peculiar going on? Anywhere, I mean? Amongst the members of your department? Between you and your employees? In your personal life?" And then he paused and waited for responses.

There were none, of course, other than a shake of the head or a muffled statement in the negative and furtive glances back and forth by the ministers who now looked at each other with suspicion and mistrust. The ministers were sensible enough to immediately perceive that it would not serve their own causes to suggest that something was amiss in their own departments, under their own watch. So the President said, demanded, "Nothing? Not one of you has noticed anything out of the usual?" Which met with only silence again.

The President shook his head as if to evidence disgust, disappointment. He turned to the wiry, slumping, unkempt individual who had come into the Cabinet Chambers with him and who still stood next to the easel and stared uncomfortably out at the faces in the room. He had seen most of the faces before, only not in person. The faces had been constantly photographed by the Department of Information Services, whose responsibility it was to keep the general populace informed of the doings of the government, to show that the government was busy at work serving the people. So he had seen most of them before in that sense: in a photograph or a news story from somewhere in the past, usually in the company of others from the elite and normally at an exotic locale in a sumptuous setting overflowing with blossoming gardens and manicured lawns and perfectly improbable trees.

"Ladies and gentlemen," the President said. "This is Dr. Valberg. Dr. Valberg works at the Institute of Health, which, as you know, is administered by the Home Secretary for security reasons. Dr. Valberg has discovered something that you need to know, that we all will need to take into account in the days and weeks and months ahead. I have refrained from telling you what you are about to learn until it could be reliably verified. As the Home Secretary and the Minister of International Affairs know, there can no longer be any question."

He took Dr. Valberg by the arm and led him up to the conference table and then pushed his own chair aside and as much as thrust Dr. Valberg to the head of the table where he faced and stood over the entire membership of the Cabinet. And then he said, "Please Dr. Valberg, tell them the news."

The Minister of Cultural Affairs could hardly contain her expectations, her anxiety. It was as though the President were toying with her. This man obviously had made a discovery of the greatest import and the President for some reason had concluded that all of her plans for the Nolebody Awards, the nominating process, the ultimate choices for that year, should be disrupted and altered at this late date just because someone had discovered one or another thing that someone else would eventually discover anyway, given enough time.

Dr. Valberg cleared his voice, twice coughing into his raised fist that stuck too far out of a shirtsleeve that was already too long and a suit sleeve that was too short. He took a deep breath and in staccato delivery said, "The Nolebody Vaccine has a half-life …," and then, after some hesitation, he added, "of thirty years."

Repeated gasps sounded throughout the room, followed by an awestruck silence. The President stepped forward. "There's more," he said, and now he looked sad and seemingly without hope.

He turned again to Dr. Valberg, who cleared his throat another time, coughing into his pallid fist, and then said in the same staccato monotone, "It also turns out that the vaccine is an inoculant for itself. It ultimately gives rise to an attenuated immunity. In other words, it can only work once on any individual."

Followed by more gasps, this time more like feeble, flatulent groans. Like the last vestiges of air out of a balloon that had already been half deflated. When the ministers of the President's Cabinet were distressed, they moaned in chorus, so it seemed.

3

It had taken the President weeks to accept the reality of the situation, to come to grips with the full implications of the tandem facts that the Nolebody Vaccine, on which the entire fabric of society was based, had a half-life of thirty years with no prospect of repeat effectiveness on someone who had been vaccinated in the past. Which meant everyone, because the governments of the world had done their very best to ensure that everyone living and subsequently born would be vaccinated via a program that involved dispersal by sea and land and air. When the startling information had been delivered to the President, he had gone through a cascade of emotional stages that began with incredulity, transformed into paranoia, and culminated with a sense of hopelessness that he had not yet shaken. He thus knew that it would take time for the members of his Cabinet to assimilate the information and make the necessary adjustments to their complacent perspectives.

But all he could give them was an hour. Because time suddenly was at the very essence of everything, with the passage of each second, minute, hour, day marking the irreversible progress of history further along the horizontal axis and up the bell curve, reminding that the immunity from violence and aggression that the Nolebody Vaccine had provided was wearing off for an ever-increasing number of people, at something approaching an exponentially increasing rate.

For the duration of that single hour, he sat and listened while his ministers asked foolish and ignorant questions of Dr. Valberg, who faithfully answered with an endless stream of responses either to the effect that, yes, that had been tried or, no, that would not work. The President finally interceded. "I hope you will not mind my cutting this a bit short," he said in a polite and yet firm tone. We—I mean Dr. Valberg and Secretary Parks and Minister Ortland and I—have already gone over the scientific issues. Ad nauseam, I might add. There is no scientific solution to be had. We are left with a social issue. And eventually we will have international issues to deal with as well."

But the members of the Cabinet would have none of it. They were still in the preliminary stages of skepticism, doubt. When the President proposed that they must prioritize the issues on a short- and mid- and long-term basis, they ignored him and asked more questions, primarily directed to Dr. Valberg, who three times had taken a seat only to stand again when someone asked another question. Down, up, down, up, down, up. And then something akin to panic set in when some of the Cabinet members began to perceive the complexity of the issues.

"I suppose that means that going forward it always will be the twenty-somethings who emerge into violence," the Minister of Criminology observed. Only to be reminded by the President that that was a long-term issue.

"We need to consider whether the Permanent Peace will remain permanent," the Minister of History chimed in. "Yes," the President answered, "that is an immediate issue."

"What about violence against women?" the Minister of Minority Rights said. "We will need to provide self-defense instruction."

"What about sports? We are going to need to institute rule changes to collegiate sport. The last thing we need is a repeat of the college series riots."

"And what about animal welfare?"

"And what about the sales of drugs and alcohol?"

All the while, Dr. Valberg, who had finally determined that it made no sense for him to stand and sit each time he was asked and then answered a question, had taken his seat yet again and slowly had sunk deeper and deeper into the unpressed folds of his threadbare suit. The President suddenly noticed him and concluded that Dr. Valberg's presence was no longer necessary and perhaps was detrimental. The President stood and interrupted the uncontrolled discussion that had deteriorated into something akin to a freshman law school class, in which the sole objective was to spot issues that arose under the stated set of facts. "Thank you, Dr. Valberg," the President said. "I don't think we need anything else from you at the moment. We, of course, will be in touch. We are going to have to make a statement to the public eventually, and we will want your assistance."

Dr. Valberg moved toward the door, his shoulders slouched and his back bent as though he alone bore the tragic weight of an impending disaster. He was about to exit the room when the Minister of Industrial Safety, who occupied a chair of middling importance, called out, somewhat rudely, "Hey, Valberg. I've got one more question for you. Why don't you and your people get off your ass and come up with some answers? That's your job, isn't it?"

By that time, Dr. Valberg was more than exhausted. He had spent the entirety of the previous day with the President and his confidants, the Home Secretary and the Minister of International Affairs, going over every detail yet another time. And then he had been unable to sleep, being already in the paranoia stage himself and not knowing what came next, from what direction. "It's rather silly to think," he began to answer, with a look that might have appeared to lack respect but actually merely reflected uncontained weariness. But before he could finish his sentence, the Minister of Industrial Safety stood up abruptly and angrily swore in language that had not been heard in the presidential residence for decades and then as much as flung his chair back against the wall behind him where it shattered one of the tall windows that looked out unto the statuary in the presidential grounds.

A long and deathlike silence fell across the room, in which everyone sat stunned and motionless, until Dr. Valberg finally observed, just before he walked out of the Cabinet Chambers, "As I said, the bell curve is merely a graphic tool to reflect when half of the vaccine will have been rendered inert. For some of us, the vaccination has already lost its effect."

4

The truth was that Philip Nolebody had known all along that the Nolebody Vaccine had a short biological half-life, as did Dr. Stalovich, who had developed the vaccine at Nolebody Laboratories so many years ago. Philip Nolebody had paid Dr. Stalovich dearly to never reveal the fact and, in turn, Philip Nolebody had reaped the financial benefits of Dr. Stalovich's reticence a million times over. Maybe more. For the sum that the warring governments of the world paid Philip Nolebody in exchange for the formula to the Nolebody Vaccine, and for the right to manufacture it and disperse it in sufficient quantity to forever alter the world's water supplies and atmosphere, was calculated not in terms of a rate of return on investment in research and development, but as percentages of gross domestic product, which happened to be rather high during that time of war.

So the governments had gladly paid the negotiated sums to Philip Nolebody by exchanges of currency and securities and precious metals and land and whatever else could be scraped together to Philip Nolebody's satisfaction, and within a month any semblance of bellicose behavior amongst humans had been eliminated on a global basis. The war, being the third world war in a generation, ended shortly after it had commenced, and the community of nations thus started out on its new footing without the need to rebuild itself in the way that had been a necessity after the previous two cataclysms of death and destruction.

The rest is known to history, except for the fact that it was only Philip Nolebody and Dr. Stalovich who knew that the planning and the eventual scheming of the various governments of the world were based on the misperception that the armies of other nations could never threaten their shores or borders again and that their own citizens' potential for rebellion and protest had effectively been neutralized by the Nolebody Vaccine. And then Dr. Stalovich died and Philip Nolebody alone possessed the secret. And then Philip Nolebody unexpectedly fell into oblivion, and the secret died with him. Into the unforgiving forgetfulness of the past.

The science relating to biological half-lives and half-lives in general was not particularly complex. The President recalled that much from his secondary school chemistry studies at which he had excelled for no other reason than that they were ridiculously deficient and simplistic. The fact that the Nolebody Vaccine had a half-life of thirty years meant that the effect of the vaccine would wear off most people in more or less that much time, and also that the effect would last longer in some people than it would in other people; or, stated otherwise, would be of shorter or longer duration depending purely on the quirks of chemistry which dictated that all things eventually were calculable, but only to the point of estimated probabilities. In any case, the expected numbers of those who would fall outside the average were few and the expected numbers at the median were high. Hence the bell curve, which the President had always believed was some kind of rounded monolith of the natural world on which all things were based.

The question that struck the President as being the most immediate was: who was on the left-hand side of the bell curve at the moment? Followed closely by the related, second question: what could be done about them? Both of which needed to be resolved before he could even get to the third question, which was what to do after that. It was for these reasons and these reasons alone that the President in his wisdom had determined to award the Nolebody Medal to Leonard Bentwood, for whom he had never had more than a passing appreciation but whom he knew to be a favorite of the working class, of the people, of the citizenry not only of the nation but to a large extent of the world. Leonard Bentwood would be his bridge to the people in this time of troubles, his palliative, his opiate if that concept was appropriate in an assuredly nonviolent world in which addictive drugs had been legalized if not promoted.

He sat in the empty Cabinet Chambers, thinking of what he should do next. The presidential dog came in and lay by his feet and slept where it often slept, on the edge of a handspun, hand-dyed, hand-woven carpet made by the indigent peoples of a southern land, with the shed dog fur of four seasons matted and felted into the carpet so that dog and carpet had, in a sense, become one. Mr. Chipper, the presidential calico, crept into the room submissively; he sharpened his already sharp claws on the teak legs of the conference table, and then came up under the President's arm and nuzzled against the President's lowered chin and commenced purring in the softest of rhythms.

"Well, Mr. Chipper," the President said, "all hell is about to break loose."

5

The advent of the Nolebody Vaccine thirty years earlier had, in many ways, an immediate influence on the organization and very function of the governments of the world. With the eradication of domestic and international violence, government planners found that much of what had been done in the past, or at least had been attempted in the name of public policy, was no longer necessary in the present and would no longer be required in the future. Armies and navies and air forces and all their minor branches and special services and corps and battalions and groups and wings instantly became obsolete; they and their endless insignias and ribbons and medals, their parades, their pomp, their tradition, their glory, all became relics of a strategic and particularly tumultuous past. And the machinery of warfare and defense and armed security fell first into idleness and then into warehousing and then rapidly into disrepair. And then the Treaty of Permanent Peace, which some called the Nolebody Treaty, made sure that is was permanently so. By international agreement, all but a few nonfunctioning relics of military hardware were to be dismantled or effectively destroyed. The role of the police and the criminal courts and the prisons were instantly minimalized, with the minor irritation of nonviolent crime being seen more as a social and psychological issue to be dealt with in a manner in which physical intervention on the part of the authorities was implicitly avoided. Wildlife populations exploded and the consumption of meats and fish and poultry came to an abrupt end, requiring entirely new management philosophies regarding public and private lands. And even more draconian changes followed once the economists and policy makers came to realize that the eradication of aggression meant also a dramatic reduction in the competitive impulse, with complacency becoming an inherently reliable trait amongst the population at large.

Industry shrank. Incomes fell. Birth rates climbed. Consumption increased modestly in some ways, and decreased dramatically in others. Health habits changed, some for the better and some notably for the worse. Some arts and sciences flourished and others came to an abrupt and seemingly irreversible end. Sport took on a new meaning. As did everything else. All of human behavior changed in the span of a dozen years.

It was for these reasons, in combination with the instinct for self-preservation, that the governments of the world adapted by enshrouding themselves in secrecy. By various forms of fiat they largely eliminated, or rendered meaningless, elections as perfectly unnecessary in a semi-perfect world; and they terminated government reporting as nothing more than a perfunctory exercise involving a waste of resources and time. And then they each after their own fashion gradually expanded their functions in some spheres in order to compensate for the decline of their usefulness in others. Like anthills on a prairie that had been swept clean by the windiest of storms, the very organization of each government was deconstructed and then resurrected in another form more suitable to the changed terrain.

In Leonard Bentwood's country, the varied departments of the Armed Services collapsed into a single minor department that aptly, and in accord with international treaty, was named the Unarmed Services. Military production was halted and the Ministry of Arms Manufacturing abolished. The Department of Border Security was transformed into the Ministry of Embarkations. And on and on and on such that an entirely new generation of governmental agencies was created, at least on paper and sometimes with profligate largesse, with the promise that in the aggregate they would ensure that the government provided the public with every form of recreational and intellectual diversion that was needed in a society in which growth in productivity was suddenly supplanted by leisure, which was perceived by those who governed to be the only commodity of real value. And, in line with government planning, public unemployment grew as incomes fell and, in many instances, were eliminated altogether.

Cornwall Vanderhoof, the famous philosopher of philosophy (as he called himself) from the pre-Nolebody era, had once opined that political philosophy is usually nothing more than the ideologue's misnomer for political expedience. According to Vanderhoof, at the inevitable postmortem stage known as history, the autopsy performed on dead governments is bound to reveal a certain congenital dysfunctional pathology that should have been anticipated if not known from the beginning. And such was the case with the government of Leonard Bentwood's nation. Because the anatomy of the government was nothing more than a hodgepodge of the past, arbitrarily intermixed with a hodgepodge of the present, whimsically combined with a forecast of what the hodgepodge of the future ought to look like. In Leonard Bentwood's day, the disassociation between the government's various appendages and the inner workings of its entrails, all separated by an inelastic and self-effacing outer skin, ensured that the monstrosity would defy the form of genetic logic and relative consistency that is required for any normal organism to survive for longer than a relatively short period in the annals of time. But these were not normal times.

And then there was the role of history. The government, which in its early years had been the unfortunate product of gratuitous revolution followed by greedy territorial consolidation embossed with civil strife, had welded itself together by its own industrial prowess and military might and then had morphed into something that looked nothing like its former self. The government's historians and politicians and bureaucrats argued otherwise. They contended, in the approved writings and in the proffered speeches and implemented policy, and even in the contemporary architecture and theory of the day, that the government was the product of a profound philosophy, bred of an erudite debate that ensured the best of governmental processes for the nation's citizenry and, of course, the world. But it was not so. The government was the manifestation of a grossly mutated millipede whose cancer-ridden organs were even more monstrous than the tangle of twisted and deformed appendages and pincers, barbs and eyes that gave it form and bearing.

In short, in the first two decades after the introduction of the Nolebody Vaccine, the government's intended operation and its actual function diverged to an even greater extent than had been the case before the Nolebody Vaccine was invented and tested and finally distributed throughout the world. The government of Leonard Bentwood's nation was meant to be perceived by the people as a purely benign organization that served as host and keeper of a fantasyland of services and entertainments that were always being improved to better satisfy the public's expectations and desires. But in truth the government was nothing more than a self-sustaining and forlorn organism struggling across a landscape so altered by unnatural change and transition that it could barely cause its mutated and diseased legs and claws to drag its hulking body forward and back from one side of the street to the other.

6

Over the next seven days following the revelation that the Nolebody Vaccine had an early half-life, the President met with his Cabinet seven times, always first thing in the morning and always in the Cabinet Chambers. Over that seven-day period the chambers slowly became permeated with a faintly detectable odor that no one could accurately describe, perhaps due to its unlikely origin in the peculiar recipe of emotionally inspired human sweat and respiration, combined with pet dander and the oils of exotic wools and woods, that all mixed together to produce a scent that was both vaguely wild and yet somehow subtly appealing.

On the morning of that first meeting after what would become known colloquially as the Half-life Revelation, the Minister of Cultural Affairs entered the Cabinet Chambers in something of a somber and irritated mood. She made her way directly to her normal place and slumped halfway into what was supposed to be her chair only to find that her nameplate had been replaced by that of the Minister of Psychology. For a moment she panicked. She looked anxiously about the room at the other ministers who were present, trying to restrain the expression of shock and dread at having been relieved of her duties, only to realize that many of the other ministers in the room also seemed disoriented by the seating, which seemed to have been altered to a considerable degree.

Those who were in the room milled about, back and forth, examining the nameplates, finding that many had been moved to a different position, but otherwise unable to ascertain precisely what had happened. As should have been the case, it was the Minister of Domestic Investigations who resolved the puzzle. "Now I understand," he announced to the others in the room. "Look. The Minister of Industrial Safety has been moved to the very end of the table. To the lowest chair, so to speak. Which means that every other one of us who were seated below him—in a manner of speaking, I mean—had to be moved up a chair or at least across the table to show the change in ranking." He wiped his hands back and forth across each other, as if to dust them off after a hard labor, and then he took his seat (which had moved up a single position) with a broad smile of accomplishment.

The demotion of the Minister of Industrial Safety had an immediate and noticeable effect on the remaining ministers, all of whom were already sensitive to the President's seating arrangements and their own relative position at the table. If nothing else, the mere alteration of the seating was enough to ensure that their conduct and demeanor throughout the meeting was particularly exemplary, although the thought crossed more than one of their minds that others amongst them were struggling to contain impulses that were suspicious at best and threatening at worst. The President called the meeting to order, the ministers quieted into an absolute and absolutely respectful silence, and then the President said, "For those of you who do not have the time to read the news, you should know that there was a shooting last night in Paradise City. No fatalities; but a shooting nonetheless."

There had not been a shooting anywhere in the nation in

over twenty years, and the news thus came as a thunderclap to those who heard it for the first time, which was just about everyone in the room. "That means there are guns on the street," the President added. "We suspect a museum was robbed, but there are other places one might get a gun if one looks hard enough." He said nothing about bullets. Did not even think about it. Nor how one could know how to shoot a gun accurately without practice and instruction.

The effects of that second meeting—which was intentionally designed by the President and his lieutenants as a reorganizational meeting in which the significance of each governmental department was reassessed in light of the pending crisis—did not become evident until the third meeting was convened the next day. Again, the seating was altered, although this time in far more significant ways. The Minister of Amateur Sport was moved from a seat that had been within six seats of the President to one that was almost totally to the rear; the Minister of Prisons was moved up almost to the same degree; the Ministers of Parks and Scenic Rivers fell four seats apiece, and the Ministers of Embarkations and Languages moved forward respectively by two and three. On this second day following the Half-life Revelation, the Minister of Cultural Affairs gained only a single seat, but it was enough for her and she accepted her modest promotion with an equanimity that masked the ripples of relief that repeatedly crossed over her when she found her nameplate and assumed her slightly elevated position.

It was at the third meeting that the President mentioned the Nolebody Awards Ceremony for the first time. The primary agenda of that meeting focused on the probable need to implement curfews in the urban areas and contemporaneously create new government programming in the media so that the public would have something to do while they remained indoors. This topic generated a great deal of thought and a flurry of ideas, most of which seemed to have more to do with reenactments of ministers' personal lives and fantasies than with the sorts of drama and entertainments that the working class were likely to enjoy. The President ultimately brought the discussion to an early termination, at midpoint in an oral dissertation by the Minister of Air Quality in which was discussed the gains to be had by having the public watch and re-watch videos of clouds passing overhead. The President stood abruptly and said, "This dialogue demonstrates why the Nolebody Awards Ceremony this year will be of particular significance. The way I see it, the Nolebody Awards have always served as the bridge between the people and their government. The reinforcement of that bridge is of greater import than ever before. We must keep that concept in mind as we work our way through the various measures that must be taken. The public should be reminded on a daily, maybe even an hourly basis that the awards ceremony is approaching and that it will be a ceremony to be remembered for years to come. For all of your information, this year's choices for the Nolebody Awards were made only after the preliminary tests strongly indicated that the Nolebody Vaccine has an early half-life. We have not been entirely idle while we waited for Dr. Valberg's final results."

At the fourth meeting following the Half-life Revelation, the Minister of Cultural Affairs found that she was only eight seats from the President, with some prospect, she thought, for yet further improvement. And she was correct in thinking so. That meeting concentrated on matters relating to the means by which to improve the general temperament of the public, to assuage the malcontent, to bring them gently round to a different perspective in which it was logical to embrace a passive approach to life in which the government acted as shepherd to the docile flock. When the Minister of Amateur Sport suggested that his budget should be enhanced so that new sporting facilities could be constructed and programs funded, the Minister of Cultural Affairs interrupted and said, "I hope my good friend the Minister of Amateur Sport will not mind my observing that it would be much cheaper to promote and advertise the existence of a few real sporting heroes than to attempt to replicate them by the millions with poor facsimiles of the real thing." To which the Minister of Professional Sport quickly agreed. When the Minister of Sciences proposed the construction of a thousand teaching laboratories to keep the adolescent mind sharp and occupied, the Minister of Cultural Affairs noted that "all that can be taught in this discipline can be taught through a single broadcast series that reaches every home." And when the Minister of Competitions argued in favor of a virtually endless number of contests that would instill ambition and preoccupation, all the Minister of Cultural Affairs had to do was to mutter a few words that included the phrase "Nolebody Awards," and the President nodded his head in agreement and reoriented the debate in another direction.

By the seventh meeting, the Minister of Cultural Affairs sat next to the Home Secretary, across from the Minister of Energy, a position that placed her not only within touch of the President but also within whispered hearing of the Home Secretary and the Minister of International Affairs, who each seemed to have come to treat her as an equal if not as a threat to their preeminence. They both graciously deferred to her every comment, encouraged her contribution in thought and suggestion. After that seventh meeting, the Home Secretary even quietly took the necessary steps to ensure that at the next meeting the Minister of Cultural Affairs would find that her chair had been replaced by one that was more comfortable and more suited to her level of influence in the government.

<h2 style="text-align:center">7</h2>

The Minister of Cultural Affairs had always thought that William Worthington was an attractive enough young man, although in a somewhat adolescent sense. He seemed different to her now. She looked deeply into his eyes from across her desk and held her stare until he began to feel uncomfortable, and then she said, "Your new beard looks very becoming on you, William."

"It's only been two weeks. It has a long way to go."

"That may be. But it is coming in very nicely. It frames your face and brings out the color of your eyes. And … well … it gives you a certain maturity."

"Thank you, Minister Frasier."

"You're welcome. Although you have nothing to thank me for."

But that was not why she had called him into her office. Or at least not the primary reason. She had become more aggressive of late, more proactive in the business of cultural affairs and more intent on ensuring that everything under her direction was accomplished when it should be, and in the manner intended.

"I remain a bit concerned about this situation with Leonard Bentwood," she began. "I understand the court has finally issued its written order and that it should have been served on

Ms. Haster by now. Have you had any confirmation?"

William Worthington twisted slightly in his chair. His hand came up to his face involuntarily, subconsciously, and he stroked his nascent beard. "No, Minister Frasier," he said with a certain apologetic tone. "I have called the courthouse and asked for the confirmation, but I can't even find anyone who knows what I am talking about or how to find someone who would know. You know how they are over there. And as I understand it, Ms. Haster does not have a phone. There seems to be a lot of that going on down there in that part of the country. No phones and such, I mean. I will have to make the trip again in order to ensure that matters have been set straight. Besides, I need to talk with Mr. Bentwood again. Under the circumstances, I think it should be done in person."

"Yes," the Minister agreed. "Sooner rather than later."

She turned her chair as she often did, so that she could look out and over and down at the manicured gardens and grounds of the Cultural Affairs Building. There were workmen along the periphery of the beech hedge that had been imported from a faraway northern island country. The men were setting up a tall fence that looked innocent enough until you focused on it and saw that it was laced and capped with some form of razor wire. And across the river, at the War Memorial, other men were hard at work. She watched their slow and tedious progress and shook her head. She turned back to William Worthington.

"I realize we still have time, William, but there is so much to do. And I'm afraid that much is going to depend on us."

He said nothing. Only shaped his mouth into a slightly compassionate smile that disguised the fact that he was unsure what compassion he had for her and her plight. For the plight of the government. He wished she had never confided the secret of the Half-life Revelation to him. Wished that he had been someone else, somewhere else, rather than there as the Assistant to the Minister of Cultural Affairs, who somehow seemed to have arrogated power to herself right at the very eve of destruction.

His thought drifted back to the desert scenes that pervaded the drive in to Leonard Bentwood's shack, how he had been overwhelmed by the stark beauty of the wild surroundings and enthralled by the sense of peaceful isolation. And he again thought how different life would have been for him had he been born out in some rural area where he never would have known the city life, where he might have learned about nature and life and himself before he decided to seek out positions in a government that only served itself.

"I think I will arrange to make the trip tomorrow," he said with a look of feigned responsibility. "I suspect it would be best to fly into the government airport and avoid the risk that something goes wrong at the public terminals. I'll get a truck there," he said.

"Yes, that's fine," the Minister answered with her back turned again as she watched the workmen raise a section of the new fence and move it into place. "But don't be getting overly paranoid about it all. Everything will work out fine. We just need to keep our eye on the ball."

CHAPTER IV

1

The plane in which William Worthington was sitting had been parked at the gate for over an hour and he had begun to think that they would never let the passengers off. He sat mindlessly stroking his beard as he looked out the window, down upon the cracked tarmac, across to Runway 7 and then beyond to where the mountains rose up out of the high desert plains to jaggedly cut the sky. He stared at the distant horizon, at the thin clouds that seemed streaked with wisps of peach and lavender, at a flock of birds, cranes maybe, heading south in neat formation. And then he glanced back down at the map that sat unfolded and open on his knees; at the mysterious greens and the red outlined road and the dotted marks that showed the trails into the inner heart of the forested mountains and wilderness.

He had seen maps in the past, of course. But they had been maps of cities and urban areas that had remained in the family car where his father, a midlevel bureaucrat, kept them so that he would not get lost as he drove from and through one sprawling city to the next in the fulfillment of his menial government tasks. Taking his family with him as though that was their family vacation when in fact there had never been a family vacation or anything else that might have exposed William Worthington to any form of outside stimulus other than that offered by rote at the public schools.

Now it was as though a new map had unfolded before him. A map that still remained to be fully defined. A map that allowed him to chart his own course away from the drudgery and linearity of the past and into a future that he could plot and design according to his own preferences despite the oppressive nature of the times. He looked down at the map that lay on his knees and he saw the greens of the forest and the empty spaces where there were no roads, no people, and he resolved to free himself of a past that never really had made any sense; to free himself from the present and his own erstwhile commitment to it.

At some point he heard a whirring sound and it pulled him out of his reverie to see that the rear exit ramp of the plane that sat at the gate next to his had suddenly dropped down to the ground. He saw also that several individuals in dark uniforms he did not recognize were standing beneath the plane. Two of them carried some form of weapon—a rifle of some sort, equipped with a sighting scope. A third talked into some form of radio. The armed men stood at the bottom of the ramp in a rigid, prepared stance—like the pictures William Worthington had seen in a history book portraying some sordid episode from the distant past. And then he watched as several other men wearing the same uniform came down the ramp leading an individual who futilely resisted while the blood from a cut lip and bloodied nose dripped down onto his shirt and the ramp and the black pavement below.

The uniformed men forced their prisoner down and then off the ramp with a notable indifference for the prisoner's well-being and comfort, and then they hurriedly dragged him to the waiting car with no care for the fact that he was unable to keep his feet. One of them pushed the prisoner's head down, roughly and almost with a vengeful thrust, and they forced him inside and slammed the door closed and drove off with the tires squealing and a hidden siren blaring as if there were a fire or some emergency to the situation.

William Worthington continued to stare out the window long after they were gone. He wondered what the man had done, who he was, where he was being taken. It all seemed so puzzling, so unfamiliar. The bloodied lip and nose, the uniformed men and their weapons, the brutality with which they dealt with their prisoner. Because none of that had been possible in the past. Neither the fact that the prisoner had apparently resisted and that the uniformed men had bloodied his nose and mouth; nor the weapons that looked so dark and futuristically insidious; nor the hard indifference, the rude shove, the ambiguity as to what had happened and what would happen next.

It seemed as though no one else on his plane had seen what he had seen. The other passengers, all of whom were government employees, merely continued to chat and patiently wait, to fuss with their belongings or read from their papers or a book. The pilot finally came on the speaker and apologized for the delay. "We have been experiencing a mechanical problem with the door," he explained in an easy voice of reassurance. "Everything is back to normal now. Thank you for your patience and please watch your heads as you disembark the plane."

2

It was the first time William Worthington had driven a vehicle that had all-wheel drive, let alone an all-wheel drive truck with high axles and ten-ply tires. There had been a time when that sort of vehicle was commonplace—back after the Nolebody Vaccine had first been dispersed and the more harmless military hardware of the Armed Services had been auctioned off to the public. Most of those vehicles, though, were no longer on the road. Over time the inoculated public had found them to be overbuilt for the type of casual driving the normal person came to enjoy. And those who had not yet been inoculated in the first wave of dispersals had beaten the machines to a slow death and rolled them in their recklessness and scavenged them to the point that very few all-wheel drive vehicles existed, even in the museums in which such things were kept and polished and maintained for the endless crowds that longed out of curiosity to see icons of the troubled past.

William Worthington knew simply by looking at it as it sat in the parking bay that he liked it. He liked the way the truck seemed designed to hug the road, like some kind of predator whose feet never left the ground, even when it was on the prowl. He admired the elevated view provided by the lifted axle and the high seat. And he found the sound of the twice carbureted engine, the way power came to it instantly with the slightest press of the accelerator, to be strangely seductive.

As he sat in the parked vehicle and waited for the engine to warm, he looked one more time at the second map he had brought—a large map of the southwest region of the country—and then he folded it up and placed it on the seat on top of the forest map, next to his pack filled with clothes and the tent and sleeping bag which he had just purchased and the sunglasses he had owned for years but had never worn. He put the truck in gear and pulled out of the carpool lot and made his way to the intersection of highways and turned onto the main highway leading west. As he drove in that direction, he slowly melded into the high commanding driver's seat until he felt in tune with the firing pistons and sensed that he was one with the road. He rolled down the window and let the warm dry air pour in like the baking heat from a ventilated oven.

At a little town with an odd name that he forgot as soon as he passed through it, he turned south by southwest. The road traversed the high plain country for miles in a perfectly straight line and then gradually and imperceptibly rose above it into a transitional landscape of rock and sage and mountain grasses in which nothing predominated and little seemed to grow. Small evergreen trees appeared, at first only one here and another off in the distance there, amid the scrubby brush and occasional yucca; and then suddenly they were everywhere, spotting neat packages of green up and down and across the brown undulating land that still rose to the west and south, in the direction he was driving. He turned on the radio, heard for the first time the rural music of that locale, twangy and filled with forlorn lyrics that seemed to strike home with a certain absurd and yet valid irony. He felt the sun beat down on his arm, which rested on the open window frame, and against the left side of his face. The isolation and the contrast of forest greens and sepia browns and the blues of the sky enveloped him. He drove on, more slowly than he realized, unknowingly keeping beat to the music with his thumbs, his sunglasses filtering the light to provide sedate and easy vistas as the land continued to rise and the scattered beginnings of forest began to appear—real pines with orange and brown bark and needles as long as pencils; thick-trunked cottonwood; twisted oaks that spread and dappled the ground with shade. Up into the mountain den of the headwaters of what had once been a mighty river.

Long before dark he pulled off the pavement and onto a dirt road marked only by a brown sign with a government insignia and a number that corresponded with a place on his forest map named Ashes Creek. He followed its course up through a winding and treed ravine crowded with tall pines and clumsy oak and locust and ash, through formations of sandstone and igneous rock, a place littered with boulders the size of small buildings that lay sunk in the sandy ground. And he was surprised to see that the road had been kept open by someone who had cut out sections of the downed trees so that a vehicle could drive through them and around the hard piles of avalanched rock and back and forth across the streambed for no other purpose than to continue to ascend into the very core of the mountains. Until, all at once the road came to an end, stopped by the narrowing of the canyon and the thickness of the trees and rubble, with barely enough room to turn the truck around. William Worthington stopped and turned off the engine and sat with the window open listening to the gurgle of the flowing creek and the playful chirping of unseen birds while the scent of the heated pine resin rose and permeated all about him like an insistent memory of an exotic incense burned but not forgotten.

For the remainder of the afternoon, he explored the terminus of the canyon, climbing up the last few hundred feet to the top of its ridge only to find other ridges where the real mountains and forest again emerged into view, peering down into the defile, sorting through and picking up rocks that caught his fancy, a pinecone, needles, leaves, feathers, an antler that had been chewed by a rodent into a stub of a would-be horn. And when he had grown tired, not of it but by it, by the primal enormity of the rock beneath and around and above him and by the staid and plangent nature of the forest and the creek, he took his rest and ate a meal of cold cereals and juice and then set his tent on a soft spot where grasses grew into the sandy bottom.

But he did not sleep within the tent, and instead only put the remainder of his food inside it. He took out his new sleeping bag and spread it out on an area of sand unencumbered by protruding rock, and then he took off his clothes and put them inside the tent, and then he nestled into the bag, naked and nakedly content, and for a long while stared up into the canyon's opening as the stars and an occasional cloud passed by, and the bats flitted this way and that in a rising breeze that carried the heat of the day up and far away.

3

He awoke the next morning to find that his sleeping bag and tent and even his beard were covered in a light dew and that a steamy vapor lifted hesitantly off the creek that fell and tumbled through the ravine like the lifeblood of a living organism. He lay in the warm comfort of his bag for a long while as the squirrels and the cliff swallows and the jays came out in number and reinvigorated the day.

When he finally rose in his nakedness, he felt the true coldness of the morning and he at once opened the tent and pulled out his clothes and boots and put them on. He filled his bottle with water from the creek, then reached back into the tent for his cache of nuts and chocolate and cereals only to find that a rodent had chewed through the tent wall in the night and had found solace in the contents of the package. He ate the remainder of it anyway, smiled at the thought of the little scurrying mice so close to his feet and body and face while he slept.

He sat by the creek. After a while he noticed a broken branch lying on the ground—a piece of pine—and he picked it up and hefted it in his hand and turned it over and over, reflecting on its size and shape and weight. He broke it into three sections of more or less the same length, and he looked at the three pieces of pine for a long time before he rose and went back to the truck where he fumbled in his bag and pulled out the new pocket knife and began to carve at the wood. He did so with some vigor for an hour or so until he had crudely shaped three different imitations of boats, one with the beginnings of a keel and another with an outrigger he had fashioned with some twigs and a separate piece of wood.

He thought to set them in the water, but then he saw that there was more opportunity for improvement. Once he had found some smaller twigs that suited his concept for design, he shaped them, and then with the knife's awl he bored holes in the center of two of the little boats and set their masts, as upright and proud as those of the great sailing ships of long ago.

He went back to the truck and dug in his briefcase. He pulled out spare copies of letters and folded the paper and tore them into pieces of the appropriate length and width and then found a way to bind them to the masts so that their paper canvasses were unfurled and readied for the wind. And then, one after another, he set sail to his little flotilla, across the calm stretches and into the treacherous boil and undertow of the mighty rapids and then over the ledge of falls of indescribable height where one by one they disappeared from sight down the waters of Ashes Creek.

With the sun still far below the rim of the canyon, he drove out, with his window open and the air as fresh within the cab as without; down the dirt road and through the same cathedral of rock and ledge and tree that now looked completely different than when he had driven in. Then, reluctantly and with one final look back into the yawning mouth of the ravine, he turned onto the paved highway that continued to climb toward a mountain pass that he could not yet see.

At the divide he pulled the truck over and got out and for a long while looked out across the vast expanse of land to the south and the southwest. Again and again his eyes followed the folds of the mountains, traced their terraces of slowly descending elevations that traded with a sure progression, from one exposure to the next, the firs and spruces and aspen for nothing but pine, and then into juniper and cedar unto the desert itself, which from that distance lay stretched out like a great seabed, dried and left exposed to sun and sky. And then he drove down out of the mountains through endless turns and switchbacks, with his foot on the brake pedal and the earth falling off one shoulder of the road and then the other into an abyss of treetop and cliffrock and mystery.

Now, for the first time, as he wound his way through the last foothills, he thought he understood Leonard Bentwood's art, how Leonard Bentwood had intellectually communed with all of nature and life, combined living and seeing into an artistic expression. He saw the mountains and the forests in his mind and he could only wish that he could find a way inside Leonard Bentwood's thought so that he could see the world with the simplicity with which Leonard Bentwood saw it. That he could shed his ties to a past that was beyond redeeming and live a natural life that had none of the constraints the government sought to impose.

The road fell down into the desert and he passed by the intersection where the highway he was on joined with the highway he had taken on his first two trips to see Leonard Bentwood. From there on, the road and the desert landscape of rising buttes and island mountains engulfed by hard arid sunburnt flora suddenly were familiar to him even though he could never have remembered it all, no matter how hard he might have tried. He turned on the radio, listened again to the plaintive tinny songs of heartbreak and remorse and, occasionally, redemption.

He drove the last ninety miles to the post office—the post office where he knew Frieda Haster worked—in a state not of confusion but of fusion, in which everything he had ever been and known and thought recombined together to create a new, more energetic form that knew nothing of its former self. A state of mind that placed value first and foremost on the peace and tranquility offered by the natural world and natural people and the ability to take each step as though it were the next rather than the last.

The hot air blew in through the open windows and he let it blow in, the dust thinly coating his clothes and even his face, his sunglasses keeping out just enough of the sun to allow him to stare into and against it as he drove on with a heart that was not light as much as it was free; free for the first time. And in the heat of it all he planned and considered and imagined what he would do once he found Frieda Haster and explained to her that he now understood Leonard Bentwood and would never do anything to hurt him.

4

William Worthington walked past what looked like a hitching post for horses and through the door of the diminutive post office only to run directly into Frieda Haster, who stood at a side counter sorting and preparing her mail delivery for that day. She looked up at him momentarily and did not recognize him and then paused and looked at him again with an unfriendly glare.

"Good morning, Ms. Haster," he said. He extended his hand, which she did not take, and so he awkwardly pulled it back down to his side. "We need to talk, Ms. Haster. Is there somewhere we can go?"

"Right here will be fine," she said without looking up, without any indication that there was reason for her to stop what she was doing.

With a single sweep, William Worthington examined the confines and stark adornment of the brightly lit one-room building, the stucco walls and clay-tile varnished floors that echoed the slightest sound, the hand-drawn posters seeking jobs and lost cats and dogs and children, the dirty unwashed windows with frames that had been painted and then painted over a dozen and more times, the gray-haired lady behind the counter and her patron who had been loudly talking but now had stopped and watched him intently. He turned back to Frieda Haster and said, "I think it should be in private. I have something I want to talk to you about."

"I thought it was against the rules for you to talk to me in private," she said, again without looking up, as if he were some form of disembodied spirit that could be spoken to but not seen.

He stood in silence, staring at her, staring and waiting until Frieda Haster finally turned her head and met his eyes. He offered a look that was meant to convey a personal disappointment in her rejection, but he saw from the angry and affronted expression on her face that she must have seen him as childish or demeaning or chauvinistic or worse. "I'm a busy woman, Mr. Worthington," she said. "I have to work to make a living. You wouldn't know about that, I suppose." She placed the last batch of mail in the wooden milk crate that had been given to her by Leonard Bentwood, and then she picked it up and walked past him, out the door and into the dusty lot where her worn pickup sat, battered and tired next to the newly styled custom deluxe model William Worthington had reserved at the government car pool.

He followed behind her, and only when he sensed that he was losing her, that she would drive off without so much as another word, he stepped up next to her and said, "I'm on your side in all of this, Ms. Haster. I care about Leonard Bentwood. We need to talk. I may be a government employee, but deep down I now know I'm a nobody. Please, Ms. Haster. I think I can help."

They had coffee in a small café located at an innocuous intersection that served as the center of the little town of Dried Well, which itself comprised little more than a mercantile, a curio shop, a hardware store, a gas station and saloon, some other odds and ends all constructed out of that same stuccoed clay block formed from the very ground on which they stood. For a long while, he talked and she listened. He breached confidences, violated rules, risked security, but he did not lie and he did not exaggerate. He told her all he knew about the Half-life Revelation, of which the public was still unaware, and of the panic in the President's Cabinet and the inevitable restructuring of the government into an autocratic fiefdom in which the public would have even less say, less voice, less function. "You see, Ms. Haster," he said as he unknowingly twisted a paper napkin into a long and tattered braid, "they think the public needs to be convinced that the only way to survive once the vaccine wears off is for everybody—everybody outside the government, that is—to give up everything. I mean everything. And let the government decide what happens next. There's all kinds of crazy talk going on, Ms. Haster. You would not believe some of the ideas that have been thrown on the table."

Finally he stopped, and his thoughts flowed and tore through the silence as would water through a broken dam. He looked at Frieda Haster and waited for her response, only to find that she had no response other than to say, "Well, isn't that the way it works right now, Mr. Worthington?" And before he could respond, she continued, "I mean, you haven't exactly described something new. Besides, I don't see why you found it so important to come here and tell me about it. I mean, I'm just a contract mail carrier, Mr. Worthington. I don't exactly have my finger on the pulse of the nation."

William Worthington sat back, leaned back in his chair, disconcerted and desperate. His eyes turned up to the ceiling, saw more of the same cracked and flaking stucco with which the entirety of the town seemed to have been faced. He sighed and said, "Maybe you're right, Ms. Haster. Maybe it sounds the same. The difference is that they think they can use Leonard Bentwood as a replacement for the vaccine. That he can be a sort of pacifier. A martyr almost. A prophet or something. I don't know exactly how to put it. They think they can claim that the popularity of Leonard Bentwood and his art shows that deep down the public should be submissive and complacent while those who are in power make all the decisions in the future. About everything. About how we all live. How the government should operate once the vaccine has totally worn off. What we eat. Everything. They think they can parade Leonard Bentwood around the country for the rest of his life and hold him up as some kind of intellectual icon upon which everything can be based."

He had become flustered and was not sure that he was making sense, that what he thought, what he had concluded, had any foundation in reality.

And he would have gone on in his rambling had Frieda Haster not cut him short. "There's something you need to know about Leonard Bentwood, William," she said in a voice that was not sad as much as it was filled with a cryptic and sentimental pleasure. "It's a little hard to explain."

5

At almost exactly the same moment at which Frieda Haster told William Worthington that there was something he needed to know about Leonard Bentwood, the Minister of Cultural Affairs, who was meeting with the President and his lieutenants, said, "There is something you need to know about Leonard Bentwood, Mr. President." But the President would have none of it. His response was imperious and definitive. "I don't even want to hear it," he said curtly, and from his tone and demeanor it was more than clear that he meant precisely what he said. So the Minister of Cultural Affairs did not tell him all that William Worthington had related to her regarding the idiosyncratic and eclectic side of Leonard Bentwood, of how he lived in a dilapidated hovel in the desert and drank spoiled water and seemed to be teetering on the edge of senility if not utter oblivion.

The President stood and paced back and forth with quick, agitated turns. He finally stopped, leaned down and petted Spangler, who lay against the silken curtains that had been a gift from a far eastern country that, in the not-so-distant past, had been a dire enemy. "We will proceed as planned," he said firmly. "There is no time left to be altering the course we have decided on. We can refine it, naturally. But our direction now is clear." There was a knock at the door of the presidential conservatory in which the four of them comfortably sat— the President and the Home Secretary and the Ministers of International and Cultural Affairs, all of them now perfectly familiar with each other and yet as officious as circumstances and their relative rank required.

"Yes," the President said loudly and without looking up, and this alone was enough for the presidential caterer to know she had been admitted. She pushed her way through the towering double doors carrying the main entrée of their working lunch on an engraved silver serving tray, much as she had now done every day for a week straight, followed by her adjutants, who pushed a large silver-plated cart filled with a selection of drinks and desserts, breads and cheeses and condiments, and an assortment of appetizers and confectionery enticements that all looked as though they had been prepared in a school of art that specialized in culinary design. They laid the food out before the President and his three lieutenants with choreographed precision and then stood in abject silence, at rigid attention with their eyes slightly toward the ceiling, waiting until the President paid heed to their effort. Which he did with an ambivalent thanks and the observation that that would be all. For now.

In the past two weeks, by her own calculation, verified by

measurement confirmed by a second scale, the Minister of Cultural Affairs had gained ten pounds, at least. And the same would have been true for the others as well—for the President who had aged a score of years in the first half of his first term in office and the Home Secretary who had been tending toward obese before she was appointed to her post and the Minister of International Affairs who dined nightly with one or another foreign dignitary on the delights of a foreign table—had they not already been acclimated to the pattern of consumption that was new and delightfully palatable to the Minister of Cultural Affairs.

She dived into the working lunch with an exquisite relish, just as she always did. And as she piled the cheeses and pastries and crumble on her plate, she muttered something about needing to start using the Cabinet Members Gym, saying it quietly enough that no one else heard her. And not really meaning it anyway.

The agenda for that day consisted of two items. The first was the question of when the public should be informed that the Nolebody Vaccine had a short half-life and that the vaccine was also an inoculant against itself. The second related to the news that on the previous night someone had broken into the old armory, which was located only a few miles down the street from the presidential residence and the War Memorial and the entire capital complex.

The issue of when the public should be informed of the Half-life Revelation had been addressed by the entire Cabinet in prior meetings, but the President had become more and more uncomfortable with the idea that the entire Cabinet should be involved in the decision-making process during the transitional period. He had slowly reduced the number of Cabinet members in whom he maintained confidence until only three remained. The Home Secretary now reiterated the opinion she had offered from the start. "Why ever tell them?" she said with something of a snide vehemence. "I mean why tell them that the vaccination cannot work twice? That will only invite chaos and rebellion. Once the public gets to thinking that they are completely on their own, who knows what will happen? I would not want to be on the streets when they let loose, I can tell you that much."

The Minister of International Affairs naturally had a broader view, given, as he was, to thinking in global terms. "You forget, Elaine," he said as he wolfed down his second piece of pie, "that the leaders of other nations sooner or later are going to realize what the situation is and they are going to make their own choices. There is no keeping this a secret forever. We need to be in the fore, even if it means that everyone everywhere learns about it at the same time. This is a time for us to lead. We cannot sit back and become one of an unruly crowd of nations. This is our time. There is about to be a power vacuum and it is ours to fill or not fill as we choose."

A wry smile crossed the President's face. "Let's stay focused," he said. "The issue isn't whether. The issue is when." He threw Spangler another bite of the potato salad and then sliced off several pieces of the blue cheese and tossed them over to Mr. Chipper, who had been sitting upright on a chair with one leg straight up into the air while he licked himself clean, apparently in anticipation of joining in the meal.

In the end, the question of when to make the announcement all came back to Leonard Bentwood and the Nolebody Awards Ceremony. The President had started pacing again, although this time he had to alter his route to avoid Spangler, who had carried a portion of a sandwich into the middle of the room and was now dissecting it so that he could eat the choice morsels first. "We must convince the public that we are with them, not against them," the President said as he paced in one direction. "In order to accomplish that objective, we must put forth someone that the public can relate to," he added as he paced in the other. "Now I do not need to remind you of the fact that the latest polls show that Leonard Bentwood is the most respected individual in the nation, inside or outside the government." He turned and paced back in the same direction from which he had just come. "There is not a single member of the public out there, other than Leonard Bentwood, that they will follow." He turned again, headed back toward the center of the room. "And once they are told about the Nolebody half-life, they are not going to be inclined to listen to any of us." Again he turned and took his paces. "Leonard Bentwood represents our last best chance. That's the phrase you people like to use, isn't it?"

He stopped pacing and bent down and picked up the slices of cucumber that Spangler had rejected. "Let's move on to item number two," he said. "What are we going to do about this armory business?"

They talked about it for an hour, maybe more, but there was no real solution there, either. Some unknown persons had broken into the nation's old armory building only to find that there was nothing there. Nothing at all. Because the entire windowless building, which consumed the better part of five square blocks, was literally empty and had been literally empty now for well over a decade. They discussed the fact that whoever committed the break-in must have presumed there was something in the armory, which meant that they had come away with at least one thing, and that was that the government wanted everyone to think it could arm itself but no matter how much the government might want to do it, it could not do so simply by going to the closet and pulling out the weapons of a former day.

"My biggest concern is that it was foreign agents," the Home Secretary said. And the Minister of International Affairs could only respond by saying, "From what I am reading in the news, it looks far more likely that it was someone from your turf. I mean, what with these panics on airplanes and the trains and whatnot. We've no reason to think there's a single other nation out there that even knows about the Nolebody half-life."

"They don't need to know about it to be getting anxious about us," the President said. "All they need to be is getting a little paranoid, which I suspect they are. I have to believe they are starting to experience incidents of civil disruption too. All I know is that there is someone out there—if they're able to put two and two together, that is—who now has reason to believe that the nation is more or less defenseless at the moment. Just like we were supposed to be under the treaty, I suppose. Although I've never believed for a minute there is a single nation on the entire planet that has honestly followed the treaty terms. And I shouldn't have to remind you that it was not just an attempted robbery. It was a break-in. They broke through three doors to get in. That means they were on the left-hand side of the curve, my friends. We've got ourselves a problem that is not going to go away. We are going to have to open Sealey Cavern. Now. There is no other way around it. I trust you agree."

To which the Home Secretary and the Minister of International Affairs readily and vocally acceded, and in response to which the Minister of Cultural Affairs, being somewhat in awe of the moment and her position in it, mumbled "yes" just after she swallowed the last piece of white chocolate fudge and even though she did not even know where, let alone what, Sealey Cavern was.

6

The dirt road leading to Leonard Bentwood's shack passed under Frieda Haster's truck like a carpet of air, the truck and driver and road integrated as one by subconscious familiarity and wear such that none of them—the truck, the driver, the road—was either predominant or entirely subservient to the other. As she instinctively negotiated her way along the dirt track, without effort and without consideration, she ruminated on her conversation with William Worthington and the strange way she suddenly felt attracted to him. She wondered whether he would keep his word; whether he would return to the capital city and falsely report to his superiors that Leonard Bentwood would indeed attend the Nolebody Awards Ceremony. She wondered whether William Worthington would fulfill his side of their agreement that everything possible had to be done to ensure that Leonard Bentwood forever remained at his isolated hideaway, away from the public eye, in the lost corner of the cactus-strewn desert in which she now drove.

"You must promise me by your most sacred vow," she had insisted of William Worthington after they had agreed on their course of action. And when he replied, "I promise, Frieda; you can trust me," she had said, "Swear on it then. Like an oath." So William Worthington had sworn the only oath he knew, which was to a god in which he did not believe, and Frieda Haster had gained sufficient comfort by it.

Based on William Worthington's assurances and represent-ations, the President and the Minister of Cultural Affairs would advertise to the nation and the world that the reclusive Leonard Bentwood would appear at the Nolebody Awards. The President simultaneously would exploit that fact by advising the world that the Nolebody Vaccine had an early half-life and then by offering up Leonard Bentwood as a kind of governmentally sponsored mascot around which the loyal and faithful public would rally in support of the government in its moment of crisis. Except that Leonard Bentwood would not be in attendance when the curtain rose.

"It will be the end of both of us, you know," William Worthington said after they had sealed their conspiracy with a warm embrace, and Frieda Haster had replied, "It would be the end of me to let them treat Leonard like a piece of human propaganda. He would never survive it." And William Worthington had answered, "Yes, I can see that you are right. If it is the end of us, then so be it." And then he had driven off in the government truck—with the wind in his hair and his sunglasses deflecting the bright sun and images of ocotillo and yucca and huge columnar cacti like scrolling film on a darkened screen—back across the desert and the dried lakebed and over the mountains to the government airport where a plane would return him to the capital city and the Cultural Affairs Building and the end of the world as he had come to know it.

Frieda Haster pulled through the gateposts that really were not gateposts, up to Leonard Bentwood's shack where Leonard Bentwood, as usual, stood waiting for her. She came up on the porch. They hugged and smiled and exchanged sincere and meaningful greetings. But she could sense that something was wrong, that he was agitated somehow, for some reason. He had known from their meeting the prior week that his mother had recovered sufficiently from her illness. And she could tell simply by looking at him if he were ill. She thought for a moment of what William Worthington had told her about the bell curve and the half-life concept, but it did not seem possible that that might relate to Leonard Bentwood. "Let me get your things, Leonard," she said. "And your mail. Your mother has sent you two letters. She must be making up for lost time."

She went back to the truck and pulled out his box of groceries and supplies and carried them to the porch and they went inside together. She saw instantly the manifestation of his mental state in the form of dozens of sheets of paper spread over the table and stuck to the walls or between books or crumpled into wads or torn into bits. They all bore writing on them, lines and fragments of words and phrases in Leonard Bentwood's unmistakable hand, with the hand-printed letters twice as large as the norm and punctuation at a minimum and more space than writing on any given page.

She put the box on one of the table chairs and looked down at the papers, saw that the writing was more frenzied than normal, and that each paper bore a heading or title that was at least related to the heading or title on the other pages she could see. They all said Will or Bill or William or Wordsworth or Wordsmith or Woolworth and other similar variations of what were plainly attempts by Leonard Bentwood to recall William Worthington's name. And below those words, Leonard Bentwood had scribbled the typical collection of only vaguely connected thoughts of words and objects and occurrences and impressions, of anything that Leonard Bentwood could think of that might serve to trigger memory and remembering.

She pulled out the items she had brought him, describing

them one by one even though it was obvious what they were. The fruit and vegetables and nuts, the bread and honey and coffee, the crafts glue and the pins and thread and copper wire all as descript and identifiable as they were when they stood on the shelf, waiting to be bought. She handed him the two letters from his mother, which he quickly placed on the edge of the table where he could not miss them, and the bottle of brandy, which he instantly opened after mumbling something to the effect that the last bottle was empty, but no newspaper, which he looked for but did not find.

He poured them each a glass of brandy, the half-opaque tumblers masking the amber color of the liquid with a milky white film of dulled glass. And then they went outside to sit on the porch in the heat of the afternoon.

They talked about his mother first. "I spoke to her yesterday, Leonard. She is fully recovered. It was the flu," she lied. She did not tell him that his mother had been hospitalized for heart discomfort, that she had had a fright, that someone in a passing car had yelled at her while she drove, and that she had become faint and that the fainting spells and panic did not go away until after she had rested at the public clinics and then her home for two weeks straight.

And then they talked about the weather and the end of the monsoon and things that Leonard Bentwood had observed during his days and during his nights—of creatures afoot and birds on the wing, the heavens the clouds the sounds of a week all recalled in a half hour of conversation—until he leaned forward and said, "What's a nobody?"

A covey of quails had just come into the yard and Frieda Haster had been watching them closely. When Leonard Bentwood said to her, "What's a nobody?" she at first did not hear it or it did not register with her; and then she did comprehend the words. "Excuse me, Leonard," she stalled. "I didn't hear you. What did you just say?"

"What's a nobody?"

"Well, I don't understand, Leonard. What do you mean? 'Nobody' means no one. Like 'there's nobody here.' Is that what you mean?"

"I thought maybe it meant something when someone says they're a nobody, like when you said it a couple weeks ago when that fellow from the government was here. What was his name? I saw it in the papers you gave me. It seemed like there was a story that was calling someone a 'nobody,' like it meant something. I just thought I'd ask you because you would know."

She looked over at the quail, at the matched adult male and female and the seven chicks that pecked and scurried their way across the sand as if there were no time for anything else, and at the lone male that followed behind, forlorn and yet determined not to be left totally alone. "As far as I know 'nobody' means no one and nothing more."

Leonard Bentwood took another sip of his brandy. And then another. He leaned back into the old unvarnished rocker and slowly rocked back and forth, back and forth, back and forth. "What was that fellow's name?" he said as he looked out at nothing, at everything.

"I'm not sure who you mean, Leonard."

"That fellow you had the letter for. I can't remember his name for the life of me. Or what he wanted. He was selling something, wasn't he?"

"Yes, Leonard. He was. Everybody's selling something these days. Except you and me."

CHAPTER V

1

The People's Hillock had stood relatively unmolested and relatively innocuous, in the center of the capital city's main park, for hundreds of years. Not that it did not have a history of its own. At one time in the distant past it had played host to swordplay between several of the early revolutionaries who founded the country and their oppressors with whom they were in all likelihood related. The revolutionaries had prevailed, the knoll was seized in the name of a country that did not yet even exist, and the vanquished retired to engage in their colonial undertakings elsewhere where opportunity was less demanding. The hillock also had been the site of various romantic interludes, both successful and unrequited, and even had once served as the backdrop to the final scene in an early movie that portrayed an aspect of the nation's history that had never really occurred.

But that had been in the distant past, which had a much more glorious aspect to it than the times that were to follow. More recently, statues had stood proudly at its highest point, but those had been erected in the aftermath of the first great war and had been taken down and carted off to warehouses or the foundries after an early post–Nolebody Vaccine proclamation required the removal of all but a single war memorial from public sight and access. Since that time, the People's Hillock had served as nothing more than a sort of bucolic pulpit from which an occasional drunk or religious convert might peacefully proselytize those who willingly stayed nearby long enough to hear more than a sentence or two of the speaker's diatribe or prophecy or whatever it was on that particular occasion. At least since the advent of the Nolebody Vaccine, the People's Hillock had never been the site of real dissension or radical pronouncement or even public agitation. Until now.

The three men who had been occupying the People's Hillock were as uniform in dress and determination as could possibly be the case. They all wore black. They all wore hoods. And they all delivered their own version of the same angry oratory that denounced the government as a body of pathological deceivers.

For three days now, and for three nights, they had stood and slept and harangued from the very highest spot on the People's Hillock while crowds of ever-increasing numbers gathered as each day wore on. Officials from the government openly observed them and recorded everything they did and said and represented, but the government did nothing to stop them. On this early hour of the fourth morning of their occupation, the three men were already at work plying and prodding the crowd that had formed an engulfing circle below them, challenging them with insinuation and innuendo and plain and simple truths.

"There is not one of you out there," the tallest of the three asserted as he pointed out to the throng and then swept his hand across it as though he could gauge their temperament and disposition with his palm, "who has not been subjugated by these government devils. Not one of you who has not been violated and aggrieved. Think about it, people. Where do they have you living, and where do they live? What do they have you eating, and what do they eat? What do they have you wearing, and what do they wear?" And when the crowd offered nothing in response, he emphatically added, "I can tell you what they wear; they wear the mask of deceit and corruption."

The second, a somewhat shorter and yet far more robust man, chimed in. "We've been here for three days now, ladies and gentlemen. And I haven't heard a peep from any of you. Wake up, ladies and gentlemen. Can you hear me? Wake up!" He clapped his hands and then clapped them again, more loudly. "What we need, ladies and gentlemen, is a rising. The time has come to rise up. Do you hear me? To cast off this 'nobody' designation they have labeled us with and to demand rights. Privileges. Equal treatment. All of it. All of the things they used to write on the statues and monuments before they decided it would be easier to just take them all down. It's already in your heart; you just need to hear it in your ears. I am telling you the time has come to rise up and take back what is ours." There was a bit of grumbling amongst the audience, but nothing that would suggest agreement with what he had said or, more importantly, joinder in what he proposed to do. There was organized movement in the back of the crowd, but he did not see it.

The last of the three men came forward to stand with the other two. He was of middling height and of lesser build, but it was clearly he who led them. He spoke in a deeper voice, calmer and yet more authoritative, laced with intellectual prowess and an eerie persuasiveness that was almost irresistible. "My friends," he said with the softest lilt in the bass of his voice, "time has become critical for us all. We must be honest with ourselves. With those we love and care about and care for. We must act now or we will never be allowed to act. We must act now or all will forever be lost. They will become too strong. They will put us down permanently." And even as he said these last words, two government security men came to the fore of the crowd and ascended the little hill and reached out to take the leader of the three revolutionaries by the arms.

The shortest of the three occupiers of the People's Hillock dropped into a peculiar stance that looked like the statue in the National Museum of an ancient god from a faraway land. In three practiced motions that blended in form and gracefulness to harness the entirety of his strength and velocity, he lunged toward the unarmed security workers with an aggressive and surgical brutality that seemed suddenly uncaged and primal and predatory. The flurry of kicks and punches and chops left his victims twisted and broken on the ground with injuries that were real and severe.

The crowd collectively gasped as it happened, as if there had been a sudden shortage of air that required them all to suddenly breathe deep and then hold their breath unnaturally. But they did not move more than a step or two backwards as they watched, riveted to what seemed to be some form of forbidden and profoundly disturbing theatre. Then more security men came from somewhere—from out of the obscurity of the crowd—this time armed with a handheld device that shocked the three revolutionaries first into writhing pain and then into unconsciousness. The crowd, which itself was numb with disbelief and awe, was dispersed with calming words and the suggestion that it would be best if all went home and stayed indoors.

2

Mary Bentwood reached over and picked up the controller. She deftly pushed the up arrow once, twice, a third time, and the enormous bed rose up on command and assumed the form of a curvaceous chaise lounge. She leaned back into the mattress and then reached behind herself to fluff the already fluffy pillows that had been made of down salvaged from another source, which itself might have relied on an even older source for the goose down that had not been produced for over a quarter century. She pushed the call button, spoke into the receiver and asked her private nurse to bring her some tea and, of course, milk and sugar, and then she reached over and picked up the little bundle of opened and unopened letters she had received over the last four weeks from her son but which she had not seen before her release from the public clinics.

She had read three of them already. As was her practice, she had opened them one at a time and had read each letter carefully and then had turned it over to thoughtfully examine the words and lines that Leonard Bentwood had scribbled on the back—the words and lines written in a large hand in tall letters widely spaced and having obscure meanings that she never could totally grasp but at least sometimes could appreciate and sometimes would read again and again and again. And then, in accordance with the system she had employed for many years on end, she would write either the word "yes" or "no" on the back of each page.

She pulled out the unread letter and carefully opened it with her silver letter opener. Gently and with a mother's anticipation, she unfolded the three pages on which it was written. She laid them out before her on the satin sheets, and then she picked up the first page and brought it up closer to her failing eyes. She noticed that it bore an earlier date than the others, that it must have been written just before Leonard Bentwood learned that she was ill. "Dear Mama," it began, and then it proceeded as most letters do, as would a conversation stuck in monologue, to talk to Mary Bentwood in voiceless words that nonetheless carried with them an intimate and subconscious portrayal of the writer. "Frieda told me you have been feeling tired," it said. And then it told her to find a way to get some exercise and fresh air. "It has been a good monsoon," it noted, followed by a long description of a particular flash of lightning, the way it momentarily lit up the sky and the cacti and the mountains and then instantly returned them to the darkness of the night. "I had a visitor who said he was from the government," it said; and the calm and disinterested way in which Leonard Bentwood had stated it did not help to minimize the sudden jolt of adrenaline that shot through his mother's system, delivering an effect not unlike an electrical shock followed by a sudden elevation in the temperature of a room. She sat in her bed motionless, staring straight forward until her heart slowed enough for her to know that she was all right, that the arrhythmia that had necessitated her convalescence had not returned.

The letter ended with a long discussion of Leonard Bentwood's thoughts on why the tarantulas only came out at night—something to do with their furry bodies and the extreme heat of the day—but Mary Bentwood could not bother to think about it enough to form an opinion of her own. She reached for the phone and began to dial a number that she could not fully recall. She placed the phone down and fumbled on the bed stand for the address book, and only then did she realize that she had not turned the pages of the letter to read what had been written on the back.

The backs of the first two pages of the letter were of little interest to her. One repeatedly referred to truck keys and a key chain and truck seat; and she wrote the word "no" on it and placed it aside. The second was even worse, for it had been used as a coaster and had nothing written on it other than the words "make coasters." But she liked the third, and it calmed her sufficiently that she read it a second time, and then a third, before she noted "yes" on it and placed it with the one other that bore that designation. It read:

three cups of coffee, three times, three
a bird, a song I do not know
cheeseburger cheeseburger cheeseburger
a visitor coming, from down the road

She took the two pieces of paper that contained portions of Leonard Bentwood's letters on one side and on the other side of which bore some of his jottings and her "yes" notations and she folded them and placed them in an envelope, which she addressed to Mr. Samuel E. Corry, an old old friend who, thanks in part to Mary Bentwood, had become an icon in the publishing business at a time when any commercial enterprise was difficult to sustain. And then she placed the envelope on her tray where the nurse would know to look for it.

She opened the address book and found Frieda Haster's name and dialed the numbers with her long narrow fingers shaking and her watery eyes tired and apprehensive. The phone rang and rang and rang and rang until a voice came on and gave her no other option than to leave a message.

"Frieda, it's Mary Bentwood," she said in awkward intonations. "I have a letter here from Leonard saying the government's been there to see him. Do you know anything about it? Please call as soon as you can, Frieda. I need to know what's happening."

She hung up the phone, dissatisfied, feeling as if she had had a conversation with someone who refused to respond or who could not understand her words. And so she dialed the number again and waited through the rings and the message before she added, "It's me again, Frieda. Mary. I hope this government business is not about the trust taxes again. I thought we took care of that last year. Would you mind verifying that everything has been switched over?" She had almost hung up before she realized that there was one last thing that she wanted to say. "Oh, and also, I have a letter here saying that our option on the three parcels next to Dry Wash has been activated. We only have sixty days to exercise our rights, so we had better get to it now. As I recall, those tracts are only three miles from Leonard. We wouldn't want the Dry Wash tracts to fall into the wrong hands. Please take care of it Frieda. And confirm when it is done."

She leaned back and sighed. The private nurse brought in the tea and some cakes. She placed the serving tray down on the bed stand and waited while Mary Bentwood mixed the milk and sugar according to her own sense of proportion, and when Mary Bentwood thanked her and told her that would be all for the day, the nursed kissed her once on the forehead and left the room.

Mary Bentwood sipped at the steaming tea and at the same time reached for the controller and turned on the television. The television slowly warmed up and a news channel came on, showing an odd scene in a park with large numbers of people milling about and several uniformed individuals hauling off three men who were dressed in black and who seemed to be resisting the authorities. She frowned once and flipped through the channels until she landed on a game show in which the contestants vied for prizes by attempting to correctly answer questions about the arts and sciences and geography and history and the like. And she sighed again and leaned back and commenced to blurt out the correct answers, particularly on matters concerning literature and plays and music and such, usually before any of the contestants could even try to answer.

3

They drove the three prisoners by a circuitous route to the Mills Ferry Prison, which had not been a real prison for many years but instead a national landmark through which hundreds and sometimes thousands of tourists trudged in relative boredom every day. Its normally open doors had been closed now for over a month, and from behind its concrete reinforced walls and the rusted barbed wire and ominous towers the sounds of construction had been heard by those who happened to pass by before someone in a security uniform had shooed them off. The tourist signs that had provided narrative and historical descriptions of what had gone on in the past in the various cellblocks and holding rooms and catwalks had been removed and replaced by colder, official signs that told what they would be now, of what would transpire in times to come. Cell Block 5. Dining Room 2. Prisoner Admittance. Interrogation. First Aid. And everything had been recoated with the brightest of white paints, as if to ensure that there would be no place to hide, that there would be no dark or even shadow, when the lights went out.

The prisoners did not know that they had passed through the infamous "One-way Gate" at Mills Ferry Prison, the gate through which so many prisoners of a different era had passed, albeit only in one direction and only once. The security men had blindfolded the prisoners even before they had been thrown into the back of the security van, which had driven away from the People's Hillock at a reckless and urgent speed. The prisoners had seen nothing and had heard nothing but the muffled and yet animated conversation in the cab of the van and the shuffling of the feet of the two security men who sat silently next to them, presumably armed with the same weapons that had shot high voltage currents through the entirety of their bodies and sent them into convulsions on the ground. So they did not know where they were being taken or what their fate might be. They knew only that their adversaries had hurt them and presumably would hurt them again with little provocation and with the same cold indifference.

They placed the prisoners in separate cells and still did not remove the blindfolds; did not even speak to them or give them drink or offer any form of comfort or explanation. And then they took them one by one and interrogated them using methods that left no scars, no visible wounds and yet were effective in their objective and expedient in their efficiency. Only there was nothing they could learn from the three men who readily gave their names and their addresses and the names and addresses of everyone they knew. Because they—the three men who had thought to incite a revolution by standing on a hill in a park and calling for the people to rise up and take back what was theirs—apparently had acted entirely on their own. They had nothing to confess except that they were in agreement on principles, and nothing to admit except that the shortest, the stockiest of the three had bought an illegal martial arts training manual on the black market and had been perfecting his forms and execution for many months.

At first the interrogators did not believe all of what the prisoners said, and the call went out to the Home Secretary's office to have the truth serums delivered and applied. But the truth serums, which had been perfected in the Nolebody Laboratories toward the end of the final war, suggested that the prisoners had nothing more to confess. "It's just the three of us," the leader of the prisoners said toward the direction of the face he could not see but only hear. "I wish there were more, but there aren't. It's just me and Harry and Ian."

"Who gives you your instructions?" the interrogating voice asked a slightly different question.

"There's no one to give us any instructions, I tell you. Unless you mean me giving instructions to Harry and Ian. I wish there was someone else. But no one seems to listen to what we're saying. No one seems to care."

"Who is your leader then?" the interrogator asked in a third variation, all in accord with the standard Nolebody method that reputedly had worked so well before the end of the second global war.

But the prisoner could only lower his head and shake it in defeat. "There's no leader," he said. "I wish there were. There's no one but us."

So they took the prisoners to Cell Block 5 and placed them in separate cells where the prisoners could not see or even hear each other. And then one of the security men, one of those who had driven the van and had not been armed with an electric shock weapon, said, almost as an afterthought, "I think we should take off their blindfolds and untie their hands. It's the least we can do. They can't harm anyone in here. What's the point of treating them like animals."

"You've got a lot to learn, Snyder," his superior replied in a tone that showed frustration and maybe even distrust. "Leave them as they are for now. I'll come back and take care of them later."

4

They say news travels fast. But that is only really true when the news has been given legs or other means of transportation. Or at least so said Leonard Bentwood in his younger years, at a time when he was more inclined to witticisms and ironic humor.

On the day following the arrest of the three protestors at the People's Hillock, the War Memorial was leveled by a man-made explosion that shattered the windows of nearby buildings and sent up a billowing cloud of smoke and dust and debris that darkened the skies over the capital city like a smudgy and indecipherable inkblot on a black and white photograph. But Leonard Bentwood never came to know about it. Because Frieda Haster had ignored Leonard Bentwood's request that she bring him more newspapers and maybe magazines too, trusting that his proclivity to forget would override and suppress his desire to know. And even had she brought him another and another of the papers with names that implied independence and reliability and consistency, it would only have been a form of adulterated news that he would read—reports and stories and renditions in which the facts were merely a vague and manipulated version of their real selves.

To the remainder of the world, to that segment that read or heard or watched the news as it was delivered to them, the explosion was explained as a planned demolition, a precursor to the construction of a more functional park in which the public could do more than read the names of the honored dead of unnecessary wars. The public read or heard or watched the story as it was presented and, having read or heard or watched it so quickly after it had happened, felt informed and current on developments, satisfied with the knowledge that news, such as it was, travels fast when given the means to do so.

"So I hope you understand, Mary," Frieda Haster repeated into the receiver for the third time. "It seemed like the only thing to do, given what Mr. Worthington had told me, I mean."

"Oh, I quite agree. I always knew the day would come, Frieda. I've said as much before. It's a mother's impulse to worry, that's all. The impulse to protect your own. I would have preferred you asked me first, of course. But I can see you had no other option at the time."

"I think we can trust Mr. Worthington, Mary. He has become a great admirer of Leonard's. In a different way from all these people who claim to be fans and who worship the Leonard Bentwood that has been portrayed to the world. Bill—I mean Mr. Worthington—has met Leonard and has an insight into who Leonard really is. I would almost say he wants to be like Leonard, if I didn't know better. Of course, now that he knows the truth …"

There was an uncomfortable and momentary silence on both ends of the line. "Well, we are left to trust this Bill of yours," Mary Bentwood finally said. "That much is clear. I suppose I always knew they would try and find him at some point. I'm not sure we are at that crossroads yet, but we might be. We can trust Mr. William Worthington, but we will need to be wary nonetheless." And just as Frieda Haster sighed, both in relief and in disappointment at the contradiction, Mary Bentwood added, "By the way, have you seen the news this morning?

There seems to be some odd goings-on in the capital, although I really can't make heads or tails of it."

"Yes, I saw it. If you mean this explosion and all," Frieda Haster said without offering any insights. She had already succeeded in avoiding telling Mary Bentwood what she had learned about the Half-life Revelation and the pending ineffectiveness of the Nolebody Vaccine, and of her own speculations as to what was happening in the capital city, and why Leonard Bentwood had been selected to receive the nation's highest honor. She was not about to tell her now merely because Mary Bentwood had seen the news that the War Memorial had come crashing down in the middle of the day in full view of half the city's population. It was enough for Mary Bentwood to know that Leonard had been named a recipient of the Nolebody Medal and that Frieda had found a way to insulate him from the implications of attending the awards ceremony. "These people running the government seem to be entirely preoccupied with parks renovations. As though better food and schools and housing and jobs wouldn't do more to make people happier," she said blithely. "I suppose the whole point is to give the unemployed more space to loiter." And then she waited to see whether Mary Bentwood would press the conversation. When she did not, Frieda Haster took their discussion in another direction.

"Speaking of parks, I have exercised the option on the Dry Wash tracts. That was the last inholding in that sector. We can now close the gates in that area and rip the roads and post the signs. That should keep intruders and snoopers out, for a while at least. I'm afraid, though, that once the news gets out that Leonard was chosen to receive the Nolebody Medal, every other reporter and dilettante and groupie and professor of this and student of that is going to come looking for him. Sooner or later someone is going to figure out where he is and attempt to take him out of the desert and into the public light."

"Yes, I know, Frieda. But that is what we have been working for all these years. We are going to have to close Leonard's road at some point, you know. I just don't know how we are going to do it."

Frieda Haster smiled wanly as she thought of Leonard Bentwood and his excursions into the desert and the foothills and to the dumps and junkyards, of his inventory of bones and rocks and metal objects and whatnot piled in heaps and set in rows against the walls of his shack. "We will have to let him go out at times, Mary. The question is how to do it without looking too suspicious. There's no way to stop him. He has a mind of his own."

"Yes," Mary Bentwood said. "That is always the question, isn't it? Perhaps your Mr. Worthington might have an idea or two. It seems our little duet has grown into a conspiracy of three."

Frieda Haster held silent again. She thought of William Worthington and how he had changed so much in a matter of a month. Of how much he might change again in another month, in another year. She wished she were younger, or that he were older, but she knew that life did not work that way, that you took what came to you or you did not take it at all.

"One more thing, Frieda," Mary Bentwood said. "I think we will still need to continue with Leonard's work. We don't want people to start asking questions, and from the looks of things, we are going to need more funds than in the past."

"Yes, I suppose so, Mary. For better or worse, we are in way too deep to suddenly stop. Is there anything new?" she asked with a sincere and yet regretful interest.

"There's always something new. At least that's the way the public sees it. I have sent two more on to Mr. Corry. I assume they will meet with his approval. They always do, you know."

5

The various remaining members of the President's Cabinet entered the Cabinet Chambers at an unusually early hour, one by one or in twos and once as a haggard threesome. The first thing they noticed was that an easel had again been set up at the head of the long conference table and that someone had placed upon it the same graph depicting the bell curve of the Nolebody Vaccine half-life. But it was not the exact same graph they had seen in the past, because it had been altered, or at least embellished, in meaningful ways. Someone had performed the task of placing a mark on the graph at each point of the curve that represented another day passed on the horizontal axis, so that the slow and steady progression of time up the curve was now delineated by a series of climbing Xs, like little stickmen sherpas ascending some great peak. And it did not require calculation to see that it would not take many more of the funny little headless figures to complete the attack on the summit.

But the eyes of the Cabinet ministers were drawn not only to the orderly column of sherpas laden with their increasingly heavy burden of portending crisis; they saw too that a large capital letter N had been written in black marker in the very heart of the bell curve, and that the word Nobody had been written below it. They saw the word Nobody written in a bold black print and all they could do was to stare at it in disbelief and look questioningly at each other and then, with a sense of urgency, seek out their seats to sit in silence and wait. Even that exercise filled them with apprehension since it was apparent, as they moved about the table in search of their peripatetic nameplates, that the table had been shortened since the last meeting to accommodate the smaller number of seats that now remained. Nor did it escape their notice that the carpenter had done a hurried job of it, with the newly cut edges of the exotic hardwood splintered and the center of the table now slightly sagging and the legs positioned in a way that interfered with comfort and decorum.

It was the first time any of them had seen the proper noun Nobody for what seemed like ages; for the use of the word Nobody—in its capitalized form—had been legally forbidden by statute and international treaty for a quarter of a century, maybe more. The word at one time had served as the ultimate expression of organized resistance against the new governments of the world that had formed and then transmuted and then nonviolently suppressed the global populace in the aftermath of the dispersal of the Nolebody Vaccine. During that early post-vaccine period, the Nobody Party had stood as the antithesis of the new social order, as the antipode of the Nolebody governments of the world. Its agenda had been peaceful, and its members were multitudinous. They wore black and only black and called themselves Nobodies and offered only passive and yet formidable defiance to the new and supposedly benign autocracies that dispensed goods and services according to the whim and directives of their leaders.

From its modest beginnings, the Nobody Movement had gained great momentum and potential and, at its zenith, by the sheer weight of its coordinated popularity, had threatened to bring down governments and the very foundations on which the new society was based. Finally, in a sweeping global edict that had no precedent and no authoritative basis, the Nobody Party had been outlawed. The use of the capitalized version of the word Nobody, in all its linguistic variations, had been banned on pain of loss of privileges, which in the end meant not only housing and clothes, but even food and the very wherewithal to live.

The excising of the word Nobody from human language and discourse had been swift and definitive, as had the prohibition of the solitary use of the capitalized letter N for any purpose, anywhere. There had even been those in the government who had advocated the legal elimination of the un-capitalized version of the word nobody from permissible vocabulary, but it was ultimately agreed that the word nobody was, in a way, indispensable to the language, and that the elimination of the proper noun necessarily must suffice. After all, there was no denying that there always would be plenty of nobodies in the world, but they would be anonymous and singular, or at least not organized or collective in any way. Frieda Haster and those like her were nobodies, but none of them was a Nobody and not one of them had dared, for a span of twenty years and more, to overtly state that they were.

Now, for the first time in recent memory, the members of the President's Cabinet were directly confronted for unknown reasons by the forbidden word. Some of them thought to approach the easel and erase or efface the offensive graffiti. Others in the room looked away, as though by looking directly at the word some mythological consequence, like blindness or worse, might befall them.

The President entered, followed by the Home Secretary and the Minister of International Affairs and lastly by the Minister of Cultural Affairs. The President's three lieutenants assumed their preeminent seats next to the throne-like chair that was reserved for the President at the head of the truncated conference table. The President himself did not sit. He walked over to the easel and lifted up the wooden pointer that leaned against the tripod, and with a swordsman's precision cut the air with a swoop of the pointer, which whacked the chart and remained motionless where it landed, on the dead center of the N.

"By now, at least some of you should have noticed that matters have gotten worse." His voice was both angry and trembling, as was his hand and the pointer, which he finally lowered to his side. "There are hints that the rising violence is organized. I know it may be too early to know for sure, but the indications are that the Nobodies have re-formed. These recent disturbances have all involved non-governmental workers. They all wear black. Their theme is to disrupt the government. They are all nobodies in the colloquial sense of the word and could easily be Nobodies in the illegal sense as well. It is for that reason that I break protocol and write and speak the forbidden term." He drew a deep breath and then continued. "We cannot deny that the Nobody Party and the Nobody Movement once existed. And in the face of the Half-life Revelation we cannot deny the possibility that the party and the movement might rise up again and wreak havoc on our nation. We must face the reality of it, ladies and gentlemen; we must take preemptive action."

Then he laid out the agenda, the plan that he and the Home Secretary and the Ministers of International and Cultural

Affairs had devised over the past weeks in secret meetings at the presidential residence, which was slowly being fortified with the limited means at hand. "We would like to mobilize an army," the President said to the shock of many of the Cabinet members. "But as you know, the treaties required the destruction of our arsenals. What you don't know," he said, and then he carefully watched for their reaction, "is that we have held back a reserve over all these years. We have no army. No trained forces. But we do have equipment. That is all I will say of it for now.

"We have devised a test to determine whether the vaccination has worn off in the person who is tested, so that we can determine who amongst us can serve usefully in the security forces and in our new military, so that, when necessary, we can determine how dangerous a particular prisoner might be, at least at any given moment. I will take the test daily. All of you and your most trusted assistants will take it weekly. As you can see," he said as he looked to the back of the room where the end of the table used to sit but where now there was only empty space, "we have already randomly applied the test to those we suspected. We will deal with positive results on an ad hoc basis. If it turns out that your vaccination is no longer effective, the manner in which you are treated will depend on what your personal tendencies would be in the absence of an effective vaccination.

"Sometime soon we will ban the wearing of black." He looked about the room, not at the faces of the Cabinet members but at their apparel, and as an afterthought added, "I'm afraid that will mean all of us. Feel free to budget in a new wardrobe. Nothing black, mind you. And please, be reasonable; we are already short of funds.

"We are working on the speech that will make public the fact that the Nolebody Vaccine has an early half-life. We expect to make that speech as soon as reasonably possible. It will be a speech of concession and conciliation. We will attempt to assuage the fears of the public. We will boost food rations and ensure that every recreational facility is open and functioning. We will announce that the cultural icon of the world, Leonard Bentwood, has been named to receive the Nolebody Medal and that he will finally appear before the public at the Nolebody Awards Ceremony. Between our efforts to subtly impose security and our efforts to placate the public by showing that we share the ultimate cultural bond, we hope to maintain public order and ensure a smooth transition in the face of the half-life crisis."

He stopped and looked out across the table to the faces of the Cabinet ministers, but was met only by a dumbfounded and naked silence. "Well," he finally said when it was clear that no one was going to speak. "Does anyone have anything to say, for or against?" Again he waited as the faces stared into nothingness or looked up with glassy eyes at the chart or down into the emptiness of their laps. Finally the Minister of Families, who now sat at what had become the far end of the conference table said, "Don't you think that maybe we are being just a bit hasty? I mean, we don't even really know that the Nobody Party has been resurrected." He paused for a moment, unsure whether it was permissible for him to speak the word. And then, when he was not chastised, he resumed. "I mean, for all we know, these people who have been arrested simply had a bad initial reaction to the vaccine wearing off."

The President sighed and shook his head. With hands held behind his back he slowly strolled across the room to the tall windows that looked out across the lawns to the National Museum. He looked out in a heavy silence while the others in the room waited and hoped. The dewy mist rose off the manicured lawns and the dawning light beamed down upon the capital complex and deflected brilliantly off the east wall of the museum, so that, through the clearing fog, he could not help but notice that under the cover of night someone had crudely painted an enormous black N on the side of the building. He reached down and picked up the birding binoculars he kept at a table near the window, and saw with the greater magnification that the letter must have been painted on the building even as the Cabinet met; that a single trail of black paint still ran and dripped from the bottom of the leg of the N, like the last feeble bleed from a mortal wound.

"No," the President said without turning. "I can assure you that we are not being hasty. If anything, we are far, far too late."

CHAPTER VI

1

There had been only one romantic interlude in Leonard Bentwood's life. Her name was Ruth. More accurately, he had named her Ruth. He had considered other names, but could find none to bring description to what she had been in his mind: not necessarily ruthless—which is what he was forced to settle on in naming her Ruth—but at least remorseless and if not that, then careless. And Remorse and Care were no names for a woman.

She was real only in the imaginative sense; she had never walked the earth, never breathed breath or spoken word. But that minor detail did not diminish her significance to Leonard Bentwood, who had envisioned and then relived the entirety of their failed relationship many thousands of times, in a thousand slightly varied iterations, from its promising inception to its stalled and awkward progression into a predictable failure that left only the crumbled and irredeemable ruins of a misconceived attempt at something less than love. A relationship undermined by the erosion of uncaring and impetuous forces. So he called her Ruth even though In or Im or Un would have been more apt. For in his construction of her, he made her insensitive and inconsiderate and immature and uncaring and unsophisticated, and in other ways instilled her with a character that seemed to thrive on those negative and self-effacing prefixes for shorter, more seductive words.

Ruth, Un, In, Im. They all carried more or less the same meaning to Leonard Bentwood. It was only that Ruth was already a woman's name. So he used Ruth when he ruminated upon the injuries he had suffered in an artificial past.

Throughout the better part of his life, she had been his best unreal friend. He thought of her when he was lonely. He thought of her when he was sad. He would pull out a piece of his unused paper and write RUTH in bold letters at its top. Then he would recall the scenes of what had never happened, with a jot of words remind himself of what he tended to forget, of the insensitivity and immaturity and uncaring manner in which Ruth had responded to his overtures of love and giving. Then, having reminded himself once again that he was better off alone, that never having loved and never having lost was better than that other alternative that always ended in the devastation of rejection, he would set the paper aside and move on to other, more productive endeavors, whatever they might be.

He had been somewhat down that morning, somewhat sad. And not knowing why, he had ascribed his depression to his isolation and the solitary passage of his life. And so he had written himself another reminder of Ruth, of what otherwise might have been.

RUTH

There is a lonesome sadness
that marks the sadness that we mark
There is a hint of tragedy
that rhymes within the workings of the clock
There was a passing moment

And so on.
As was the norm, the words scribbled in his large hand

served their purpose, relieving him of the weight of loneliness that, after all, came only rarely and only when something else of even more subtlety was at the core of his frustrations. He placed the paper with the others that waited to be exploited for some other purpose, for making lists, for cleaning windows, for letters to his mother. And he went outside to work on projects and bask in the pleasures of his life.

2

The four men stood at the base of the mountain and stared into the dark nothingness beyond the mouth of Sealey Cavern, each with their own thoughts and each with a different view of what they saw: a suggestion of perpetual depth and condemnation; an eerie and surreal veil drawn from a promising foreground of rising mountain and lightly colored rock; an intriguing abstraction of pitch and tar; an ominous threat to the bright blue sky above. Until that very week, the cave had been closed and sealed so tightly that not even a scorpion could have flattened its venomous little body into wafer thinness and found its way inside. But a presidential directive had come down and the mining equipment from the nearby government mines had been commandeered and the cave had been reopened and its contents exposed again to the air and seeing eye.

The grayest and by far the oldest of the four men, a paunchy and gentle-looking fellow with a goatee and longish graying hair, stood in the middle of the others in a collegial pose that seemed to invite discussion and exchange. He formerly had been the Minister of History and before that a professor of history at the National University, but the President had recently assigned him to head the newly established Ministry of Defense and had moved his seat at the ministers' conference table from a position in the rear up to the veritable front. Against his better judgment, he now wore a gray jumper of the sort used by government-contracted flight mechanics and custodians throughout the nation, on the shoulder of which someone had hastily pinned some bronze stars to indicate that he was in charge, if not command. At the moment, he was trying to explain a point that he thought he had already made quite clearly. "I have previously explained to you, Mr. Wiles, I am not a general and do not want to be referred to as such. I don't really care what you call me, as long as it's not general. You may call me by my first name, Bob, if you like. And you may refer to me as Minister, if it makes you feel better. But I am not a general and do not want to be a general and I thus do not want to be called general. Now let's go over where we stand. I need to know what is available now and how long it will take us to mobilize."

"Yes, sir," the man named Wiles answered smartly. And it was all he could do to refrain from adding, "General Anderson, sir." And then Wiles turned to look at one of the others—a timid and bookish-looking individual who held in his hands a bound set of papers. "Braley here has got the information you want. Explain it to him, Braley. In summary, I mean."

The man named Braley, who worked as a clerk with security clearance at the National Archives, opened the binder and held it up so that the others could see the individual pages, as if he could avoid explaining anything by simply displaying the information and letting the others divine what the papers said and what they meant. The pages, which had browned and in some cases cracked and chipped with age, flipped over randomly in the breeze, so that not one of the four men could have possibly read the various inventory sheets that showed column after column of items and their quantities and even, in some instances, their model and serial numbers. So Braley finally offered up the information in a summary form. "From what I can tell, Minister Anderson, everything was stored with no thought to using it again. All that is mentioned here are the assets themselves. There is no indication that anyone saved any manuals or spare parts or fuel, not that it would have made sense to leave fuel sitting around for thirty years. It does appear that there is ammunition, though. In fact, from the schematic of the inventory system, it appears that the munitions are in the front of the cave where they can be got at quickly."

The Minister of Defense, who preferred to be referred to as Professor Anderson and who signed his signature with that appellation and who even answered his phone with an announcement to that effect, frowned in disgust. "Well the idiots had it all figured out in advance now, didn't they? We've got forty-year-old planes and forty-year-old tanks and forty-year-old artillery pieces and forty-year-old half-tracks and forty-year-old this and forty-year-old that, but no idea how they work and no way to make them move—at least on their own—and no one who knows how to load them and maneuver them and fire them even if we can find enough men who would be willing to do it."

"Oh, we've got men who are willing to do it, General," Wiles said with a snide, almost predatory grin. He reached out his foot and crushed a small spider that scurried across the sand beneath his feet. "The Ministry of Psychology has got that one figured out. I've seen how they do it personally. We'll have the men we need coming in by the truckload before you can say lick it or spit."

"Well I hope you're right. Because it is going to take an army to pull this stuff out of this cave and figure out how it works and then get it, and the men who will operate it, into decent enough shape for it to even matter."

The four of them walked into the cave, past the guards, whose faces wore a still-life mask of intensity, and the electricians who were setting up generators and stringing wires and lights across the high and multi-colored ceilings of undulating rock that seemed too smooth, too soft to have been made by nature alone. And they could not help but sense the life-giving humidity that invested the cave from unseen sources within the very rock itself, and see the spiders and other insects that moved along the walls, wary of the incoming light and the threat of change that had befallen them.

The Minister of Defense and the others who followed closely behind him walked up and down the long rows of military hardware, flashing their handheld lights this way and that across row after row of machines that had been designed to kill and which in some instances actually had killed in the very wars on which Professor Anderson had written and opined and even critiqued. The first thing the flashlights revealed was that the weapons of war that stood in waiting ranks were more than mere mechanisms designated with cold serial numbers and made of colder metal; they were, in some way, animate, even though they had long been entombed in that remote and heartless cave in a lost sector of the desert mountains. Because many of the planes and tanks and cannons and even the troop trucks and vehicles had long ago been given not only names but personalities, life of a sort: names of loved ones, names of those already dead, names of fighting units, names of gods and goddesses, maybe even names of pets. And as if to ensure their immortality, many had been personified with depictions and caricatures of living beings—women, dogs, a snake, a shark, the very devil itself, as if to remind others, and perhaps themselves, just who and what they were.

The men came back out into the open air, to the light of day. Each of them spontaneously looked up, up at the overwhelming height and breadth of the mountains in which the cave was situated, and up further into the sky, at the wisps of cloud, the depthless heavens. The Minister of Defense shook his head and looked back over his shoulder into the blackness of the cavern. "The first thing we'll be needing is fuel for these things," he finally said with resignation.

Wiles, who stood erect and proud with his shoulders back and his stomach in, said, "They are already on their way, Minister Anderson. Gasoline and diesel and lubricating oils for the whole division."

The Minister of Defense turned and looked directly and sternly into Wiles' eyes. "All of this stuff was supposed to have been destroyed, you know. Under the terms of the Nolebody Treaty. We agreed to destroy all of it. And we even provided evidence that it had all been destroyed."

"Yes," Wiles answered, again with that predatory grin that must have been ingrained congenitally or at least from a very early age. "That's the beauty of it."

3

William Worthington sat in a dark booth set in the far corner of the pub, facing the wall and all but hidden beneath the obscurity of a dim and artificial yellow lantern that was meant to contribute to the antiqued aura of beveled glass and darkly stained pine. He had come there because he knew that it would be safe and that it would be quiet. He had been there before. He had been there before alone.

He needed to think. There were things he needed to sort through. He felt that something was happening to him, but he was not sure whether it was an emotional reaction to the moment or the first signs that the vaccine was wearing off, that he was about to plunge into a hellish world in which a new and terrifying reality unfolded, layer after frightening layer, before his eyes.

He had already ordered and drunk down one of the dark ales that the bartender drew from brass taps emblazoned with swarthy and colorful figures from the past, an ale that bore a name that meant nothing to William Worthington but which others might have recognized as the brew of an ancient highland clan. He drank it down in steady, but not voracious draughts, each time wiping the foam from his lips with a napkin, and then his lips and his mustache and beard with his hand, and then his hand with a swipe or two across his pant leg.

His mind returned again and again to Frieda Haster. He could not reconcile the fact that he thought he loved her and that she was twenty years his elder. It was supposed to be otherwise, he thought. The woman he would share a life with would be younger, less worn with time and less burdened with the personal trauma of a past, more like he was or at least once had been. And he worried for Leonard Bentwood; with each draught of the ale his resolve to protect Leonard Bentwood became more and more entrenched, more determined with each passing reminiscence of what he had seen of Leonard Bentwood, of what he had learned. He thought of the Half-life

Revelation, of the manner in which his body and his mind gave hint that the vaccine in him was wearing off, of the flashes of heat and discomfort he was having in the middle of the night and of the sudden desire to strike at something, to damage something, to do some kind of harm if only in the name of something good. He wondered whether the Nolebody Vaccine was even real, or if it had been conjured up in the imagination of some government-paid psychologists who persuaded the leaders that if you tell enough people that something is true they will believe that it is true and then conform to the new reality.

The waitress returned. He looked up at her through the pallid light and thought how foolish and demeaned she looked in her colonial dress, the low-cut silky blouse and bouncy pleated skirt, her braided hair held back by ribbon and bow. "You want another one?" she repeated when he did not hear. He nodded his head and she turned away with a flip of her pigtails and a bouncy step. The step of a youthful nobody who knew no better.

There was talk from the booth behind him. A group of government workers from some administrative department that dispensed funds for this and collected funds for that. He did not want to hear them, but they were loud, offensive, impolite. "I don't see why the government needs to cater to these people," one of the voices said, too loudly, too sure of itself. "Cater is the right word," a second answered. "You'd think we were here to serve them dinner and wash their clothes. What we ought to do is shut down the government services for a month or two and let them think about that." "The problem," said a third, "is with letting them think at all."

Without intention, by sheer impulse, William Worthington

turned his head slightly aslant and angrily gritted his teeth and raised his fist, all in a single coordinated reaction that should have culminated with him slamming his clenched hand down on the wooden table and maybe even with him confronting the speakers, who did not even realize that he was there in the next booth beside them. Except that he froze with his hand raised, and then he slowly calmed, just as the waitress returned. He drank down the second tankard of the dark and tepid ale in a matter of minutes, fighting through the foam that he did not like and not even bothering to wipe his beard and mustache between one draught and the next. And then he ordered a third and drank it down too, while the three government clerks solved the world's problems with effortless displays of ignorant intolerance and indifferent greed.

He paid his bill and over-tipped the waitress then went outside into the fog of the humid night. He made his way through the security barriers, flashing his identification with disdain at the security workers, who looked at him first with distrust and then with obeisant condescension when they saw he worked at the highest echelon of the government. He came to the central area of the capital complex and walked for a long while until he finally entered the immaculate gardens that surrounded the Cultural Affairs Building. He sat down on the park bench that faced his window and, higher up, the floor-to-ceiling windows of the office of the Minister of Cultural Affairs.

For a long time he sat in the misty nocturnal haze that gradually subsumed and transformed the dark into something less insidious, into something more surreal. He found anonymity in the fact that he could see little other than the outline of evergreens and bushes that had been shaped in sensuous and unreal forms and the façade of the building in which he worked and which towered over him like a white and impenetrable castle wall. He tried to summon up anger, but he could find nothing more than frustration and sadness in the heart of his being. He held his breath and tensed his body, but could not draw up the adrenaline that rested somewhere within him, in wait for a greater need.

He leaned down to the ground, picked up a stone, cast it aside. He picked up another, felt it for smoothness and shape and cast it aside also. He picked up a third and finally found what he sought. He stood and looked up at the panel of windows that marked the office of the Minister of Cultural Affairs and then did nothing for a long while as he gauged the distance and gathered his mental strength so that he might give his theory a valid and determinative test. Then, with great effort, he imagined that the glass was not glass but rather the still and gentle surface of a country pond. He saw it shimmer in the light of an unknown source, and he saw it ripple from the current of an unfelt breeze. He stared and sensed and knew and desired that it was a pond, a pond unlike any other, but a pond nonetheless. And then, with great exertion and perfect aim, he threw what he imagined to be the perfect skipping stone across the glassy surface of the water; he watched it as it sailed through the air and as it skipped, skipped, skipped effortlessly across the surface. He watched it in a sequence disassociated from real time and reality as it glided and skipped and defied, until the surface of the pond, as imagined as it was, itself intervened, and the rock penetrated the still and illusionary surface of the water. And he saw it shatter the Minister of Cultural Affairs' window and, unbeknownst to him, come to rest on the Minister's high-backed chair.

4

Before he even walked up the first of the broad granite steps that led to the Cultural Affairs Building, he knew he had been caught, that he had been seen or filmed breaking the window, or that the circumstantial evidence was enough to convict him as a calculating vandal and a traitor to his own. And yet he knew enough of the government's subtle approach to security issues not to be surprised when the guards did not stop him as he walked by the front desk and up to the elevator bay. As he waited for the lift, he repeated over and over in his mind what he would say when he was confronted by the Minister of Cultural Affairs. "I will make it easy for you, Minister," he would offer. "Yes, I did it. And I'm glad I did. I'm a nobody, Minister Frasier, nothing more."

When he came to his office he found that they had already cleared him out, that his furnishings and certificates and pictures and files and even his personal effects, his books and knickknacks, the dull and average rocks he had picked up as he drove out of Leonard Bentwood's remote corner of the desert, the dried seed pods of yuccas and the dried skeleton of a cholla, all had been removed. He looked at the bare walls, the empty room, the marks on the carpet where his desk and chair and credenza had sat, and he thought how like life itself the room now was, empty and barren, cold and denying. He turned, not knowing where to go next, thinking not of the days to come but of the inevitable moments he now had to endure, only to find himself face to face with the Minister of Cultural Affairs, who held in her hand the embodiment of the perfect skipping stone, which she smoothed over repeatedly with an almost sensuous caress.

"I will make it easy for you, Minister," he almost said, but she was quicker to speak. "You're late," she said. "Again, I might add." He stood before her, muted as he again tried to summon the words of confession. "I told them to pack without waiting for you," she said. "They've moved us to the presidential residence. To the Situation Room. We are going to have to work in close quarters for the next few weeks." She hefted the skipping stone and softly smoothed it over again and again. "There were several breaches of security in the capital complex last night. This little present was delivered personally to me, straight through my window. I'm glad I wasn't there at the time. Whoever threw it had a perfect aim. I might have been killed."

It was Wednesday, which meant it was again time for William Worthington to submit to the Nolebody Vaccine test that the Ministry of Psychology was administering weekly to government personnel with the highest clearance. "I'm supposed to be at the testing center at ten o'clock," he said in an unsure voice.

And she answered, "Yes, I know. You had better not be late with them. They might not be as patient as I would be."

They walked out together, past the security desk that now was staffed with twice the number of people, and down the wide granite steps that led in every direction to the buildings of the capital complex. "I am assuming it will be the same drill," William Worthington said. "They seem to be efficient enough at it. I should be over to the presidential residence by eleven. Where should I meet you?" he asked without enthusiasm.

"Just show your badge at the entrance. They'll give you an escort to the Situation Room. It's quite secure. Three floors down, encased in reinforced concrete. You'd never find it on your own, even if they let you try."

He made his way to the Psychology Center, past the guards, who scrutinized his credentials closely and with an unfriendly attitude, with a practiced emphasis on the serious nature of the business that was conducted inside. Up the narrow flight of stairs, into a waiting room that offered nothing other than cold plastic chairs and a water fountain—no magazines through which to browse, no pictures on the wall, no windows through which to gaze. A test of his patience, he supposed.

After a while, the unmarked door to the interior examination room opened and a lanky middle-aged male with a sallow face exited. He stared straight ahead as he looked into the room, his eyes twitching with what might have been fear or, if not that, the still-vivid memory of real or imagined pain. He walked past William Worthington without acknowledgement, perhaps without even knowing that William Worthington was there, past him and through the door that led into the hallway and beyond.

The door to the examination room opened again and a severe, sturdy-looking woman with cropped hair and squinting eyes came out. "William Worthington," she called out, as if there were anyone else in the room other than him. He walked through the door and she shut it behind him.

They performed the tests in much the same way as they had on the prior occasion. He was insulted, verbally and by displays of material he would never have wanted to see. He was slapped when he did not expect it. His life, his credentials, his curriculum vitae, so to speak, were demeaned beyond exaggeration. He was subjected to pain, which they knew could be imposed with the least of pressures once one knew where and how and with what aids; he was forced into corners that allowed for no further retreat. He was pushed to the wall.

He bore it all with a passive reaction that made no suggestion of resistance, let alone defense. They proceeded through their ritual with a punctilious and practiced precision, with nothing to suggest regret or even sympathy on the part of the supervising technician and the director of the program. And he endured it all not only in acquiescence, but also by making it even easier for them, if and when he could. For twenty minutes exactly. Twenty minutes of what some might call torture but which they called an examination. And the irony of it was that he could have stopped it at any time, or at least defended against it; not because the vaccine in him had reached its half-life and had worn off. Because it hadn't. But because he now knew that the vaccine itself was not foolproof. A nonviolent individual could commit acts of violence simply by pretending that what was done was not intended to be violent. By imagining that the act was not one of aggression but merely something involving benign intent. Like the imagined throwing of a skipping stone, with no other motivation than to see how many times the laws of physics would allow you to make it jump over the surface of a pond before gravity and friction took over and sank it beneath the tranquil water that was merely the figment of an illusory vision.

5

The Situation Room in the presidential residence had not been used for its originally intended purpose for decades. Instead, it had served as a convenient storage facility for the endless accumulations of the five presidents who had lived in the residence since the advent of the Nolebody Vaccine. No one could remember who first proposed to use the room as a place to store the diverse and unwanted assortment of gifts and apparel, the photographs and plaques and awards, the bribes and inducements and remembrances of each succeeding presidency. In the end, it proved to be the wrong place. The ventilation system, which had been designed to accommodate a throng of sweating and anxiously respiring people working under intense pressures, relentlessly sucked the humidity out of the room without abatement, drying and splitting, cracking and crumbling the storied treasures and memorabilia of yesteryear as if they had been left atop the highest of desert mountains.

It had no windows, of course. And no skylights, naturally. No living plants. No suggestion of decoration or decor. And while the air was as sterile and purified as one would hope, it certainly was not fresh and, scientifically, was only air in the sense that it contained the appropriate proportions of oxygen and nitrogen to pass for the same thing that circulated outdoors. The room recently had been returned to a semblance of its former self, but nothing that was needed was available, the original equipment was long gone and long outdated, and compromises had been made. A variety of electronic maps had been commandeered from the Department of Meteorology and had been installed high up on the walls. With the push of a button, the operator could scroll the maps from hemisphere to hemisphere, continent to continent, sea to sea; but no one had found a way to eliminate the happy suns and frowning winds and clouds with puffed up cheeks that rolled across the map like flying ghouls and cartoonish weather gods. And that was not all. Inaccurate globes from a local elementary school also had been brought in and placed in two corners of the room, like fraternally twinned planets from a solar system in a sister dimension. Dozens of incompatible phone lines and television screens had been rigged and cross-rigged and jury-rigged and their wires had been strung across the room like the broken multicolored web of a phantasmagorical spider. A phone would ring and then others would follow. A television screen would come on to display a closed-circuit picture, only to turn off when the video shunted to another screen. Desks and tables of varying height and width had been placed in awkward rows and face to face, creating faulted topographies that might have been bred out of a series of diminutive earthquakes. And on and on until there was little space to stand or sit and no promise of comfort or functionality to be found in the room anywhere, at any time.

Not one of the ten or so people in the room had had any direct experience with matters concerning crowd control, let alone military conflict or armed rebellion. That sort of background did not qualify you to act on behalf of the government in the post-Nolebody epoch even if you were the Home Secretary or the Minister of International Affairs or Defense or Psychology. There was no standing army to defend against a nonexistent enemy, no flotilla of naval vessels to stand watch over a coastline that had no need of protection, no air forces because there had been no need to employ force in the air or, for that matter, on the ground or even beneath the sea. And so there were no generals in the room either. No admirals. No commanders, no colonels, no privates, no seamen, no airmen, even though in the last month the government had begun, secretly and in violation of treaty and diplomatic promise, to create a complete array of military forces, all conceptualized in the minds of the President and his most intimate counselors, all of whom were now assembled in the Situation Room.

William Worthington had come to the presidential residence directly from his examination at the Ministry of Psychology and had been admitted to the Situation Room while its occupants were in the midst of heated debate. The guard opened the four-inch-thick steel portal that was more like the door to a bank vault than anything else, and the first thing William Worthington heard was the President say, "That's absurd."

The guard gave William Worthington a gentle nudge in the back, pushing him forward enough so that the guard could swing the heavy door back to its closed and locked position. William Worthington found himself standing side by side with the man the President was addressing—Robert M. Anderson, III, Professor Emeritus, former chair of the History Department at the National University, and dean of the Anderson school of military theory—someone that William Worthington had long admired and often read.

Anderson's *The After Math of War: Recalculating War's Cost in Hindsight*, which was by far the most highly acclaimed of his many works on the internecine human struggle that had engulfed the world in the period immediately preceding the Nolebody Vaccine epoch, rightly placed Professor Anderson as first amongst a competition of peers that included many military officers-turned-academics who had tried to find new meaning for their lives once war had come to a permanent end. Anderson's treatises on military history were remarkable not only for the surgical precision with which he deconstructed the origins and execution of war and warring nations, but also for his merciless assault on the institution of war itself, for which he offered no quarter and granted no mercies. There was a particular line from Professor Anderson's final work—

Unwarranted War Rants—that had always impressed William Worthington as the perfect summing up:

> All wars are failures from inception, not because they fail to accomplish what they set out to accomplish, but because what they seek to accomplish cannot be accomplished by war.

At the very pinnacle of his academic career, Professor Robert Anderson breached the ramparts of the mandatory retirement age of sixty-four, and it was thus at the very height of his intellectual prowess, and all in strict accordance with the pension laws, that he surrendered his employment as a university professor. His forced retreat was a modest disappointment to academia, and much more so to the consuming public who read his works with an almost nostalgic fervor even though most of his readers had no personal recollection of the periods of which he wrote and even fewer comprehended much of what he had to say. He slowly faded from the public eye and into the twilight of his days until, just a month or so ago and for reasons that remained unexplained if not obscure, the President had appointed him to the newly created post of Minister of History and then, just weeks later and in utter secrecy, as the head of the Ministry of Defense, the very existence of which was publicized only on a need-to-know basis.

Professor Anderson had no interest in the Ministry of Defense post, and he had told the President so. "What you need, Mr. President, is a younger man. Someone with enthusiasm for action and excitement." When the President replied by telling him he was confident the professor knew better than anyone how an army should be run, the professor had added, "That is not what we academics do, Mr. President. We do not live in the real world. We live in the theoretical world in which nothing is real. Ours is to opine on the sublime, Mr. President, not on the mundane. We collate and distill the wisdom and lessons of the past and postulate philosophical wisdoms and lessons for the future. Our product has no practical application, Mr. President. I mean, other than for intellectual learning." But the President would have none of it, and Professor Robert Anderson had dutifully assumed his role as the Minister of Defense.

The President had just characterized something Professor Anderson had said as "absurd," and Professor Anderson would not stand for it. "'Absurd' is a word that should not be used lightly, Mr. President," he lectured. "'Absurd' means ridiculous or unreasonable and I hardly think it is ridiculous or unreasonable to state what is a matter of pure and rational fact. It is clear from observation that most of those who can fly the planes or operate the tanks and artillery are either too old or have no present inclination to use those objects forcefully against other humans. I have gone over this with the Minister of Psychology, who has confirmed for me that there is no way to cause these men and women, no matter how loyal they are to you and the government or how biased they might be against the nobodies of the world, to take up arms against other men and women until such time as the vaccine has worn off. And, as I have now said repeatedly, by the time it wears off in enough of them, whenever that might be, in all probability it will be too late. I have not left anything out, have I, Minister?"

He turned to the Minister of Psychology, who icily smiled in agreement with his statement and shook her head no.

"I do not mean to say," Professor Anderson added, "that we

are unable to find men and women to bear arms. There are plenty of foot soldiers to be had. Why, I have one sergeant who spends the better part of his day searching for insects he can squash. So you can have an army if you like. The problem is in finding leaders." This last statement gave him reason to pause, reminded him of something he had written long ago, but, on reflection, he thought better of mentioning it to the others in the room. "And as we know, an army without adequate leadership is nothing more than a mob."

"What you are saying then," the President said, ignoring the reference to a mob, "is that your people cannot even be made to drive the tanks? To fly the planes? Even if someone else is pushing the buttons that drop the bombs or shoot the guns? Is that what you are saying?"

"It's an indirect effect of the vaccination," the Minister of Psychology chimed in. "It seems that an attempt to induce the subject to be involved, even indirectly, in an act of violence excites the temporal lobe, which, due to its elevated state of activity, interferes with the cortical neurons sufficiently to render the subject incapable of doing much of anything." All of which was what was known in the colloquial as hogwash, because the Ministry of Psychology had not actually statistically verified the premise and certainly had not identified its cause. "It is a sort of defense mechanism the brain uses to ensure that the host does not circumvent the vaccination," the Minister of Psychology continued in her self-aggrandizing lie. "As far as we can tell, it is foolproof. Meaning, there is no way around it."

"Then what you are saying," the President capitulated, "is that we cannot count on the Ministry of Defense to provide any assistance in the days and weeks to come."

Which is not what Professor Anderson had said, and he thus interceded in one last effort to make clear what he thought he had made clear from the beginning. "It depends on what we are trying to accomplish," he said as he shook his head in frustration, as if all of his years of scholarship had gone unheeded. "It might do well to recall the words of the ancient philosopher Annealius: 'The only purpose of war is to eliminate war and the only way to eliminate war is by waging war; it thus follows that if it is one's wish to eliminate war he should wage war with vigor and without hesitation.'"

William Worthington listened to it all and said nothing, but he knew that they were wrong. He knew that the nonviolent could be trained to commit the very acts that apparently would suffice to keep the government in power as the crisis and the unknown unfolded before their very eyes. He looked over at the Minister of Cultural Affairs who had listened to the debate with interest. He knew that for her the outcome of the discussion was that her role over the next few weeks had become even more significant and determinative. And he saw how she continued to examine and sometimes even caress the skipping stone, as though, with enough of hope and care and mystical belief, it might grant her every wish or answer her every question.

CHAPTER VII

1

At the most, a week passed. Six or seven of the little headless sherpas gained on the peak of the Nolebody half-life bell curve. The cartoonish gusts, the smiling sunny face, the fluffs of cloud with happy eyes and billowing cheeks moved back and forth across the maps in the Situation Room without regard for the direction of the prevailing winds, with no relation to the actual rise and fall of temperatures across the globe. The video screens captured narrow images of narrow scenes and missed all else that transpired out of view and out of range. The President moved toward the verge of panic. His counselors schemed and lied and failed. William Worthington's beard grew and he kept it long. Even Leonard Bentwood began to feel the press of change, pangs of frustration, a discomfort bred of restlessness and something else—something new and undefined.

He had run out of paper. He had gone through ream after ream and scrap after scrap noting any thing, any idea that might cause him to recall William Worthington's name. It was as though the interior of his little barnboard shack had been wallpapered in a nouveau decorative style that evolved each time a piece of tape failed or a breeze knocked a page from off a shelf, from off the wall. But the lack of paper had not stopped him. He had resorted to writing on old magazines, on the table, on the floor, scribbling nonsensical words that did not entail recollection but only a fantastic search for something he should have known all along. Until finally, having failed to recall William Worthington's name or any other trigger that might stimulate memory of who the visitor had been and what he had wanted, Leonard Bentwood gave up.

It was not the first time that he had failed to remember something despite repeated and vigorous effort. But it was the first time that it really mattered to him, even though he did not know why it mattered and could never have explained what had driven him to attempt to recall the name that had been lost with scores of other names somewhere in some repository of his mind.

He went outside, into the morning cold that had finally come with the approach of early autumn. Into the unbelievable chorus of birds that gathered in greater number, on the edge of migration or on the cusp of newly fledged wings and flightful ambition. He sat into his rocking chair, eased himself down as though a great labor had been completed, and gently pushed back and forth, back, forth, as he rolled a cigarette and then smoked it in its entirety. All the while he drank his coffee, considering what he might do now, now that his preoccupation with the unknown name had been exhausted. The smoke from the cigarette and the steam from the coffee curled into the air and commingled and dissipated in wispy humid fragrant clouds up through the miniature leaves of the mesquite and palo verde that had fully rejuvenated after the monsoon rains.

Something, perhaps the song of a bird he could not identify, caused him to fret again over what he could not recall, and that thought then turned to his last conversation with Frieda, just a few days back. She had come to deliver the mail and his supplies and his mother's letter. When she learned that he had no letter to send to his mother, and when she saw that he had been wildly preoccupied with his struggle to recall the name and purpose of William Worthington, she had become impatient with him. She had become impatient with Leonard Bentwood for the first time that he could ever remember. "You have become obsessed with this, Leonard," she said with gentle admonition. When he asked her if she recalled his name, she said abruptly, impolitely, "No, Leonard, I can hardly remember his face." He had not believed her; and he wondered why. "You need to get off of this," she had said harshly. "You have better things to do with your time than waste paper on something that doesn't matter."

The birds sang and chirped and whistled and fussed and cooed for an hour, and then the sounds subsided back into the more reasonable, complacent norm of the maturing day; the sun rose above the desert floor and bore down upon the porch until it achieved a great intensity, as if it had been focused by a magnifying glass to burn on that spot alone, until it became too hot to bear and Leonard Bentwood finally rose and went inside.

He had decided that he needed to get away, that the time had come for him to go up into the trees, for at least a few nights— up high amid the aspen and pine and fir, into the thinner air and cooler breeze where he might clear his thoughts and bring back the calm on which he depended, on which he thrived. He found the duffle bag and packed what he would need. Some changes of clothes. A sleeping bag. Food and water bottles. His knife. A book of poems and a frail and damaged pair of reading glasses. His forest map, if only he could find it. His compass, which he did not know how to use, and his tobacco and rolling papers, which he did and would. The bottle of brandy. Matches. Some paper to kindle a fire. The little miniature binoculars Frieda had given him years ago. A good knife for whittling. A pillow for his head.

He went out back and dug in the inventory of metal and rubber tires piled in a heap beneath the spreading mesquite that shaded his truck. Digging carefully through the bramble of metal and detritus to avoid the spiders and scorpions and centipedes that waited in the cool moisture for a victim, for a meal. He pulled out the rusted and fraying metal cable he had scavenged somewhere in the desert along a long-abandoned road, a road that someone had intentionally blocked and bermed to keep intruders out. He dug some more, now toward the edge of the pile where he recalled something, an old sign, that would serve his purpose. He pulled that out too—a foot square piece of aluminum which on one side said in fading reddish words: KEEP OUT, Missile Testing Site.

He dragged the cable behind him with the sign stuck underneath his arm, around the corner of the house, scaring off a collared lizard that all but flew across the heated scrabble of sand and rock in flight of terror from the grizzled biped whose metallic tail whipped across the ground like a braided scythe. At the porch, he stopped, put the cable and the sign down and dug into a collection of scrap wire that lay in a wooden box, pulling out six or eight varied lengths, leaving the rest for another time, another project. He went inside, found a little bottle of black acrylic and a brush, came back out and painted the words Closed, Gone Fishing on the shiny side of the sign. Then he picked up the cable and the sign and the little bundle of bailing wires and carried them all to the gateposts on which a gate had never been hung and dropped them to the side. He went back to the shack, secured the door, but never thought to check the windows. He threw his duffle in the truck and drove the truck through the gateposts, where he stopped it. He got out and strung the cable between the posts, wired the sign to the middle of the cable and then stood there, looking back at his shack with something of a broken heart, as though he were leaving home forever.

2

There had been a time far back when Leonard Bentwood regularly had made his way up into the mountains and the forest wilderness, back when he was young or at least still youthful and it was his body rather than his mind that required exhilaration and appeasement. With an old army rucksack on his back, he would explore the most remote of trails if trails they even were, cutting his way into and through the very heart of the mountain den, to the rugged heights, near the tree line where the forks of what would become river formed from seep and stream to cut their way down, cascading through rock and fallen tree and tumbled boulder into great canyons of sandstone and feldspar and intrusive igneous rock. From morning to evening, for days on end, he would trod paths once used by indigenous natives, inhaling the same resinous sweetness of the pine, immersed in the same contradictory stimulations bred of convergent desert heat and rarified mountain air, sharing the pristine wild with the squirrels and deer and elk, the bear and lion and even the few remaining wolves, throughout the tranquility of each day and the vulnerability of each tentless night. And at times he almost imagined that he could see them, the native peoples who long ago had built their mud-walled dwellings into the canyon cliffs and who had spent long days gathering their paradise unto themselves, watching the carving river pass.

But he had not been there for many years, and he knew

that now it would be different, that he would barely be able to penetrate the edges of the primitive wilderness because he could no longer hike it; because he would have to settle for his dependency on his truck, which meant he must rely on roads, and roads could not mean wilderness under any definition. He drove slowly up the winding highway that rose up through what now were foothills but which eons ago had been root and base of a massive range, looking the whole while for a forest road or trail that might suit his need to be alone, away from the sounds of the highway, alone with tree and rock. Up through the spotted hills of pinion and juniper and yucca. Down into ravines where water once had flowed but where it seemed it might never flow again. Higher into the mountains, until the shaded, mostly northern slopes showed scatterings of pine, stunted and gnarly and staid. Around bends, up switchbacks, along narrow ledges; up and into the unfolding tangle of long-needle pine and corkbark fir.

Finally, he saw the hint of what he sought—a two-track trail that led into the gaping mouth of the beginnings of a canyon. He stopped his battered and rattling truck and sat there for a while in silence, listening and looking, wanting to be sure. He heard nothing but a few jays, the chatter of a squirrel; saw nothing but the canyon walls and the pines and sycamore and cottonwood swaying in the gentle breeze. He turned on the ignition and the truck sputtered back to life and he drove slowly up the dirt road, ignoring the sign that purported to tell him where he was—another name for another place on a map filled with unnecessary names and marks and designations. With the window down and the sun breaching the canyon walls and the water in the creek flowing at a steady gurgle and swollen by the monsoon rains that had fallen there in even greater fury, he drove into the mountain canyon sanctuary so adorned with spires and altars of stone and ledge, side-canyon apses and buttressed walls, that to another eye it might have been the ruins of a great sandstone abbey of an earlier era, on another continent.

All that day and all that night Leonard Bentwood absorbed the calming salve of his mountain retreat. He had brought with him a tattered book of poems, written by a poet from a long-past century, written in a time when the romantically and the lyrically inclined were more willing to yield to the seductions of nature to evade the cruelties of struggle and strife. He put on his broken reading glasses and picked through the poems like a buyer at a fruit stand, relying not only on the titles to decide which to read and which to avoid—poems of love and poems of family, odes to friends, laments of war and battle— but squeezing them and plying them first before he made the choice of what he would read and reread and reread yet again, after his own fashion and style. And the poems, which rhymed and metered along in differing moods and differing tone, with great regard for structure and form, brought to him a sense of calm and reassurance by their sensibility and sentiment.

He slept that night as one could almost always sleep at that time of the year in the great southwestern mountains. Open to the air and yet with tarp strung up beneath tree and limb so that as last resort there might be a place to retreat and yet remain outdoors. He slept well, better than he had for many months and maybe many years, waking to see the stars casting overhead and fading back into dream despite the stomping of hoof or the snuffling of some creature along the ground nearby. He slept and he dreamt and he woke to the early morning light with little recollection of anything other than the distant cry of a coyote, far off and deeply emoting, late into the night.

The morning brought with it new sounds that seemed alien and out of place to Leonard Bentwood. The distant sound of thunder, he thought at first; the irregular boom, boom, boom of giant drums in the land of giants. When it did not stop, but instead increased, not in volume but in frequency, he decided he would spend his day in search of what was causing the sound of drums when he had never known of such a sound before.

He breakfasted on fruit and bread and honey, drank down cup after cup of coffee grounds mixed in the stream water, which he warmed on the tiniest of fires. Then he packed some items and picked his way up the western slope of the canyon, up the broken rock walls and across slides of scree that gave way beneath his feet, holding on to branches that sometimes cracked and gave way even before he could place his weight upon them and sometimes stabbed and cut with thorns he had not seen. Gradually and carefully up the longish ridge, only to find another higher ridge beyond the first. Up that ridge too, with his first bottle of water already consumed and his old legs tiring and then tired and his old heart wearied by the work that seemed far too great for far too little progress. To the top, only to see yet another, higher ridge beyond it, although this time clearly the last ridge because there was something to it that said that from there the earth fell away into nothingness, down into the lower elevations.

He paused and drank again, and he thought how odd it was that everything could be obscured by the last little slice of obstruction; that you could climb up slope and ledge and canyon wall, gain hundreds and hundreds of feet in elevation in an effort to see what lay on the other side, and you could make all but the last few steps and never learn what was there for you to see beyond, as though only the last step really mattered. So he savored the last ten feet, stopping and eating from his mixture of raisins and nuts and seeds, drinking more of the precious water, catching his breath, regaining his strength before he crested the top, so that when he came over the ledge and caught the vista he would immediately benefit from the rigor of his labors. He drew one more breath then pulled himself up and made the crawl to the peak.

Below him, spread out at the base of the mountain at the beginnings of a vast desert of gypsum flat and gypsum dune, he saw what reminded him of something he had seen in his youth. A television documentary, perhaps. Something about movie sets and actors and how movies were made. When he pulled out his bird glasses, the tiny binoculars that Frieda had given him with the explanation that the lack in aperture was more than made up in one's ability to hold the glasses steady, he confirmed in his mind that it was, indeed, a movie being produced there below him in the brilliant white-sanded desert. A movie of war and war machines. A movie of the folly of humankind.

There was so much to see that he could never have taken all of it in, but he saw enough to conclude that it must have been a farce, a comedy of sorts that they were filming, for no one in reality could have been as inept as the characters he saw with sufficient clarity through the magnifying lenses of the binoculars. They drove airplanes in circles on the ground and sometimes ran into other objects they should have been able to avoid. They swerved tanks this way and that, jackknifing trailers and artillery pieces when they tried to back up and reposition their armament in rows or columns on the road.

They zigged and zagged with no rhyme or reason, jerked here and there in hopeless disassociation from what the others around them did. He watched them, noted their lack of improvement and their lack of cohesion, for the better part of an hour, and he thought how much they were like shrimp larvae he had once seen as a child at the public aquarium, directionless and mindless, struggling to survive without any sense of purpose or orientation.

Had he been able to see more closely, though, with greater magnification, he would have seen that it was not fiction that he was observing, but life itself being practiced in advance of its occurrence. For the artillery shells that set off the thunderous booms, and which continued even as Leonard Bentwood watched, were real, as were the rounds being fired with poor aim and to no effect by the tank cannons and mortars and rifles and guns. Which could never have been the case on any movie set in that day, in that age in which such things were not supposed to even exist. And had Leonard Bentwood been able to see with even greater magnification, had he owned the sort of field glasses that at that moment were draped around the neck of Sergeant Wiles, who stood far below him barking and personally reinforcing orders without relent, he would have seen that there were those amongst the actors who had brought more than a dramatized portrayal of violence to the scene, that there were those amongst the cast who, in fact, had no need to act at all.

He watched for a while longer, all the time smiling and twice even laughing at the ludicrous aspect of what he saw, with the gridlock and futility of it all as obvious and engaging as one could wish for in any entertainment. And then he made his way down slowly, back into the canyon, which looked far steeper in descent than in ascension.

By the time he made it back to the canyon floor, he was all but exhausted. He thought that he might reward himself for his effort, for having achieved such a great elevation and for having found the means to enjoy something of the humorous side of humanity. He rolled two cigarettes, nicely and thickly filled with tobacco, and pulled out his bottle of brandy. He walked a ways down the creek, found a large boulder along the water's edge, perched high and on the eastern side so that it still caught the late afternoon sun. He sat there listening to the water and smoking first one cigarette and then another and partaking in the brandy with the rock beneath him warm and the canyon walls lit a bright yellow by the westering sun.

He became light-headed from the combination of tobacco and brandy and the weariness that had descended upon him, and it heightened his senses, his imagination. He saw a butterfly lilt by on the wafting breeze and thought how like a magic carpet with head and legs it was. He saw the trees bend and then lift their branches in the lightest of winds and thought how they were servants to the canyon god, fanning their lord with the gentle sweeps of their pine needle fronds. He saw a place where the creek waters dropped off a ledge and down into a little pool and thought he saw the vestiges of a tropical scene, with sandy beach and stranded outrigger canoe. And when he rubbed his tired eyes and the vision did not go away, he rose and moved over to the spot and lifted the broken remains of a diminutive water craft out of the wedge of rocks where it had jammed and stuck.

Leonard Bentwood looked at the paper sail that had been lashed to the mast with a twisted curl of beargrass and he could not believe his eyes. In raised black ink, the sail said

William Worthington
Assistant to the Minister of Cultural Affairs

It was as though an electrical storm of scattered recollection had been set off in Leonard Bentwood's mind. In momentary flashes of light and dark, he remembered first William Worthington's name and then a face, albeit both pale and shaved and tanned and bearded and lastly, fragments of a conversation, something vague and unclear, relating to nobody, and to the nation's honor, and something more. But he could not recall the remainder, not then, not there with the sun gloriously illuminating the canyon and the creek waters flowing and a weariness such as he had not known for years creeping over him like a long-awaited dream.

3

It was the most important speech of his political career—perhaps the only important speech of his life—and the President thus indulged his counselors by accepting their advice that the speech be scripted and edited to perfection. It took two days to produce, and in the end it consumed enough film to stretch a ribbon from the capital city to the westernmost coast. The President made his delivery of a sentence or two, or a paragraph or two at the most, and then they stopped and reviewed it and cut it and revised the words and his manner of delivery and then they recorded some of it again, and then integrated what they liked into what they had already accepted. By the end of the first day, only half of the speech, which itself would prove to be only fifteen minutes long, had been recorded to their satisfaction. So the President had retired for the night and they had started anew on the following morning, again figuratively snipping, delicately inserting, peremptorily withdrawing, recording again and again the same or similar words until they got it right. To those who in later years closely scrutinized the video of the speech, it was like watching something in accelerated time, with the President visibly tiring with the passage of only a few minutes and his beard growing darker and then the President suddenly shaved and rejuvenated, albeit with a newly raised blemish that popped up from out of nowhere and which all the makeup in the world could not fully obscure.

Mary Bentwood watched the speech from the comfort of her lounging chair in her sunroom. She had been viewing a rerun of her favorite daytime drama—something involving a cast of overaged and oversexed overachievers in a highrise building in which all of the attractive tenants knew each other intimately, for thirty stories in all directions. An intriguing episode was just reaching a particularly climactic moment when it was interrupted by an announcement that the President would speak to the nation on a topic of the utmost importance. The screen went blank and whatever it was that transpired between Richard McClarendon and Vanessa Poplar, both of Paradise Terrace, remained unknown to those who had not seen that particular episode on one of the twelve occasions on which it had been previously shown.

The television screen flashed into navy blue and then cut to a scene that looked like an interior view of an opulent palace from a bygone era but actually was a tunneling close-up of the grand foyer of the presidential residence. For a while nothing happened and the screen showed nothing else, until in the far background a figure appeared and slowly strode toward the foreground with a parade-like cadence in his step, with a theatrical confidence that was belied by his inherent lack of dignity. It soon became evident that it was the President, dressed in a dark suit that had never before been worn and which had been pressed so thoroughly that it would not admit of wrinkle or fold. He approached the podium, on each side of which were posted enormous flags—the flag of the nation and the presidential banner, both of which sported the long-familiar war eagle whose talons tightly gripped the weapons of former times. He looked into the camera, seemingly waiting for a signal that all was ready, and when he did not receive one he finally said, "My fellow citizens . . . My fellow citizens of the world."

He spent a solid ten minutes—two thirds of the entire speech—discussing the fact that scientists had recently determined that the Nolebody Vaccine had an early half-life and how the vaccine would reach its half-life sometime the following week. "For some of us," he said, "the vaccine has already worn off, whereas others of us will have to wait." He attempted to describe the science of molecular decay, its inevitability and randomness and the remotely potential quirks of probabilities and chance. And then he discussed the known science of vaccines and immunizations and the unavoidable implications in light of the Half-life Revelation and the fact that the Nolebody Vaccine was a vaccination against itself.

Many, if not most of those who heard the first portion of the President's speech were not even sure what he was saying. Yes, the population of the world generally knew about the Nolebody Vaccine and how its dispersal via water and atmosphere had inoculated the world from the disease of violence. But the concept of a half-life was not so easy to grasp. Words like "nucleotide" and phrases such as "synthesis inhibitor" were unusual, to say the least. A life, after all, was a life; a half-life seemed like a peculiar proposition, an oxymoron, since something was either alive or not alive; dead or alive, if you like. In a strictly grammatical sense, the President's explanation was clear enough. But it presupposed that his audience was thoughtfully listening and that his audience was sufficiently astute. Both of those suppositions were baseless in a world in which inattentiveness and ignorance had been fostered by the very government that the President ran and sought to perpetuate far into the future. Fewer than half of those who heard the first two thirds of the President's speech understood it, more than half of those believed it was untrue, and the majority of the remainder thought little more than that the speech was an artifice for some ulterior motive the President would not reveal.

"In the days to come," the President said as he summed up the first portion of his speech with a paternal look of benevolent sincerity, "we are going to have to look out for each other. We will need to remain calm and we will all need to control our emotions." He explained that when the time came for any particular person, the vaccine would wear off instantly, but that no one could know how any particular person would react after that. "All we know," the President said, and now he spoke sternly and with a fervency that was as staged as it was strong and assertive, "is that criminal offenders will be dealt with harshly. There will be no tolerance for crime in the days to come. Any disturbance of the peace will be dealt with by immediate imprisonment without trial under the mandate of martial law." And so the people knew at least that it had come to that.

Mary Bentwood listened to it all and grew more and more concerned; she worried what the implications were for her son and whether he could be kept secure in his hidden desert sanctuary in a future in which fences and signs might not be enough to keep trespassers out. She wondered whether the government would seize the enormous swath of land that she and Frieda had slowly purchased and aggregated over the years, over decades, and placed under the protective covenants of the LB Trust. She wondered whether they had already done it, whether the government had plans to turn the land into a bombing range or a military training ground or a site for something even more insidious. She suspected that might be the very reason why she had not received a weekly letter from Leonard. She wondered if Frieda had known. She picked up her glass of freshly squeezed lemonade and drank it down in gulps as she stared at the President, whom she noticed sometimes moved with jerks and spasms, like the actors in her daytime shows when the weather interfered with the reception and the picture froze and then leaped ahead.

The President waxed sentimental. "We must remember we have common bonds, that we share the same needs and desires, the same goals and objectives, that we all love life and its simplicities. It is for that reason," the President said, now with a look of kindness and concern that almost pleaded for cooperation, "that I am so pleased to be able to announce that Leonard Bentwood, in whom we all have found comfort and solace in our times of need, to whom the nation and indeed the world has always been able to look for emotional guidance and insight, the only living human being who can rightfully claim to be a citizen not only of our nation but a citizen of the world and of the entire universe, has agreed to come to the capital city, to come out of seclusion at our time of need, and to accept the Nolebody Medal which, as you know, is the nation's highest honor." The President proceeded to remind the listening audience in great detail of Leonard Bentwood's many contributions to the arts and social and philosophical thought and consciousness. And to everyone who heard it, the President's announcement had the instantaneous effect that comes with the delivery of the sudden and shocking news of some great historical event; it carved indelible pathways into the living memory of the listener and the observer, as if the recollection of who and what and where you were when the news of it came would still be recalled after all else was forgotten.

Frieda Haster heard a crackling rendition of the speech on the radio of her truck as she made her mail delivery. She had known in advance that it was coming. William Worthington had even given her the time at which it would occur. And she knew what the President would say because William had read the speech verbatim to her in the course of the last of their daily phone calls that had become more and more personal and intimately confiding. But she could never have prepared herself for the effect it had upon her. She cried when the President mentioned Leonard's name, and she feared, just as Mary Bentwood simultaneously feared, for Leonard Bentwood and the world.

William Worthington watched it live on television. He stood in a cramped corner of the Situation Room with the remainder of the crisis team and watched one of the twenty-seven screens that showed the speech in varying resolutions and in varying magnification. When it was over, he felt worn with exhaustion, as though his heart had sunk deep and irretrievably into despair. The remainder of those in the room turned to the President when it was over and as if on cue broke into applause. The President smiled weakly, shook hands all around, and when he came last to William Worthington he said, "The rest is up to you, Bill. You and Leonard Bentwood."

4

Leonard Bentwood did not hear and did not see the President's speech. He owned neither radio nor television and, in any event, was far too preoccupied at the moment to have wasted his time on the triviality of the news and politics. He had come down from the mountains in a plummeting descent that was uncontrolled and all afire. From the first early hour of his return to his desert shack, he had immersed himself in a frantic search for the final pieces of the William Worthington puzzle.

The answers he sought had only slowly emerged as he consumed page after page of the scraps of paper he was forced to scavenge and tape together to provide the platform for his work. It was on his tenth or eleventh try that he made real progress despite the fact that his tired eyes seemed to blur the words he scribbled before he even tried to read them. He again wrote William Worthington's name, William Worthington's title on the top of a page, and this time it reminded him of Frieda, although he did not know why. He built on inspiration, wrote words and phrases that reminded him of Frieda, but to no avail, toward no apparent end. His mind strayed, his emotions wandered to his mother, of the guilt he suddenly felt for failing to take the time to compose his weekly letter to her. A sadness of sorts enveloped him. In a moment of idleness, he wrote Letters to Mama beneath yet another taped-together sheet on which he had again already written William Worthington and Cultural Affairs. It made him pause, but he could not learn anything useful from it. He thought of Frieda again, and again of unwritten letters and of his mother and of Frieda's admonitions. He thought how much he admired Frieda and cared for her and needed her, and how it made no sense that she could think she was a nobody when she did so much, no doubt, for so many. That thought, too, made him pause. In bold print he idly wrote: a world filled with nobodies. Then he wrote the word nobody again on the line below it. Suddenly, as if he had never forgotten, he saw with perfect clarity in his mind William Worthington's letter, exactly where he had placed it many weeks ago, under the wax-encrusted brandy bottle that had served as a candleholder for years and years on end.

He rose and walked over to the shelf and lifted up the bottle and took up the letter and unfolded it and quickly read the words that he now already mostly remembered. Of how they had chosen him, Leonard Bentwood, from among all the other nobodies of the world, to be awarded the nation's highest honor; of the fact that the ceremony was only days away; of the requirement that the attendees wear a tie the color of black; of the place; of the time; of the particulars one would need to know.

At just that moment, Frieda Haster pulled her truck up to Leonard Bentwood's shack. He heard the screech of the steering hydraulics as she came in through the gateposts and he came outside into the blaring sun to greet her. The radio in her truck was still on as she opened the door—a newscaster or someone else speaking in a serious tone—and when she saw him she quickly reached over and turned it off. He thought she might be sick, so pale and drawn and bloodless were her face and lips.

"Good morning, Leonard," she said as brightly as she could. But it did not matter, because Leonard Bentwood was already cheery and vibrant in a way she had not seen for many years, if ever once.

"Frieda, my dear," he took her by surprise. "You're early. I was just about to write my letter to Mama."

"Yes. I am early. I know. My schedule is a bit confused today. How are you Leonard?" she asked. "I've been worried about you."

She brought in his groceries, his letter from his mother, a new bottle of brandy. They had their glass of it despite the hour. Mostly they talked of nothing, but all the while she probed the edges of the conversation, searching for clues or hints of whether Leonard Bentwood somehow had learned the news. "You know, Leonard, I just realized the other day that I have not brought you batteries for your radio for over a year now. Are the old ones still working?"

Leonard Bentwood frowned. "I don't have a radio, Frieda. Remember? I traded it to old Hoaggie at the yard in exchange for those wooden window frames he salvaged from that fire they had. Got the better of that trade, I can tell you that much."

"And what have you been doing? Are you feeling well?"

"Couldn't be better, Frieda," Leonard Bentwood said. "I gave up on trying to figure that fellow's name, and I took down all that paper mess I was making." Which was true enough, because in his search to find the scraps of unused paper he needed to complete his quest, Leonard Bentwood had removed and examined every single sheet of paper and then had piled them all in a heap in the corner of the shack.

"I'm so glad, Leonard," she said. "It's like I said. You've got better things to do than to be worrying about some trespasser."

Leonard Bentwood answered, "There's no need to be worrying about me, Frieda. I feel fit enough to climb a mountain."

She left him with a smile not only on her face but on his also. He watched her drive off and felt no remorse for not telling her what he had done and what he was about to do. She had always been a bit overly protective, he thought. But he had humored her, not only to be nice, but because he cared for her more than anyone in the world, except perhaps his mother.

She drove out slowly but still in a cloud of inevitable dust, and he immediately turned to assembling his clothes and pulling out his wad of money and putting his things in the cab of the truck. He went back inside, found the little bottle of metallic acrylic and the brush and pulled out the sign and cable that he had hid away. He picked up the sign and painted out the words Closed and Fishing so that the sign just said Gone. He threw the cable and the sign in the truck bed and drove through the gateposts and stopped. He restrung the cable tightly between the two posts, hung the sign on it, got in his truck and headed out.

CHAPTER VIII

1

To the members of The Committee, the news the President had delivered was as bitter as it was sweet. The public acknowledgement that the Nolebody Vaccine had a short half-life and could not be used twice on any person had merely verified their general conclusion that something had gone radically wrong with the vaccine. They had known that much for months and, in their egoism, believed they had known it even before the clowns in the government could have come to the same conclusion. The Half-life Revelation had showed that the very basis for the autocratic government had failed, and it had only served to embolden The Committee's resolve to resurrect the Nobody Movement and the proud display of the capitalized letter N, to throw down the government and reestablish a democratic republic more in line with the governments of the past. And yet for all of that, Leonard Bentwood's willingness to come out of seclusion and to throw his full support behind the government represented a potentially fatal blow to those who felt the time had come for the Nobodies to rise.

The Committee had attempted to do much in the twenty-four hours that had passed since the announcement had been made. But it had realized little progress. Just as it had made little progress with its prior forays into rousing the public and laying the foundations for revolt; the fiasco at the People's Hillock and the destruction of the War Memorial and the countless other little plots it had masterminded and sanctioned had all proved ineffective in their execution or their objective.

And as they met yet again in the dark and ill-lit confines of the basement apartment of Member 4, in the west ghettos of the capital city where the government's security men still were afraid to roam, the members of The Committee all knew that time was running short. Time, in fact, had already run short and they had less than two days before everything, everywhere changed.

"They are cunning enough to be worthy adversaries, I can see that now," Member 2 said as he poured cheap black coffee for himself and for anyone else who wanted it. "They know we need unity amongst the people in order to be successful, so they enlist the one man who can thwart that objective. They know we will try to stop them, so they find someone they know that we can't stop. Because to stop someone, we have to find him. And they know we can't find a man when we don't even know what he looks like." He stopped and sipped at the scalding coffee, looked over the edge of the cup to his fellow committee members, to the glum and haggard faces, the slouching bodies dressed in black. "It doesn't matter how many agents we have inside the government," he said. "And it doesn't matter how many agents we have looking for Leonard Bentwood. Either someone tells us what Leonard Bentwood looks like, or we'll never find him. I mean, for all I know, one of you is Leonard Bentwood."

Member 5 took a cup of the thick syrupy coffee, added some powdered milk and remained standing. "Are you saying there's no information at all? That no one can even give us something to start with? Like where he used to live or where he last was seen or what he looked like when he was younger? That doesn't make sense."

"That's exactly what I'm telling you. Unless you want a photo of him when he was sixteen. We've got that from his mother. But she claims she hasn't had a word from him in thirty years. I know it seems strange for someone so well known. I mean, think how rich he must be. I have no idea how someone can be one of the most famous people in the world and yet be totally anonymous."

"Maybe the government made him up," Member 7 offered. "Maybe there is no Leonard Bentwood. Maybe they pulled his name out of a high school yearbook years ago and paid his mother to use his name and made up the rest. You know, just to keep everyone happy."

Member 1 laughed caustically. She had personally assumed the responsibility for reading and cataloguing intelligence as it came in from their people in the field. "From what our agents are telling us, the problem isn't that Leonard Bentwood doesn't exist. The problem is that there are dozens of him. We've had reports of Leonard Bentwood sightings in every city in the nation, sometimes two or three in different places at the same time. Or two or three in the same place at the same time. We've even had claims from people stating that they are Leonard Bentwood. We've done what we can to check each story out, but it poses dangers for our people. And besides, you can pretty much tell from reading the reports that most of them are baseless. I've got one report from the charity center down south of the western regional airport stating that an old hobo driving a jalopy came into the shop claiming to be Leonard Bentwood, and that all he wanted was to buy a used black necktie. So that's where we stand. No one knows the slightest thing about what Leonard Bentwood looks like or where he lives or how his voice sounds, but everyone has seen him in the last twenty-four hours."

"Kind of like God," Member 9 said with a contained smile, but no one laughed.

"So you're saying we may have to deal with it at the ceremony," Member 2 said. "It won't be easy, you know." There was a pause, and an uneasiness spread throughout the room, making the cold unadorned concrete walls even colder, imbuing their dampness with a different sort of chill. Then he added, "Let's hope there's a clean shot. We wouldn't want to make a mess of it. And we'll probably only get one."

Member 1 frowned as she envisioned how it might unfold. "That's not what I am saying at all. I've given it some more thought. I still think the best thing to do is to get our hands on him before he can say anything to the public, before the public can even see what he looks like. We need more than ever to find someone inside to do that. But I still think it's the best approach. The last thing we need is to make a martyr out of someone who is already a hero. We kidnap him and we never let anyone know his fate."

"And what fate is that?" Member 3 interrupted. "If I may be so bold as to ask."

2

The arrangements for the traditional Recipients Cocktail Party had been in place now for many weeks. It would be held, of course, when and where it was always held—on the eve of the Nolebody Awards Ceremony at the prestigious Colonial Club, just blocks from the presidential residence. The guests would be feted in the same memorable surroundings where they always had been feted, in the marvelously restored Cardroom where centuries earlier the founders of the nation had supped and drunk before the enormous granite hearth, beneath oil portraits of themselves and canvassed portrayals of their many deeds. And, as if conduct too were a tradition that need be followed, the guests and their hosts would behave much as their forebears had behaved so many years ago; they would smoke and toast and joust for rank and position, exaggerate this accomplishment and embellish that, propose one solution while debasing others; subtly, and with little regard for consequence and logic, they would arrogate unto themselves the glory they rightly deserved.

The soirée, naturally, would feature the same opulence as it always had in the past: the string quartet from the National Symphony, the imported hors d'œuvres and exquisite champagnes and aged wines and malted whiskeys, jewels of incomprehensible craftsmanship and value, dress of indescribable taste, the power, the wealth, the very guest list of dignitaries and former Nolebody awardees, all to reinforce the people's confidence in the government and the government's satisfaction with itself. But the party this particular year would nonetheless differ from all others due to the dramatic developments revealed in the President's speech about the Half-life Revelation and the fact that the ceremonies had never before involved an individual of the stature of Leonard Bentwood. It was a privileged occasion not to be lightly ignored and, with the exception of Leonard Bentwood himself, the invitees had thus responded with unanimous affirmation that they would indeed attend.

William Worthington had struggled for days with how he would deal with the fact that Leonard Bentwood would not show up. He had considered flight, but that would not do. He had other plans, plans that included Frieda. And Frieda would not arrive until tomorrow, the day of the ceremony. He had considered various complicated fabrications, but when he practiced the lies in his mind and even before the mirror, he found that they were too easy to cross-examine and expose, that he was not believable, that he did not even believe himself. He thought of sabotage but, in the extreme circumstances he now faced, he did not sufficiently trust his passive side or his theories on how to defeat the Nolebody Vaccine. He wanted to run, to hide, to be someone, somewhere, sometime else.

He dressed slowly, pulled out the tuxedo and laid it meticulously on the bed with the music from his stereo playing a somber dirge softly in the background. He tightened the waistband and then the tie with anxious and aggravating tugs. The day would come, he thought, when he would never again wear a tie of any sort. He grimly smiled when he saw himself in prison garb, in a shirt without buttons, with clothes devoid of anything one might wind around a neck. He tied the shoes too tightly, put on the jacket, which over the past year had become too snug. He combed his hair, which had grown longish and wavy, and his mustache that curled slightly outward at the ends. He exited his condominium and took the fire escape stairs in order to avoid unnecessary conversation and encounter.

Outside, under the foggy yellow streetlamps, the preparations for the Nolebody Awards Ceremony were fully in progress. After much debate, the President had determined it would be a mistake to radically alter the custom of the past since the ceremony had always represented the one day that the public had been invited to the capital complex en masse. The Home Secretary had argued that the enormous viewing screens and the park stands and parking lot bleachers should not be set up at all. Professor Anderson had agreed and had proposed that the ceremonies be shown in lecture halls and classrooms and theatres across the city instead. "It will have more of an educational air that way," he had contended without success. And even the Minister of Psychology had asserted that the best way to contain potential disturbances was to close the streets down and keep the public at home where they belonged. But the Minister of Cultural Affairs would not have it and after much consideration and prolonged debate the President had agreed. "The whole point of the ceremony is to show a common bond between the government and the people," he observed. "And that objective is now more important than ever. What good is Leonard Bentwood if the people can't see him? Think about it. They've never seen him before. It is our gift to the people. It shows we are in this together. We must not squander the opportunity now." So a compromise of sorts had been offered, in which the public would be given access to the capital complex but would be restricted to the streets, so that, as the President observed, "They can be herded in and herded out in the quickest possible way."

The workmen had lined the streets with fencing and signs and arrows pointing to the nearest viewing screens. They had mounted the huge screens wherever convenience or necessity required, at intersections where they could be viewed from varied strategic directions, on defaced walls where the banned letter N had been painted clandestinely in hurried and uneven lines, on every street and corridor they could find between the river and the Center for the Public Arts. And then they had installed security checkpoints at every crossroads and entrance, like valves from which the flow and pressure of humanity could be controlled by the mere shutting of a gate or the turning of a wheel.

William Worthington walked under the dull vapor lights with the uncomfortable sensation that the roads and sidewalks were being prepared for a great funeral procession that would be captured on closed circuit and rebroadcast, live, back to the ground even as the people watched the real thing and cried and wept for the deceased. He hurried along with the pant legs and the cummerbund of the tuxedo constricting and the rain beginning to fall.

He came to the Colonial Club and showed his credentials and was admitted through the seemingly ancient iron doors into the hallway. An elderly gentleman in colonial dress took his overcoat and stiffly directed him to the rear of the reception line where the President and many of his Cabinet members and their spouses stood, bowing and nodding, kissing hands and prolonging handshakes, receiving all those who entered with gracious smiles and redundant gestures of appreciation and respect. As the line moved in unsynchronized jerks, William Worthington moved with it, down the queue to shake the feeble hands and kiss the powdered cheeks until he came to the end of the line and found himself being greeted by the Minister of Cultural Affairs and the President.

An impulse moved him, inexplicably. He leaned forward so that he came up close to both of them. "I've some bad news," he whispered. "I've just had a call from Leonard Bentwood. He's been delayed. Just briefly," he added when he saw the President's eyebrows rise and the Minister flush. "He won't be able to make it in until tomorrow. Something about his travel arrangements. A mistake by his assistant, I think. He seemed to be in a hurry. That's all he told me." When the President said nothing and instead looked back and forth at him and then the Minister of Cultural Affairs and then back at him and then back at the Minister with incredulity, William Worthington added, "He said there was nothing to worry about. He'll be at the center long before the ceremony begins."

There was a long pause in which the three of them stood totally still, each immersed in a personal debate of doubt and indecision. "All right, William," the President finally said. "You might as well go in and enjoy yourself." He placed his hand on William Worthington's back and gently and yet surely pushed him into the room and away from the line. Then the President and the Minister of Cultural Affairs talked in whispers.

William Worthington went to one of the three bars in the room and asked for a double martini and drank it down in long narrow sips and fast swallows, in between which he overheard one of the new category awardees, the architect A. Winston Feldston, explain to a group of admirers how he had convinced the government planners that they could increase available public housing space by slanting the floors on the project highrises that proliferated in the capital city. "You see," Feldston proudly explained, "a one-to-ten pitch actually means you increase the living area significantly. Roughly speaking, you can get as much as 10 percent more people in the same area as you would with a flat floor. Of course, one has to secure the furniture and rugs and things; but that is a minor inconvenience compared to the savings involved."

William Worthington asked the bartender for another martini and drank that one down too while the music played and the rich and famous mingled in little circles where acquaintances held strong and where safety was better ensured. He watched the menagerie with an uncertain fascination—the past and present category award winners reveling in their glory, the few Nolebody Medal awardees, supplanting all the rest with their preeminent status and sense of higher accomplishment, and the remainder of the guests, who, to a number, considered the idea of one day receiving their own award to be totally below them or far beyond their reach. William Worthington thought how absurd it would have been for Leonard Bentwood to be there at the cocktail party, how it would have been like throwing a mouse into a river filled with piranhas.

The crowd transitioned; one coterie formed and another dissolved. Katrina Solatairie, another category award winner, entranced one circle by her description of her latest foray into the extra-sensory sciences—something having to do with trans-evolutionary communication by which the progenitors of a former species were able to exchange thought with successor species of another era. Another clutch of listeners stood in awe as Wexford Thropingham explained how he had conceived of the now well-established sport of Courtesies, in which the sole objective was to outdo your opponent with strategic displays of sporting etiquette and decorum. In yet a third circle, Boswell Slatterly, the category award winner in botany, described how his hybrid tulipgrass provided a psychological benefit to the small plot owner who now could have both the garden and the lawn of his or her dreams.

After a while, the President assumed a position in front of a microphone that had been set up to the left of the hearth. He tapped it twice to gain the attention of those who had failed to see that he desired to speak. "I have an announcement. If I may have your attention, ladies and gentlemen." He cleared his voice and explained in the most regretful terms and with the most apologetic tone that Leonard Bentwood had been delayed and would not be able to attend the cocktail party.

There was some disappointment, certainly. But not much. No one in the room except William Worthington had ever met Leonard Bentwood and it was not as though old friendships awaited rekindling and reminiscence. Nor was there much reason for any of those present to desire to be preempted by the famous Leonard Bentwood who, after all, had given everyone there at least some offense by refusing to show the slightest degree of interest in being amongst them anywhere, at any time. He would have his moment in the limelight at the ceremony on the morrow. That seemed more than sufficient exposure for the reclusive Leonard Bentwood. And besides, it made for a better party, one at which no one had to fawn over a guest of honor and express admiration for his many accomplishments and infinitely sublime achievements.

The President bid the guests an enjoyable evening and then announced that he would retire early, in preparation for the festivities of the next day. The guests acceded to his every wish. Throughout the night, they drank and smoked and danced and lied; they postured and cajoled and manipulated; they tired and sagged and they said many things against their better judgment; they intentionally and quite by accident insulted and praised each other and themselves, not only far into the night but into the next morning as well. And in an effort to assuage any concerns the Minister of Cultural Affairs and the President might have, William Worthington joined in with his own particular brand of vengeance, which favored martinis chased by highland ale.

3

The phone rang, and he let it ring. It rang and rang and rang and rang until he finally picked it up just to stop it. "Hullo," he mumbled. He looked at the luminescent numbers on the clock, which said it was not yet six in the morning.

"William," the voice on the other end said. "It's Minister Frasier. We've had some developments. You need to get over to the Situation Room. Now."

He fumbled for the light switch, knocked over an empty bottle of Guardsmen's Ale, tried to focus his eyes in the darkness of the room.

"William. Are you awake?"

"Yes, Minister Frasier," he said as he continued to grope for the light which seemed to have been moved from its normal place. "I was in the shower. I'll get there as soon as I can."

"Get here in thirty minutes," she said.

He said, "Yes, ma'am," just before the receiver clicked dead.

He sat up in his bed, slid his legs over the side and placed his feet on the cold hardwood floor. He rubbed his eyes and found the light switch and the room instantly was illuminated a sedate yellow color that somehow differed from the color of his designer lampshade and the designer color of his textured walls. He reached for his robe and put it on just as he heard a knock at the door. God Almighty, he thought. He moved to the vestibule and opened the door in a stupor, thinking that it would be the Minister of Cultural Affairs, which made no sense since moments before she had been on the phone, calling him. And there, in the glaring hallway light, stood the Assistant to the Minister of History, whom he knew from university and whom he had seen more recently at several lower ministerial functions.

The visitor greeted him with a tone of apology before William Worthington could react in irritation. "Good morning, William," the visitor said. "I know it's early." He looked furtively over his shoulder, as though someone might be following him. "May I come in?" he asked. His bloodshot eyes pleaded with desperation.

William Worthington showed him in, wearily, without speaking. He closed the door and turned to the visitor so that their faces were only a foot apart. "Do you have any idea what time it is, Wayne?" he said.

Wayne Scanton, the Assistant to the Minister of History, answered. "Yes, I do, William. I've come here at great risk. In a way, my life is in your hands."

William Worthington led the visitor into the receiving room of his condominium and showed him a chair. He excused himself and went into the kitchen to put on the coffee and then stepped into the water closet to comb his hair and his beard. He returned to the embarrassment of the cluttered room, the scattered empty ale bottles, the discarded newspapers, the half-eaten instant dinner of potatoes and beans and rice.

His visitor had not moved. He sat on the edge of the chair, leaning forward, fidgeting with his hands while his eyes darted nervously about the room.

"What is it, Wayne? What do you want? I need to be somewhere in fifteen minutes."

"It's about Leonard Bentwood," the visitor said uneasily, with a wince, as though he were about to be struck and could do nothing about it other than to take the blow.

William Worthington sighed heavily and leaned back into

the deep cushioning of the couch. "If you're looking for tickets to the ceremony," he said, "I don't have any. You ought to know as much."

"No. It's not that, William. It's about the future. You see," Scanton said, and then he stopped and waited into the silence until he knew that waiting would not save him. "You see, I'm a Nobody. I mean I'm a member of the Nobodies, William. With a capital N. I even have a number: Member 227. We have reformed the organization. We have risen. We need to find Leonard Bentwood and stop him, William. And we believe you might be the only person who can help us to do it." He leaned further forward, watching for William Worthington's reaction. When there was none, he said, almost in a whisper, "We know you're sympathetic. We've been watching you, William. We know you've committed your own acts of protest. That you are one of us." When William Worthington said nothing, he added, "Please, William, everything depends on our stopping Leonard Bentwood."

William Worthington almost said something in answer, but he caught himself before he said it. Because he could not, ever, reveal what he knew about Leonard Bentwood. And then there was Frieda. "You have nothing to worry about," he said cryptically instead. "You're right. I'm on your side, Wayne. But I can't explain it all to you. I can tell you this much: It will not work out the way the President wants. Leonard Bentwood will not be there. They think he will be, but he won't. You can tell your people I said so. That I've made sure of it. You can tell them that I guarantee it. But that's all I can say. I can't explain further. It's like you say, Wayne. There are lives at stake." He got up and went into the kitchen and came back with two cups of coffee. He gave one to Wayne Scanton and then he sipped at his several times before he said anything more. "I guess we're in the same boat now, Wayne. My life is in your hands too, now that I've told it to you. All I know is that your people can't let the secret out. It would ruin it. This is the best way, Wayne. That's all I can tell you."

Member 227 asked for more—for where Leonard Bentwood was and who else knew and what he looked like—but William Worthington would not give it to him. So the visitor left, armed with information he had not sought and which he was not sure that he could believe.

William Worthington hurriedly showered and hurriedly dressed and then made his way down the lamplit streets that led to the capital complex and into the heart of the complex itself, past the cordons of security guards and the random security checks, the newly installed fences and gates and into the rear entrance of the presidential residence where the guards had come to know and like him. He went down in the iron-plated elevator that moved so slowly that one could not be sure that it moved at all and through the bank vault door, and into the room that now was alive with radio operators and video screens and the translucent maps from which someone had finally removed the cartoonish weather figures and replaced them with little figurines of army men and ships and planes, as if a great war had been waged between the weather and humanity, and humanity, the victor, had eradicated the weather entirely, or at least exiled it to another planet or another time.

The Minister of Cultural Affairs intercepted him as he entered the room. She took him firmly by the arm and brought him through a hidden door he did not know existed, into a small conference room with table and chairs and nothing more. Already seated were the President and Professor

Anderson and a third person, a wrathful-looking man in a new army uniform whose face seemed stamped with a vicious and permanent snarl.

"Sit down, William," she said, coldly, with a certain authoritarian flair. "We've had a security breach."

The President looked over at the fierce army officer and said, "Let's go over it again, Captain Wiles. From the beginning."

Captain Wiles rose to stand and the President told him there was no need, so he sat back down, uncomfortable and self-righteous in the presence of the President. "Like I told you," he said curtly, as if the need for repetition were a waste of precious time. "We'd been told the site at Sealey Cavern was totally secure. The Great Gypsum Desert has been fenced all along its periphery for ten miles square. We've had it sufficiently manned from the beginning to know if a peccary tries to get through, let alone a human being. So that's not where the breach occurred. Where the security boys made their mistake was in concluding that the mountain itself was secure. That's what we were told anyway. That no one could ever possibly see us from the mountain side of the base."

"As I understand it," Professor Anderson interrupted, "that is not exactly what they said. They said there was one spot from which the base could be seen and that it was so far off the beaten path that there was no chance that anyone could ever find it. That's why we did not bother with it, Wiles. Let's keep to the facts."

"Yes, sir, General. I stand corrected, sir," Wiles said. "That's what they told us. But they were wrong. I caught someone spying on us three days back. Picked up the glint of a glass or mirror or something coming from way up on the very top of the ridge, right where those security boys said no one would ever make it. I even saw him through my own glasses, a tall gangly looking fellow, long gray hair and a beard, all dressed in black, if you catch my meaning. It took my boys a whole day to figure out how it was done—used a little track of a road that goes way up into a little crack in the mountains on the other side." His mouth twitched and his lips pursed like he was about to spit. And then he turned and looked directly at William Worthington. "And here's what they found." He half stood. He leaned across the table to a cardboard box that sat in front of him and he pulled out an object and placed it on the center of the table.

William Worthington looked at it and his face flushed a crimson red. The remainder of those in the room also stared at the object even though they each had already seen it at least once—a crudely carved canoe-shaped boat, about four inches long, single-masted with a sail emblazoned at the top with the words, William Worthington, Assistant to the Minister of Cultural Affairs, followed by several spaces and then, to the left, the words, Dear Mr. Bentwood.

It was the President who finally spoke. He dismissed Captain Wiles with a "thanks," and then stood in silence until Wiles was gone and the door was closed. "So, William," he said. "What have you to say about all of this? The way we are looking at it, you and Mr. Bentwood are the only two people who logically would have been in possession of such a letter. Either way, it gives reason for pause, if you see my meaning. Especially with Mr. Bentwood failing to appear last night."

"I suppose so, Mr. President," William Worthington answered apologetically. And he was thankful that this time he did not have to trust in a lie, or at least not much of a lie but instead only a slight twist of the truth. "It's my fault. But it's not what Captain Wiles thinks. The answer is really quite simple. It's almost funny. I had some annual leave left over from last year, so I took my camping gear and spent a night in the mountains before my last visit to Leonard Bentwood. The boat ... well I carved that," he said with some pride. "And the sail ... well I had to use something, and the extra copies of the Bentwood letter were all that I could use. I suppose it's silly, but I wanted to see if I could make something that would hold up in the creek. How far it would sail. That's all there is to it, Mr. President. I hardly meant to do any harm."

The two ministers and the President looked at him with a questioning stare as if what he had just said made absolutely no sense. So he added, "The Youth Corps, and all that, you understand. I used to do a lot of that sort of thing when I was a kid." And when no one said anything yet, he continued, "As for someone finding the cavern, I wouldn't be too sure. The sun plays tricks up there in the mountains you know. There was a major aurora while I was there. Besides, I wouldn't be too confident in anything Captain Wiles says. He strikes me as being just a bit too aggressive for his own good." To which Professor Anderson wholeheartedly agreed.

So that was the end of it. At least to the four people who remained in the room. In a way, William Worthington had even come out a bit ahead, because the two ministers and the President now looked at him with a higher level of respect, given as how he was the first person they had ever met who had slept out under the stars at night, at least intentionally and alone.

But it was an altogether different matter to Captain Wiles, who had left the building still thinking about the figure of a man he had captured in the field of his glasses—the way they both had seemed to hold the other in their respective gazes for many minutes, like untiring duelists armed with nothing but their own contending wills. And he thought also of William Worthington, whom he suspected of the worst kind of perfidious treason a human being could commit.

4

They were all idiots. They were all fools. That much and more was obvious to Captain Wiles, who now knew what must be done. He had warned the inept Professor Anderson that the military installation at Sealey Cavern was subject to detection and he had alerted him to the fact that there was a way around the Nolebody Vaccine conundrum, as Professor Anderson liked to put it. But the Professor would not condone the use of indiscriminate force and the captain's recommendations thus died a paper death in a memorandum that went no further than the professor's desk. General, my ass, Capitan Wiles thought angrily as he drove toward the prearranged rendezvous point where he knew his own lieutenants were waiting. Goddamn idiots and fools.

He drove past checkpoint after checkpoint where the guards waved him on with grim looks and awkward salutes, and then he parked the government sedan at the train station and walked into and through the station and out the other door. He meandered for several miles, directionless, verifying he was not being followed. He took the metro to the riverfront and walked for a long time along the riprapped and littered banks until he came to the bridge. He looked about, then ducked under the abutment where his men were waiting for him.

"It's just as we expected," he told them. "The cavern was

detected days ago. It's a good thing we got our boys and equipment out when we did." He looked at their anxious faces, and he saw something in their eyes that he did not like. "It's just as we planned, men. Just remember your orders. And remember; it's your country you're fighting for. Your country and your honor. Now, are we ready?" He slapped the one nearest to him on the back, too hard, with unwarranted familiarity.

One of the others answered his question in a whispered voice, "Yes, sir. Four platoons, sir. Locked and loaded, sir."

And Wiles responded, "Good. Good work. All of you." He paused, as though he had a sudden thought, a sudden worry. He looked at the four men and knew he had no choice but to trust them. He shifted uncomfortably. "I'll let you know what the placements will be once I see how they plan to manage the crowds. Keep your men out of sight for now. And keep 'em quiet."

So low was the abutment that even on their knees Captain Wiles and his men might have touched the tires of Leonard Bentwood's truck as he passed over them, had they only been able to reach through steel beam and rebar and concrete. Leonard Bentwood passed over them and over the river and came into the capital city which was shrouded in a hazy smog that the rising sun could not penetrate but only lighten in color and shade. He passed over them and into history without Captain Wiles ever knowing it. Then Captain Wiles left the meeting place, furtively looking over and back across his shoulders as he crawled out and retraced his steps. The others left also, one at a time and in all directions but not until they had talked some more together.

Only minutes later, Frieda Haster crossed over the bridge in the same direction as Leonard Bentwood; not pursuing Leonard

Bentwood but rather her heart, heading toward William Worthington, to be at his side at his final hour. Followed only minutes later by Member 227, who had made his report to The Committee and who was now rushing to assume the pretense of attending to the affairs of the Ministry of History.

And the whole while, the river flowed in a somber steady stream of effluent and decay, past the burnt ruins of the War Memorial and by the fenced enclosure around the People's Hillock, and through the capital complex where the security forces still were installing the viewing screens and signs and barriers, past the industrial estates and the crumbled tenements and wire fences and broken streets, the smell of asphalt and diesel and sulfur, and out into the relative freedom of the countryside, curving through hills and harvested fields and the few remaining forests of the heartland, onward toward the delta and the sea.

At a point somewhere not far from the bridge, Captain Wiles found a public phone. He dropped in the coins, one by one, with a cold mechanical precision. The phone acknowledged its receipt of each coin—ding, ding, ding, ding—and then Wiles waited as the phone rang and rang repeatedly. When no one answered, he tried another number, and then another, and then yet others, until a call was finally answered by a suspicious voice that said, "Yes," and then waited in a deathly silence.

"Rodgers. It's Wiles. What's going on there?" Why doesn't anyone answer their phones? You're the first person I got to answer in eight tries."

More silence on the other end, only listening, then the voice finally said, "They've come for us. They've taken us down, Wiles." There was a muffled sound, like someone trying to talk through their hand, and the receiver clicked off.

"Shit," Wiles said. He pulled out more coins and tried other numbers, other names. He picked up his hand radio, pushed the button to talk. "Paxton. It's Captain Wiles. Do you read me?"

"Yes, over," came back a crackled reply.

"They've taken out the camp. Do you read me? We're on our own. Over. Paxton. Do you read me? Anyone? It's Captain Wiles, over. Goddamn it. Bailey. Krisner. Bultono. Can any of you hear me? Over …"

CHAPTER IX

1

Leonard Bentwood drove over the bridge and into the city proper and the first thing he found was that the number of signs had increased fivefold. The one in front of him said No Unauthorized Cars Beyond This Point. The next one, just yards beyond the first, said Awards Ceremony Public Parking, 1 Mile Ahead, so he followed the arrows and pulled his truck into the public lot and parked it there. He looked at the clock on the dash, which showed it was not yet noon. He pulled William Worthington's invitation out of his pocket and looked again at the appointed time for the ceremony, which was at the first evening hour. He frowned. Through the windshield he could see a gray mass of buildings and, beyond and above that, a hint of the heart of the capital complex, which seemed to bristle with antennae and radio towers. He thought how like old Hoaggie's dump it looked with its bramble of glass and metal and wires all piled atop each other like a work of modern art. He picked up his old tweed sportsjacket, which he had laid across the passenger seat, and the faded black wool tie he had bought at the store many miles ago, and the shoes that were resting on the floorboard—being the best shoes he owned, a pair of loafers, slightly scuffed and rather in need of a polish. And he got out of the cab and put on the shoes and the jacket and stuffed the tie in his pocket and set out to follow the signs and arrows that led in the direction of the capital complex.

When Frieda Haster came over the bridge minutes later she encountered the same signs. She pulled into the same parking lot and instinctively parked in the same section where the few other cars had parked, at the front and center where escape could be quick and easy. Leonard Bentwood's truck sat next to hers and yet she did not notice it at first, and might never have noticed it were it not for the fact that it bore the same regional plates as hers, bearing the same symbol of sun over mountain, set against a cloudless sky. As her eyes trailed up from the license plate to the tailgate to the truck bed to the cab, she knew unmistakably that the truck was Leonard Bentwood's. "Oh, no," she said aloud. "Oh, Leonard."

There were no pay phones nearby and it took her almost a half hour to find one. She dialed Mary Bentwood's number and, after a single ring, Mary Bentwood answered in a frantic tone, saying, "Yes. Who is it?"

"Mary, it's Frieda. I'm in the capital. Leonard is here somewhere. I just saw his truck."

All Mary Bentwood could say was "God help us" again and again until Frieda Haster told her that she had urgent things to do and would have to call her back. She did not know why she had called Mary Bentwood in the first place, and now she wished that she had not called her. She made her way down the streets she did not know, through the strange coldness of the clutter of the city, along the fenced corridors and the signed roads and the shuttered and barred windows and doors and storefronts and the stained brick and mortar of the apartments until she was uptown where the buildings suddenly had bright curtains and little yards with crisp landscaping. She finally found William Worthington's street and then his apartment and she went up the stairs to Number 45.

He opened the door, hoping it was her but expecting to find someone else, someone armed or someone angry, someone he did not know but who knew of him. "Frieda," he said. And she said, "William, thank God you're safe," and then they fell into each other's arms and did not let go until he thought better of it and took her inside and closed the door.

All the while, Leonard Bentwood strolled through the streets of the capital complex like a penniless child at a carnival, looking at everything with wide-eyed amazement and aching curiosity but having no wherewithal to do more than to observe from a distance. How unlike the desert the city was, he thought. How unlike the desert and the mountains where one could not help but touch and feel and experience and be part of all that was above and beneath and around you. And yet not entirely unlike the desert, for somewhere in the depths of Leonard Bentwood's subconscious thought he sensed that a monsoon would soon break upon the city just as it did in the desert, with the same unpredictable assuredness once it had laid its figurative foundation of heat and humidity and seasonal flow in proper combination.

For hours he walked at a varying pace, strolling up and down and across the capital complex that seemed to have risen up out of the plains like a great mausoleum of the past, stopping only long enough to admire from the streets the colonnaded buildings and marbled monuments, the fountains and stonework and gardens and lawns. When hunger finally got the better of him, he bought two sandwiches from a street vendor who had staked out his territory early. After consuming them both in large, voracious bites, he grew tired, and a kindly security guard saw him and helped him over a fence so that he might sleep on a park bench under newspapers that he did not read but which mentioned his name on the first page and the last, and on several in between.

When Member 227 came over the bridge, he did not park his car in the lot used by Leonard Bentwood and Frieda Haster; instead, he drove on until he encountered a barrier where he showed his identification to the guards, who were bored almost to death. They took one look at him and his identification and waved him on like a whiff of bad gas, failed to even consider the possibility that there were weapons in the trunk, that there were weapons on the floorboard beneath the seat. And Member 227 breathed only slightly easier as he drove the remainder of the way to his apartment on the high side of town. He parked his car and with some effort removed his contraband and got it inside where it would be safe for at least the moment.

By various incongruous directions, Captain Wiles made his way back to the train station where he had left the government sedan. He drove it to a lonely spot in the abandoned sector of the industrial estates, where the streets were particularly gray and particularly empty. When he was satisfied he was alone, he opened the trunk. He pulled a few of the smaller, more concealable items from the miniature arsenal he had assembled over the past week, all of it as compact and efficiently sinister as he could have hoped for in that day and age. He removed the car plates and tossed them in a garbage bin overbrimming with stale trash. He tried his radio again and again. Again, Bailey and Krisner and Paxton and Bultono did not answer. He found a phone and called the offices at the Ministry of Defense and left word to the effect that his car had been stolen, that some of his possessions were missing, and that he would be delayed.

At two o'clock sharp, the Minister of Cultural Affairs called to order the final meeting of the Nolebody Awards Planning Committee. She half assumed William Worthington would not be there, but she was wrong by half. After much deliberation, he and Frieda had decided that they had no choice but to prepare for the fact that Leonard Bentwood might appear at the awards ceremony, in which case one of them had to be there to deal with that ambiguous eventuality should it come to pass. They had laid out plans for William's escape, such as they were, and then they had set out on their separate ways— Frieda in search of Leonard Bentwood and William directly into the fray.

The President paced the halls and corridors, the offices, the library, the conservatory, the conference rooms and meeting rooms of the presidential residence for hours on end, all the while accompanied by the presidential retriever who, unbeknownst to the President, had picked up a swarm of fleas from somewhere outside and now was periodically depositing new colonies throughout the residence with an occasional flick of his ears or the scratch of his paw. "Well, Spangler," the President said as they passed through the beveled double doors that led to the billiards room. "Things are about to change, whether we like it or not. The best thing for us to do," he said as he bent down and affectionately roughed up Spangler's head, "is to keep everything as neat and tidy as we can. And then hope for the best."

2

The planners had assumed the public turnout for the awards ceremony would be somewhat larger than in the past. Beyond that they had failed to bring any insight to the calculus. The fact that public participation in prior years had been negatively influenced by extraneous factors—the weather, competing sporting events, a nasty bout of the grippe—was never even considered. Nor was the possibility that some would view this year's ceremony as if it were a festival of sorts, a circus, a masquerade to be attended at all costs and in all fashion of garb and costumed dress. The planners had underestimated the political factor and undercounted the numbers of lower level government employees who would have an interest in being on the streets at such a time, in such a place. And no one within the government was even aware that The Committee existed, let alone that it had distributed many thousands of leaflets, reinforced by the authority of a facsimile of the governmental seal, offering free food and drink to any who attended. The planners failed to add some factors and subtract others, they divided the wrong streets and squared the wrong circles, and then they multiplied their own mistakes by pure miscalculation. The fault lay primarily at the doorstep of the Minister of Psychology who had insisted that the job of administering the crowds fell within her purview but who detested mathematics as something as foreign to the human mind as was hearing to the deaf. Even as she watched the situation unfold, she wrongly concluded that it added up; to her, the successful totality of her efforts seemed as easy to verify as it was to add two plus two.

By five o'clock, the capital city was in utter gridlock. The allotted parking proved insufficient and cars and buses loaded with people were backed up in long jams that extended from across the bridges and then fanned far into and even beyond the outer confines of the city. Some abandoned their vehicles where they sat, so great was their ambition to be physically close to the Center for the Public Arts and the viewing screens that had been set up on the boulevards nearby. The barriers and the fences were overrun, in some places with tactical precision and in others by the sheer weight and mass of humanity that continually pressed into the capital complex until the security precautions literally burst at their fragile seams. The parks filled. People's Hillock was taken by an enormous and extended family from the east side who had marched in with blankets and coolers and even a grill and charcoal and preparations for a feast. The statues, the fountains, the steps and marbled promenades became draped with human beings, many of whom could not even see any of the hundreds of viewing screens that had been set up throughout the city, and many of whom wore black.

By five thirty, it had become clear to the Minister of Psychology that the only way to clear a path for the arriving ceremony invitees was to employ bulldozing equipment, which she had already ordered in and left at the rear. With some trouble and some injury, the roads were sufficiently and briefly opened; the crowds were pushed temporarily deeper into the parks where they were never meant to be, and the limousines and private cars carrying the lace and flower of society poured through. Then the crowds collapsed back into the streets behind them, as if the seas momentarily had been parted only to regain the seabed that only they could fairly claim.

Before the grand entrance of the Center for Public Arts,

the crowds were parted again and a great red walkway, made from the tightly woven and elaborately dyed fiber of a rare species of llama, was rolled out from the edge of the street, along the entire course of the walk and up the broad steps that led to the grand entryway. One by one the limousine drivers deposited their cargo of the glamorous and the absurd, stopping their vehicles so close to the edge of the curb as to eliminate any risk that their passengers could possibly step upon the scabbed and broken pavement of the streets of the capital complex. The limousine would stop and the passenger doors would remain closed while the driver got out, walked around to the rear, opened their doors and guided them out. Women in lavish gowns and men in awkward tails stepped out and twirled and posed and postured and preened until they were moved on by the associates of the Minister of Cultural Affairs who were assigned the duty of ensuring that everything moved reasonably apace. By seven, all of the invitees had been ushered out of their limousines and up the crimson carpet and into the atrium of the Center for the Public Arts. All, that is, but one; Leonard Bentwood was nowhere to be seen, not even by William Worthington, who alone of all those in attendance could identify Leonard Bentwood if and when he saw him.

A voice came over the address system and flooded the atrium with soft and lilting instructions that asked the program participants to come to the private receiving area toward the rear of the theatre and for the audience to enter the theatre and assume their seats. The murmur of the crowd died, but only a little. The evening's awardees filtered out and toward the back of the theatre, like selective grains of sand in a discriminating hourglass. The members of the audience slowly trickled into the lavish, curtain-draped theatre where long-tailed ushers showed them to their sections and rows and velvet seats.

William Worthington had been one of the last to make it up the carpet and into the center. He only had time to lift a cocktail off a passing tray and gulp it down before he heard the call over the address system. Slowly and regretfully he made his way toward the guest reception area behind the stage. He drew a deep breath and straightened his tuxedo before entering the room where the President was meeting with the awardees and the Minister of Cultural Affairs and Professor Anderson. The President turned his head as he entered. "Nice of you to come," he said coldly. He looked over to two members of his security team and nodded his head. They came over to William Worthington and took him by the arms. "Keep him here," the President said. And before William Worthington could speak the lie he had prepared, the President said, "I don't even want to hear it. If you cannot assure me with definitive proof that Leonard Bentwood is on his way, I am not interested in what you have to say."

William Worthington said nothing in return.

The category awardees looked at William Worthington with icy looks and haughty airs, conveying that it was not only him that they found to be despicable, but also Leonard Bentwood, who had affronted them for the last time, ever. The Minister of Cultural Affairs ignored him entirely, as if he did not even exist. She gave the category award winners their last instructions, reviewing the manner in which the program would unfold and reminding them each of the limited time and latitude they had for accepting their award and offering their thanks. "Now," she said, "I will ask you all to come on stage and take your seats in the order we have just discussed."

With a great exhibition of courtesy and decorum, the

awardees moved toward the stage entrance, stepping aside to allow another to enter first, holding out a guiding hand, bowing and nodding and smiling and shaking hands so that they looked like marionettes performing the well-practiced artificiality of a puppet dance. Some of them ignored William Worthington completely as they made their way onto the stage, but others could not resist one last opportunity to exhibit their disdain. Katrina Solatairie held him in the most intense of stares and, having done so, divined the pathetic frailties of William Worthington's subconscious thought down to the last sordid detail. Suzanna Kay Ralston, who wore a most exquisite dress of satin and threaded gold, took one look at his wrinkled tuxedo and bleary eyes and lifted her chin and forehead as though by so doing she might avoid the taint of something decidedly unpleasant and particularly crude. And Wexford Thropingham, whom William Worthington had long admired and long desired to meet, simply said, "Bad showing, old boy," as he gracefully strode onto the platform with all the coordinated confidence in the world.

The President turned to the Minister of Cultural Affairs. "I suppose we should begin," he said with a look of immense sadness and disappointment. "Do you still think I should refrain from saying anything until the end?"

The Minister of Cultural Affairs was on the brink of tears. She looked over at William Worthington who remained firmly in the grip of the President's men and who could not even look into her eyes. "Yes, Mr. President," she said. "I do. Let's save the news about Leonard Bentwood for last and hope that everything else goes as well as it might. Besides, it will give Minister Anderson more time to get his people in place." Professor Anderson nodded his head in agreement.

The President took the stage, assumed his familiar posture behind the podium that had been dressed with roses and sided by the flag of the nation and the presidential banner, and on the front of which had been placed the presidential seal, bellicose eagle and all. The President adjusted his posture and readied himself as he and the awardees stared directly into the closed curtain, as though they were the audience, waiting for the show to commence.

In the orchestra pit front and center beneath them, the National Maestro raised his baton and held it aloft for what seemed like minutes, and then, with a sudden aggressive swoop, he introduced a lonely horn that commenced the first passage of the National Anthem. The curtain slowly rose in a multiplicity of complicated and sensuous folds until the entire stage was visible to the anxious audience and the remainder of the world.

3

The audience erupted in a vigorous ovation, which the President endured with a practiced modesty. It refused to end for a long while, continuing like the consistent patter of heavy rain on a tin roof. All the President could do was to smile and look out across the expectant audience that numbered in the thousands and periodically nod his head or hold up his hand, as if he really wanted it to stop.

When it finally did, when the last resistant applause faded into nothingness, the theatre grew absolutely silent; so silent and anticipatory that the President became disconcerted. He forgot his opening lines, became overwhelmed with the thought that at some point he would have to confess that

Leonard Bentwood would not be present. Seconds passed and they seemed like eternities and the President continued to stand motionless before the audience, paralyzed and stricken and mute. The delay that at first was merely an embarrassment became prolonged and inexplicable, and an uneasiness arose amongst many in the theatre audience. That, too, frightened the President. He wondered who amongst them might be capable of a volatile and unexpected act of violence, and he easily might have guessed that it was even worse amid the masses outside, who watched the distorted screens on the streets and in the parks and along the sidewalks with growing impatience and agitation. Because the faces of the people sitting on the stage were more than familiar enough to the theatre audience and the public at large for them all to quickly and collectively realize that despite the President's promise, Leonard Bentwood was not there. For if Leonard Bentwood had been there they would not have recognized him, and by that perversity of logic they would have known that it was he.

"We have a very full slate this evening," the President finally said with the artificiality of the master of ceremonies on an afternoon variety show, and the crowds inside and out grew more restless still. From somewhere outside could be heard a faint chant—"Leon-ard Bent-wood, Leon-ard Bent-wood"—and it continued and continued to rise in volume until Professor Anderson, who stood side by side with the Minister of Cultural Affairs watching the President from behind the stage exit, picked up his radio and spoke to someone and the chanting came instantly to a stop.

"As you can see," the President continued, "we have with us some of the greatest luminaries of the nation. They have joined us at this critical time in our nation's history, at this critical juncture in the history of the world, to unite us in our common bond." But even as he said it, he knew it was not enough. He knew that the public felt no meaningful connection with the people on the stage. They needed Leonard Bentwood. Just as he needed Leonard Bentwood. He needed Leonard Bentwood to be there and tell the public that it was all right, that if they followed the government's lead things would work out for the best, that they could survive the Half-life Revelation and continue on as a nation, as a civilized society. The President's mind wandered again as he grappled for more to say, and the nervous tension inside the theatre rose and tightened more until, again, from outside could be heard the chant, "Leon-ard Bent-wood, Leon-ard Bent-wood, Leon-ard Bent-wood, Leon-ard Bent-wood."

Professor Anderson and the Minister of Cultural Affairs could only stand and watch and grow increasingly anxious and distracted. For the Minister of Cultural Affairs, the unfolding disaster meant no less than the beginning of the end of all her aspirations. But to the professor, it was something altogether different, an opportunity to observe and catalogue and analyze a unique moment in the history of humankind—the last gasps of a failed empire, the last hour aboard a sinking ship.

There was a sudden abrupt noise behind them. The Minister and professor turned to see that the door into the side room had been kicked open by Captain Wiles who, with one hand, held an elderly looking, bearded, and poorly dressed man by the collar while his other forced the barrel of a military sidearm into the prisoner's back. Wiles looked at the professor and the Minister with a vindictive and vindicating sneer and said, "I caught him trying to sneak into the ceremony." And when the Minister and the professor did nothing other than to continue to stand and stare blankly at him, Wiles added with an air of utter accomplishment, "This is the scum I saw spying on us through the binoculars. This is the radical that breached the professor's so-called security arrangements at Sealey Cavern."

His prisoner looked over to William Worthington and smiled. "Hello, William," he said.

And William Worthington carefully answered, "Hello, Leonard. I didn't think you'd make it."

The Minister of Cultural Affairs looked at the prisoner with a startled and doubtful expression. She looked at his long gray hair and his unruly gray beard, his tattered jacket and the faded tie. And then she recalled William Worthington's description of Leonard Bentwood. "You're Leonard Bentwood?" she asked.

"I'm *a* Leonard Bentwood," Leonard Bentwood answered just as William Worthington affirmatively nodded his head.

Captain Wiles looked frantically at the professor and then at the Minister just as Professor Anderson gestured to the two security guards who still held William Worthington. "You've got the wrong man," he said. "Relieve Captain Wiles of his toy and take him into custody." The guards seized Wiles and wrestled the pistol from his hand. Professor Anderson looked directly into Wiles' eyes and mouthed the word Idiot as the guards led Wiles away.

In seconds, the Minister of Cultural Affairs straightened herself out. She plumped her hair and ran her hands down along the sides of her satin dress and flung the side curtain fully open and strode rapidly out onto the stage to interrupt the President, whose impromptu speech had evolved into nothing more than a desperate plea. He at first failed to see her and continued in his meandering statement regarding culture and science and the arts and how it all connected to the working class. When he spotted her from the corner of his eye, he stopped and looked out at the audience with a nervous smile. She approached him hurriedly, placed her hand on his shoulder, leaned into him and whispered in his ear. The President brightened and nodded his appreciation while she strode off with a dignified attitude of accomplishment.

The President turned back to the podium and leaned into it, almost too casually, the presidential raptor seemingly bearing the entirety of the President's weight. "Ladies and gentlemen," the President said in a revitalized and buoyant voice, and in the suspension that followed he drew the deepest breath of his life and announced, "Leonard Bentwood has just arrived."

<h2 style="text-align:center">4</h2>

They brought another chair onto the stage and with a point of his finger the President directed that it be set apart from the category awardees. The Minister of Cultural Affairs led out Leonard Bentwood, her arm entwined proudly with his. She brought him to the podium and left him standing next to the President so that they both faced the audience. The applause went on and on and on until it seemed interminable. Tears came to many in the crowd and some openly cried and there were few who were not moved by the sight of Leonard Bentwood and the President standing together. Outside, under the putrid yellow of the vapor lamps that lined the thoroughfares of the capital complex, there literally was dancing in the streets.

Throughout it all, Leonard Bentwood stood perfectly still. He looked out into the audience and thought how odd it was that they should pick a simple man to honor in such a way, how odd that they should pick him, of all the people on the

Earth. It sends a message, I suppose, he thought to himself. By honoring me, they honor everyone.

"Ladies and gentlemen," the President said again and again into the microphone, which screeched and whined under the voluble weight of the noise. He finally gave up, stepped back and waited and waited and waited until the audience grew tired of itself and quieted. "Ladies and gentlemen. Fellow citizens. Citizens of the world. I give you Leonard Bentwood." And the applause and the celebration returned with even more jubilance and emotion.

Mary Bentwood watched the President's introduction from the comfort of her chaise lounge. She watched the Minister of Cultural Affairs escort out the man she had not seen for many many years but whom she knew instantly to be her son. She watched in awe as he stood, erect and dignified in his own way, despite his faded black tie and worn jacket and wrinkled pants and scuffed shoes, next to the President in the hour of the nation's need. And when the President said, "I give you Leonard Bentwood," Mary Bentwood wept as only a mother can weep.

After a long while, the President finally spoke again. "Ladies and gentlemen, as you know, we have a long ceremony before us." And this brought unexpected boos and hisses from inside the theatre and no doubt from the outdoor throngs, none of whom had the least interest in the twelve luminaries who sat quiet and humbled like sinners in a pew waiting for their turn at expiation and forgiveness. "The procedure for the Nolebody Category Awards will be the same as always." More boos and louder hisses. "I will describe a particular award category, I will announce the winner of that category award and describe that individual's accomplishments, and the awardee will come forward and offer his or her remarks. There will be a ten minute intermission after the first six awards are given." Dissension in the crowds, disturbance in the streets. "We will begin," the President continued, but then stopped, because the audience would not permit it any longer and the chanting outside the center—Leon-ard Bent-wood, Leon-ard Bentwood, Leon-ard Bent-wood—had become so loud that the walls inside the theatre shook and no one could hear a thing.

At some point, and without being asked to do so, Leonard Bentwood had left the President's side and had taken his seat. He was weary from the drive. His walk had tired him even more, as had his nap on the park bench planks. In his effort to be on time to the center he had struggled against the crowds like an old salmon battling its way up a flooding creek cluttered with too much stone and too much ordeal, and that too had worn and tired him. And then there was the angry man in the military outfit who called him all sorts of names and twisted his arm and waved his gun about like a broken plastic rudder on a little plastic boat. The words of the President lilted in the air and he did not hear them, or at least did not comprehend them. He looked over at the others who sat in the row of chairs across the stage and wished that he could sit with them. He turned and looked up at the stage set behind him and read, with his vision slightly blurred, the banner overhead stating TWENTY-FIFTH NOBODY AWARDS CEREMONY and below that another sign stating Honoring Leonard Bentwood, and he felt almost giddy with exhaustion. The President signaled to the Minister of Cultural Affairs, who came onto the stage again, again proud and dignified in her moment of glory with her eyes unable to determine on which target—the President, the audience, Leonard Bentwood—to rest. She came up to the President and the President drew her closer and said, "Bring the other six awards out now. I am going to do it en masse."

"But …," she began. But when she looked out at the crowd and realized that she could barely hear what the President said, she understood the wisdom in his approach.

Many blocks away, Frieda Haster had come to an awestruck standstill when she saw Leonard Bentwood suddenly appear on the screen that had been set up high above the walkway that ran along the Justice Center. She stopped without even knowing it and stared up at the face that she loved and she guessed what was about to happen, that the ceremony would be truncated so that the President could focus on Leonard Bentwood. She pressed ahead, thrust her way through the crowd, which seemed to have aggregated into a single body that pulsed and throbbed in reaction to everything that evolved upon the screens. She dug down into her pocket and pulled out the information William Worthington had given her. As she pressed onward she said the names of the streets again and again in her mind.

The President pulled out the list of the category awardees and managed to quiet the crowd enough to gain their attention. "We'll do it this way then," he said. "I will read off the names of all twelve category awardees at once, and then the category awardees will arise in unison and form a line at the podium in the order in which their names were announced and I will hand out the awards that way." The twelve category awardees were aghast at the idea, but no one else cared and they did as they were told. They lined up in the order they were called and then the President identified each category and mentioned the respective names of the winners and then handed them all one of the little figurines that, themselves, were nondescript and virtually featureless. The President signaled once again to the Minister of Cultural Affairs, who now had become accustomed to being before the crowd. She came out again, this time with her eye contact steady and fixed on the audience. She smiled brightly as she led the chagrined awardees off the stage.

By now, William Worthington had made his way out the rear exit of the theatre only to find himself in an alley tangled with a mass of people. As much as he tried, he made little headway in finding a way out.

With the stage cleared of all but the President and Leonard Bentwood, the crowd inside the theatre quieted. It was as if a long-awaited event were about to occur and no one knew what to expect. The President reached under the podium and pulled out four massive tomes, a four-volume set comprising many thousands of pages, all four of them finely bound and embossed with a raised print that glittered and flashed in the light as only gold can glitter and flash. He set the four volumes atop the podium, all in a row, and then reached into the inside pocket of his tuxedo and pulled out a sheet of paper.

"Ladies and gentlemen," he said into the quiet that was pervasive and absolute. "I would like to begin by reading you some Leonard Bentwood."

5

"This first reading," the President said warmly, with real sincerity, "will be a treasure for all of you. But it will be an even greater privilege for me. I have the honor of introducing tonight, to everyone across the globe, Leonard Bentwood's most recent poem, which will appear in the next issue of the prestigious *Journal of World Poetry*. I am told by the publisher that even his typesetters have not seen it."

Leonard Bentwood watched the President with curiosity; he found the President's words strange, and he wondered what he meant by them. He suddenly suspected that he might have been mistaken for someone else, that maybe there was another Leonard Bentwood who was supposed to be there instead of him.

Inside the theatre and on the streets, the crowds waited in anticipation. The President put on his reading glasses and then pressed the creases out of the paper that had been in his pocket. He cleared his throat and read,

> three cups of coffee,
> three
>   times
>   three
> a bird, a song
>   I do not know
> cheeseburger cheeseburger cheeseburger
> a visitor coming,
>   from down the road

The President put the paper down on the podium and looked up. An immense silence hung within and without the theatre, almost as if time itself had stopped and now held everything in abeyance. Then an enormous heartfelt cheer of approval and fulfillment rose up, everywhere and of a sudden.

Throughout it all, Leonard Bentwood sat motionless, trying to conceal his confusion. It seemed he knew the words from somewhere, but he could not be sure. They reminded him of many things, of a coffee-sodden moth and the little school desk behind his shack, of the song of a bird that frequented the desert. At the same time, he was embarrassed: embarrassed by the fact that for some reason the President and the audience faced him while they applauded and smiled and applauded and smiled. It caused Leonard Bentwood to blush, not out of modesty as much as out of his inability to understand.

When the crowd finally quieted, the President turned back to the podium. He reached and picked up one of the four volumes that he had set in a row on the podium and then he laid it down in front of him, still closed. "Over the years," he said into the microphone, and now his tone was more serious, more practiced, "Leonard Bentwood has been our guiding light. Who amongst us has not turned to the wisdom and insight of Leonard Bentwood when times seem darkest, when even hope seems to have abandoned us?" He opened the book and turned to a page that had been marked by a strip of paper and read:

> A lost razor
> storms coming today
> old faces

> new faces
> the rain washed all the dust away

The audience, the crowds on the streets and in the parks stirred, and many turned to their nearest neighbors to confirm that they knew the poem, that it had always had meaning to them. The President looked up over his glasses to focus on the faces in the audience that now seemed overwhelmed by the significance of the moment. "Leonard Bentwood teaches us," he said with absolute confidence in his interpretation of the lines he had just read, "that we must not lose our way, that we must be aware of the present and remain prepared for the future. We must remain sharp, and if we do, if we stay united and resolved in our mutual purpose, we will prevail and prosper together."

Again, Leonard Bentwood heard the President's words and found no sense in them at all. His mind wandered to the day many years ago when he had whimsically decided to shave off his beard only to discover he had misplaced his razor, for which he searched for many hours while a monsoonal storm passed through and wiped the desert clean.

The President looked back down at the volume and turned many pages ahead to the next place that had been marked. And he read,

> Coveys of quail
> Flocks of sheep
> pods for whales
> > and packs for wolves
> colony
> > gaggle

<pre>
                    pride
              or schools
        but never brood
              brooding
                brood
</pre>

The President looked up over his reading glasses and spoke to the nation and the world. "Leonard Bentwood teaches us that all living organisms must act collectively if they are to prevail against adversity. We must remain together and work together. We must rely on each other and do no harm to each other. We cannot brood over the triviality of our own individual troubles when it is society as a whole that requires our caring attention. Like the pack of wolves or a flock of geese in flight, we must remain cohesive and recognize our leaders and move forward as one."

But all Leonard Bentwood could do was recall a day long ago, a morning when he sat in his rocker on his porch in the early summer heat and watched a large band of peccaries come in and gather under a mesquite tree and for an hour eat the seeds from the dried pods; how he had watched them jostle for position; how the little ones squealed and stayed clear of the aggression of the larger males; how their musky scent lingered forever in the air and of the way their bristly hair raised up on the napes of their necks; how, as he watched them root along the ground, he had tried and tried but never did succeed in figuring out what a group of peccaries was called.

It went on that way for a half hour, maybe longer. Again and again the President turned more and more deeply into the open volume and read aloud the words that had been printed on the selected page and then each time offered his explanation of what Leonard Bentwood had intended by his artistic and philosophical expression. And each time, the President assured the audience, the nation, the masses who viewed the ceremony on the screens or on televisions or listened to it over the static of radios on every band, on every continent. He assured them that the meaning of the poem had deep significance to a world that teetered on the threshold of the abyss of the Half-life Revelation. And each time, the reading caused Leonard Bentwood to recall a little snippet of his forgetful past.

The President closed the book and stuck it back in the row with the others that stood on the podium. He took off his reading glasses and looked out across the crowd. "Ladies and gentlemen. Allow me to be frank. The time has come for the peoples of the world to face the reality of our times. The Nolebody Vaccine has served its purpose, but we cannot rely on it any longer. In times such as these, governments must be allowed to perform their jobs, to protect the public, to ensure a stable future. It is in times of crisis that society must stand behind its government and give support to its government and validate its government. We must heed the words of Leonard Bentwood and unite under the banner of our heritage and history. We must remain as one."

He turned to Leonard Bentwood who had grown more than weary and who had become more and more confounded by what was transpiring. He now very much regretted that he had come.

"Leonard," the President said in a tone that was beyond deferential. "May I ask that you read two or three of your works to the audience? Something that expresses your feelings at this historic moment. Something that will inspire us and give us support and hope for the trials to come." And then he bowed awkwardly and moved away from the podium and swept his hand in an invitation for Leonard Bentwood to step up.

The audience stood and applauded and the crowds in the streets stared in fixation at the screens. Those who had cameras photographed and filmed and those who had recorders held them up high, as if the words to be spoken could only be captured at a particular elevation. And Leonard Bentwood eased his tired body up and walked over to the podium and stared out into the insanity of the world.

For a long time he stood behind the podium in silence while the audience applauded and applauded until, at last, one and then several people in the balcony and then on the main floor sat down and slowly, reluctantly the remainder of the audience took their seats. Leonard Bentwood looked down at the four volumes that stood in a row on the podium and then over at the President and the President nodded his head. So he randomly chose one of the volumes and pulled it out and set it down on the podium in front of him. The cover of the book was printed with the words The Collected Works of Leonard Bentwood— Volume III. By accident he turned to the Table of Contents, which listed categories from which the reader might choose items with a particular focus or subject matter. When he saw the words Poems to Ruth, he instinctively reacted and threw open the volume to the range of pages where that material apparently could be found. He looked down at the words and then doubtfully up at the President who stood off to the side. When the President said nothing, he read aloud,

RUTH

Woman
　　　of a memory
far beyond these years I now am living
absorb this desire
　　　　　　I have of giving
still
　　　my love to you

　　And his heartfelt reading shattered the audience by its sensitivity and rich emotion. It was met by an absolute silence, followed by polite and yet contained applause by the audience, which exhibited a respectful caution in the manner in which it reacted to something so intimately personal and private. They could never have known that to Leonard Bentwood, the words carried little meaning. He had never loved the fiction that was Ruth. To him, all she represented was the reminder of what an unpleasant memory would be like; that it is best not to have unpleasant memories, whatever the cost.

　　Leonard Bentwood turned the page. He looked back up at the crowd and then back down at the page and read,

RUTH

A world
　　　so grand
that it destroys
　　　the illusive vision
　　　of hapless boys
dissolves the oils

> and canvassed joys
> of a scene
> I'd paint
> for you

The crowd became choked with emotion. Even the President, whose eyes also had become moist, found it momentarily difficult to swallow. But for Leonard Bentwood the writing meant something altogether different. Because even as he read it he remembered quite clearly the day a decade and more ago when he sat down to write himself a Ruth reminder, only to accidentally knock over his only bottle of royal blue paint, and how it ruined his plans that day to finish a little three inch square painting he had been working on for a week.

But it did not matter. It did not matter what Leonard Bentwood thought. While he did not know it, he now had the crowd fully within his control; the audience and the crowds in the streets had fallen, mesmerized, under his sway like an unknowing participant from the audience who has been caught by the hypnotic spell of a master charmer. Leonard Bentwood looked up at the theatre audience and farther back into the cameras and microphones that captured and rebroadcast his every word to the people on the streets, in their homes, driving in their cars while they listened on the radio. It was as if his word had become their command.

The President approached the podium and pulled Leonard Bentwood aside so that the President could whisper to him beyond the range of the microphone. "That was wonderful, Leonard," the President said respectfully. "But I wonder whether you might not read one or two of your poems that relate to something other than love, and all of that. I mean,

I think they are beautiful poems. Don't mistake me. It's just that we would like to conclude on an upbeat note. Something about harmony between the people and the government. You see my meaning, don't you?"

As Leonard Bentwood bent his head to hear the President's whispered words, he could not help but see the background staging—the banners of the same color as those on the government seal and on the government flags, the gold braided tassels, and, far above the stage, the blurred sign proclaiming TWENTY-FIFTH NOBODY AWARDS, Honoring Leonard Bentwood. And it seemed to him that it would only be appropriate to do what the President had asked, especially in view of how kind everyone had been by selecting him for this year's award. "All right," he answered, with the hope that the ordeal might soon be over. "I can say something like that. Do you want me to do it now?"

And the President answered, "Yes, I think so. Now is as good a time as any."

6

For twenty minutes, William Worthington had struggled against the sea of people, and in that much time he had gained only perhaps three hundred feet. He knew now that all was lost, that there was nothing he could do for Leonard Bentwood, that the only thing left for him was to find Frieda and for them to flee together. So he had pressed forward through the crowds, progressing at a snail's pace past one person at a time, sometimes taking them by the shoulders and pirouetting such that he and the other exchanged positions before his erstwhile partner even knew what had happened, forcing his way down the alley with an increasing sense of resigned urgency, just as Frieda was making her way into the alley from the opposing angle of the street.

They met in the alley into which the overflow of crowds seemed to be injected by some contrary law of physics that said the pressure must be relieved by venting it through the narrowest of alleys and passageways. There almost was not room for them to embrace when they finally came together, holding each other so tightly and so closely that the gray of her hair and the dark brown of his seemed to grow out of the head of a single human being. "Did you see him?" she said with tears streaming down her face. "Did you see him?" And he said, "I'm sorry, Frieda. It's my fault. There's nothing we can do."

In desperation, they agreed to try the other end of the alley, to attempt to make it to the back side of the capital complex even though it would take them further from Frieda's truck, from their only means of escape. So they turned in that direction, frantically pushing their way back through the crowd, back toward the direction from which William Worthington had come and against the tide of enthusiasm that exerted itself against the theatre like an emotional buttress of hope and adulation. Suddenly William Worthington felt someone ram a hard narrow object into his ribs and he turned in pain and reflex to find himself confronted by the angry face of Member 227 who jammed the pistol even deeper into William Worthington's side and said angrily, "You lying son of a bitch."

Member 227 pulled a radio out of his pocket and fumbled with it as he viciously jabbed the pistol into William Worthington again and again. "Member 10, come in. This is 227, over."

"Read you, 227. Are you in?"

"There is no way in. But I've got Worthington. Request instructions. Over."

"Hold onto him tight, 227. We might need hostages," said the frantic voice on the other end. "Things don't look good. Watch the back theatre door. You know what to do if he comes out."

"Understood," 227 said into the radio. And then he shoved it back into his pocket and jammed the pistol even deeper into William Worthington's ribs.

Inside the backstage area of the theatre, on the other side of the fire exit and only yards away from the spot outside where Wayne Scanton held William Worthington, the Minister of Cultural Affairs readied herself for the ceremony's denouement. Every preparation had been made to ensure that the final moments would be beyond forgetting—the fireworks displays, the light show that would follow, the celebratory music that would flood the streets, the confetti and balloons, the release of the doves and the unfurling of the banners all testament to the advent of a new era, bright and uplifting and all involving her. And all the while, Professor Anderson stood with her, mentally noting her every movement as she paced this way and that, attempting to divine her emotional state and her place in history as he watched her lips mime the words of the poems even as they were being read first by the President and then by Leonard Bentwood.

The crowds, too, seemed to ready themselves for the final act, albeit in different ways. While there was a uniformity of admiration for Leonard Bentwood in the crowds both inside and outside the theatre, their similarities mostly ended there.

To those in the theatre—to the cream of society that wallowed in the luxury of privilege and excess, and to the highest ranking members of the government, who enjoyed a disproportion of wealth—the ceremony represented their greatest hope that the status quo would be maintained, that they would continue to bask in the lavishness of life and the rewards to which they surely were entitled. Whereas to the vast majority of those who had stood for hours in the dirty and poorly lit streets, craning their aching necks for a better view, straining to hear what was said above the din of the noise and the increasing intensity and charge of the crowd, the world stood on the very knife edge of doom, with only Leonard Bentwood and the whim of fate between them and the darkness of the unknown.

Committee Member 1 had watched it all unfold with her typical uncanny ability to perceive and comprehend each change in the probabilities of success and failure. To her deep philosophical disappointment, the ceremonies had played out more or less as had been planned by the President and the Minister of Cultural Affairs. Yet she knew that permutations remained viable, that in at least some ways, some of the plans of The Committee had been realized due to the dramatic number of the people who had now been freed of the influence of the Nolebody Vaccine. With each passing minute, the skepticism and mood of the outdoor crowds became bleaker, more unsure. The very mien of the people slowly and unidirectionally changed from one of hopefulness and optimism to the anxious and furtive face of distrust. When she saw that time was running out, she picked up her radio and spoke the word "Nobody" again and again—the code for which her associates had long been waiting—and the crowd instantly and literally began to turn blacker as various members of the movement pulled out black T-shirts and put them on and then reached into the sacks they carried with them and distributed the shirts by the scores and then by the hundreds and then by the thousands. Within minutes the street was filled with an army of men and women and children all wearing black and all boasting on their fronts and on their backs the luminescent and illegal letter N, which stood out so boldly and brightly that the streets seemed filled with a population of prisoners who all bore the same anonymous prison number, in the form of a letter that stood for no particular person.

The President had asked Leonard Bentwood if he could wrap it up by saying something upbeat, and Leonard Bentwood had answered that, yes, he could do that, and the President had said now was as good a time as ever. So Leonard Bentwood turned back to the podium and looked back out at the audience and up at the cameras. He looked at the four volumes that stood in front of him and on which someone, for some reason, had typed his name. And he concluded they must be a gift.

The President had asked him to close by reciting a few poems about harmony between the people and the government, but he did not know any poems. He tried to think of a saying that might be suitable instead, but he did not know any sayings either, at least not for such a purpose. He looked back at the President who seemed anxious and impatient.

He leaned toward the microphone and again a silence fell over the audience, over the crowds in the street, across the world. And Leonard Bentwood said, "I'm not sure what to say. Other than thank you, I mean." But he could see that that was not enough. That the audience expected more. So he said, "I never expected something like this to happen to me. I mean I like poetry and all of that. But I've never really understood it. I really don't even read much, to tell you the truth." And that confused the crowds some and many in the audience looked at him oddly. He looked back at the President one more time, hoping for some guidance or that the President might relieve him of the burden of speaking to the audience. In his weariness his eyes roamed across the stage and again back up into the staging rafters and the blurred sign that hung above him. He looked at the banner and he thought back to his conversation with Frieda Haster weeks ago, and suddenly it all became clear. He turned again to face the audience.

"The President has asked me to close by saying something about the importance of harmony between the people and the government," he said. "Now I don't know all that much about politics and such. All I can tell you is that I'm a nobody. And, to tell you the truth, I'm quite content being a nobody."

Some of the members of the audience gasped and others turned to their companions and whispered in hushed voices. The Minister of Cultural Affairs caught hold of the curtain at the side exit to steady herself. On the streets, everyone and everything stopped. Even the gun in William Worthington's side eased back, if only a little.

Now Leonard Bentwood felt comfortable, because as he understood it this was what the ceremony was all about and this was why he had been selected. Because he was just an ordinary human being in a world filled with ordinary human beings and the government had enough sense to realize that it would be a good thing to occasionally honor someone like him because that was a way to honor everybody. It was ordinary individuals who made everything work in the first place. Like the leafcutter ants in the desert, who worked in perfect harmony as they trooped out in long work columns and steadily and as a group harvested the leaves in which they were in need and then marched them back to the hill, which had been maintained by other workers day into night into day. So he said, "I'm a nobody and I've always been a nobody and I'm sure I will always be a nobody." And then he thought of the banner that hung over his head and he added, "I'm a nobody with a capital N."

All pandemonium broke loose. The audience rose almost in unison, but it was already too late. A frightening noise came from outside, a noise that welled up from the ground like a single collective shout, like the earth itself had yelled "Hurrah!" in a single victorious cheer that had no end. Within seconds, the doors at all ends of the Center for the Public Arts came crashing down and the crowds, many of them wearing black T-shirts emblazoned by the letter N, came rushing in.

Most of what followed in the next hour was a blur to Leonard Bentwood. A swarm of the black-shirted public rushed toward him and hoisted him onto their shoulders and carried him jubilantly outside. There was the noise of gunfire, but only sporadic and perhaps fired only in reckless celebration. The members of the theatre audience screamed and tried to flee, but there was nowhere to run, nowhere to retreat to, nothing left to do other than to press themselves against the walls and watch in terror as the government came crashing down.

The President stood with a certain dignity on the stage as the crowds rushed in, moved not one inch until they were upon him and then had him in their custody, went down with his ill-fated ship like the captain he always wanted to be.

The Minister of Cultural Affairs froze into a sort of petrified stupefaction and was taken prisoner by a squad of Nobodies that came in through the side entrance door. Professor Anderson recorded it all, if only in his mind, the emotions and numbers and even the expressions and apparel of the competing combatants, carving his perception of it deep into the depths of memory from which he could retrieve it all later when the time came for him to assess and critique and expound.

They marched down the streets of the capital complex. Past the Cultural Affairs Building and the National Museum and the Ministry of Psychology and the Justice Center, all of which had been taken by squadrons and then battalions of Nobodies and from which, through the open windows and open doors, and atop their roofs, could be seen hoards of people dressed in black, waving their hands and cheering into the open air. They went on to the presidential residence where the doors had been thrown open and the hallways and even the ramparts secured by members of the public. They carried Leonard Bentwood on their shoulders the entire way, past the supporting crowds and under the din of the chant that would not fade and would not stop: "Leon-ard Bent-wood, Leon-ard Bent-wood, Leon-ard Bent-wood." Like the steady beat of an old chieftain's drum, announcing that the tribe was returning with shields still in hand.

At the entryway to the presidential residence they finally put him down so that Leonard Bentwood could be greeted by several members of The Committee who were still recovering from the emotion of the moment. Member 1 came forward and stuck out her hand and took that of Leonard Bentwood and shook it warmly and then only reluctantly released it. "Mr. Bentwood," she said with almost a religious deference. "It is my honor to thank you on behalf of the people. On behalf of the entire Nobody Movement. We always knew you were one of us. And now you are a part of us. You have come to lead us."

Leonard Bentwood looked at her and at the crowds around him and then out through the windows to where the presidential lawn was illuminated by the sporadic flashes of light from the fireworks that were being set off somewhere in the distance. Only then did he feel the dryness in his throat, a thirst unlike any he had known for many years. "May I have a glass of water?" he asked.

Member 1 directed someone to get the water and then asked if there was anything else he would like or that he would like to say. Leonard Bentwood chose to answer the first of the two questions. "Yes. I would like to talk to William Worthington. Do you think you could find him for me?"

They got Leonard Bentwood some water and by the time he drank it down, Member 227 arrived leading William Worthington and Frieda Haster at his side. "I apologize again," 227 said to William Worthington and William Worthington said, "I told you, it's okay, Wayne," and then 227 left the room and William Worthington and Frieda Haster came toward Leonard Bentwood. First Frieda and then William began to tear, and Leonard stood and smiled through his weariness and came over to them. "Hello, Frieda," he said with a look filled with compassion and reminiscence. "Hello, William." And Frieda Haster and William Worthington both knew what Leonard Bentwood wanted without him even having to say it.

7

The three of them drove out of the capital city in Frieda Haster's truck and not one of them said a word for a long time, Frieda Haster driving and William Worthington sitting next to her with his arm over the back of the seat and around her shoulder and Leonard Bentwood at the passenger window; all three of them staring out the windshield and into the future and trying somehow to avoid the silence. They drove out at first slowly and cautiously, past the dwindling crowds and the broken tenements, and then with a hurried acceleration through the industrial estates where the carbon- and sulfur-ridden smog now somehow seemed slightly less oppressive, less ominous. Not one of the three of them dared even to look at one or both of the others for fear that the one or both of them might say something that would fracture and destroy what still seemed like a fragile and ill-defined fantasy or dream. They drove for over three hours that way, into a silence that was not as much interminable as it was both vacant and yet heavily laden with doubt and wonder, until they were forced to admit they required fuel and that there also was need of coffee and a break so that they could continue on without having to really stop and lose the momentum they required to return Leonard Bentwood safely to his desert home.

They pulled in and out of a gas market as quickly as they might and continued, this time with the radio tuned to a station with nothing but music. William Worthington suggested that they open the windows to bring in the revitalizing air, and the wind and coolness of the night blew soothingly through their hair and against their faces as they drove and drove and drove until the country began first to empty of people and then to spread and then finally to rise. The silhouettes of foothill and even mountain began to gain outline and form as a faint hint of dawn rose up from behind them to separate sky and earth. Still they drove without talking, without even thinking too much of any one thing, be it the disaffection of the past or the instability of the present or the ambiguity of a future that would be improbable no matter what eventually came to pass.

The light of the new day flooded down upon them just as they came out of the darkness of the forested elevations, and the beginning of the desert again declared itself in ways that were familiar and warm beyond mere warmth and familiarity. The land itself now wide and open and undulating and illuminated with a thousand shades of shadowed brown and the darkest hints of scattered green amidst rock and ravine, the rise and fall of the earth.

A song came across the radio that somewhere in a past now long lost to Leonard Bentwood had reminded him of something youthful and invigorating. The song began with introductory chords that had once connoted to Leonard Bentwood a theme of newfound freedom amid desert and canyon and mesa. And then a male vocalist sang the opening words—opening the tale of a lost soul wandering through a historical past now long forgotten—that were etched in the back of Leonard Bentwood's memory. Leonard Bentwood drew in the very deepest of breaths—the inhalation of a sigh—and he instantly became lightheaded with tiny brilliant asterisks of light flashing before his eyes. Then the entirety of his body shuddered uncontrollably as the vaccine inside him lost its effectiveness and his metabolism struggled to adjust. In the indescribably brief interlude between one moment and the next, the matrix of Leonard Bentwood's mind and being was rewired and rewound. Hidden tendencies toward anger and volatility sought pathways to replace those of complacency and quiet. A primal instinct for preservation returned itself in full. At the base of his subconscious thought and desire, something new was now deeply rooted. A need, perhaps. A demand. A subliminal insistence on survival in an existence in which nothing survives forever. William Worthington could not help but feel him shaking.

William Worthington turned to Leonard Bentwood and he thought by Leonard Bentwood's expression that he might be in some form of pain or discomfort. "Are you all right, Leonard?" William Worthington said. But before William Worthington could turn to Frieda Haster and say, "Pull over Frieda. Quick," Leonard Bentwood said, "It's all right. I'll be fine."

Leonard Bentwood turned and looked out the open window, at the passing desert and mountains, the rising sun. He sighed and deliberately took in another breath, deeply filling his lungs with the fresh and arid morning fragrance, and then he let it out as slowly and calmingly as he might. And when the tension in his back and shoulders had sufficiently eased, he turned to look at William Worthington and Frieda Haster and said with a simple and affectionate smile that only Leonard Bentwood could have smiled, "Let's the three of us go home."

About James Gaitis:

James Gaitis is an author of fiction and non-fiction, an editor, a former trial lawyer, a part-time university academic, and a nationally recognized arbitrator. He obtained a BA in English Literature from the University of Notre Dame and a JD from the University of Iowa College of Law where he was an editor of the *Iowa Law Review*. He is a specialist in energy law and arbitration and a member of the Global Faculty at CEPMLP, University of Dundee, Scotland. Publishing credits include *A Stout Cord and a Good Drop—A Novel of the Founding of Montana; The College of Commercial Arbitrators Guide to Best Practices in Commercial Arbitration*, on which he served as co-editor and co-author, and numerous articles published in prestigious law journals. He and his wife live in the Sonoran Desert.

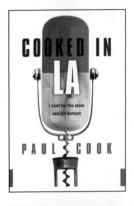

Cooked in LA ■ Paul Cook

How does a successful young man from a "good" home hit bottom and risk losing it all? *Cooked In La* shows how a popular, middle-class young man with a bright future in radio and television is nearly destroyed by a voracious appetite for drugs and alcohol.

Non Fiction/Self-Help & Recovery | US$ 24.95
Pages 304 | Cloth 5.5" x 8.5"
ISBN 978-1-60164-193-9

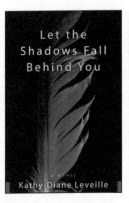

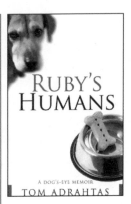

Against Destiny
■ Alexander Dolinin

A story of courage and determination in the face of the impossible. The dilemma of the unjustly condemned: Die in slavery or die fighting for your freedom.

Fiction | US$ 24.95
Pages 448 | Cloth 5.5" x 8.5"
ISBN 978-1-60164-173-1

Let the Shadows Fall Behind You
■ Kathy-Diane Leveille

The disappearance of her lover turns a young woman's world upside down and leads to shocking revelations of her past. This enigmatic novel is about connections and relationships, memory and reality.

Fiction | US$ 22.95
Pages 288 | Cloth 5.5" x 8.5"
ISBN 978-1-60164-167-0

Ruby's Humans
■ Tom Adrahtas

No other book tells a story of abuse, neglect, escape, recovery and love with such humor and poignancy, in the uniquely perceptive words of a dog. Anyone who's ever loved a dog will love Ruby's sassy take on human foibles and manners.

Non Fiction | US$ 19.95
Pages 192 | Cloth 5.5" x 8.5"
ISBN 978-1-60164-188-5

The Unbreakable Child ■ Kim Michele Richardson

Starved, beaten and abused for nearly a decade, orphan Kimmi learned that evil can wear a nun's habit. A story not just of a survivor but of a rare spirit who simply would not be broken.

Non Fiction/True Crime I US$ 24.95
Pages 256 I Cloth 5.5" x 8.5"
ISBN 978-1-60164-163-2

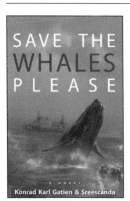

Save the Whales Please
■ Konrad Karl Gatien & Sreescanda

Japanese threats and backroom deals cause the slaughter of more whales than ever. The first lady risks everything—her life, her position, her marriage—to save the whales.

Fiction I US$ 24.95
Pages 432 I Cloth 5.5" x 8.5"
ISBN 978-1-60164-165-6

Screenshot
■ John Darrin

Could you resist the lure of evil that lurks in the anonymous power of the Internet? Every week, a mad entrepreneur presents an execution, the live, real-time murder of someone who probably deserves it. *Screenshot*: a techno-thriller with a provocative premise.

Fiction I US$ 24.95
Pages 416 I Cloth 5.5" x 8.5"
ISBN 978-1-60164-168-7

The Short Course in Beer
■ Lynn Hoffman

A book for the legions of people who are discovering that beer is a delicious, highly affordable drink that's available in an almost infinite variety. Hoffman presents a portrait of beer as fascinating as it is broad, from ancient times to the present.

Non Fiction/Food/Beverages | US$ 24.95
Pages 224 | Cloth 5.5" x 8.5"
ISBN 978-1-60164-191-5

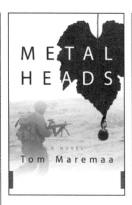

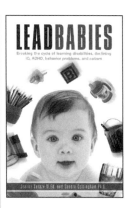

Under Paris Skies
■ Enrique von Kiguel

A unique portrait of the glamorous life of well-to-do Parisians and aristocratic expatriates in the fifties. Behind the elegant facades and gracious manners lie dark, deadly secrets

Fiction | US$ 24.95
Pages 320 | Cloth 5.5" x 8.5"
ISBN 978-1-60164-171-7

Metal Heads
■ Tom Maremaa

A controversial novel about wounded Iraq war vets and their "Clockwork Orange" experiences in a California hospital.

Fiction | US$ 22.95
Pages 256 | Cloth 5.5" x 8.5"
ISBN 978-1-60164-170-0

Lead Babies
■ Joanna Cerazy & Sandra Cottingham

Lead-related Autism, ADHD, lowered IQ and behavior disorders are epidemic. Lead Babies gives detailed information to help readers leadproof their homes and protect their children from the beginning of pregnancy through rearing.

Non Fiction/ Health/Fitness & Beauty | US$ 24.95
Pages 208 | Cloth 5.5" x 8.5"
ISBN 978-1-60164-192-2